carol coffey

The Butterfly State

POOLBEG

Crimson

This novel is entirely a work of fiction. The names, characters and incidents portrayed in it are the work of the author's imagination. Any resemblance to actual persons, living or dead, events or localities is entirely coincidental.

Published 2009
by Poolbeg Press Ltd
123 Grange Hill, Baldoyle
Dublin 13, Ireland
E-mail: poolbeg@poolbeg.com

1 3 5 7 9 10 8 6 4 2

A catalogue record for this book is available from the British Library.

ISBN 978-1-84223-397-9

Typeset by Patricia Hope in Sabon 10.2/14
Printed by
Litografia Rosés, S.A., Spain

www.poolbeg.com

Note on the author

Carol Coffey grew up in Dublin and now lives in County Wicklow. She has a degree in Education and has worked in the area of special education for over twenty years. *The Butterfly State* is her first novel.

Acknowledgements

Thanks to Paula Campbell of Poolbeg Press for the opportunity to publish this book. Thanks also to Gaye Shortland for her wonderful editing and to all the staff at Poolbeg who have shown such interest in this book and to T & C who encouraged me all the way.

For Dave, for his endless support

Chapter 1

1981

Tess Byrne had thought it would be a sleepless night until she awoke to the sound of the cleaners mopping the long corridor outside her room. It was a comforting sound that she had become used to over the ten years she had spent at the institution. She placed her bare feet onto the cold tiled floor and walked gingerly across her room to look out into the bright, frosty February morning. This was the first thing she did each day. Tess enjoyed the ritual of seeing the same things: traffic passing by on the road, cyclists taking a short-cut through the grounds on their way to work, nurses arriving in taxis or on foot. However, this morning was different because this was the last morning she would ever see these things, this was the last day she would ever spend in this place. Today she was going home.

Tess dressed slowly and methodically, carefully

unfolding each item of clothing separately. She took her small suitcase from beneath her bed and packed in silence. She did not have much to pack, mostly her drawings and coloured pencils along with a few clothes. When she finished she sat on the bed and stared around the sparsely decorated room. Apart from her bed and locker, the only other piece of furniture was an old wooden wardrobe that smelt of mothballs. The walls of the tiny room were painted white, which made the quiet room appear colder than it was. Apart from a few of her own drawings that she had decided to leave behind, there was nothing on the walls except for a round white plastic clock and a large wooden crucifix that she had taken a long time to get used to. What she liked most about her room was the large shuttered window, which had a deep windowsill in which she often sat and painted.

Tess settled down to wait to be called for breakfast which was more than half an hour away. She took a small notebook from her suitcase and opened the first page. Written there in large red letters was a list with the word "Apologise" written neatly above.

Apologise

Seán

Kate

Ben

Dr Cosgrove had asked her many times what the list meant but she would not tell him. It was her secret and you had to keep secrets. She put her list back into the suitcase and took a deep satisfying breath. Today was the first day of her new life. She was going home and she had work to do.

Dr Martin Cosgrove lowered his large body into the black leather chair in his stuffy office overlooking the institution's exercise yard. He leant forward, his thin blond hair falling over his dark-rimmed glasses, and watched as rows of children played under the watchful eyes of two orderlies. He sighed as he thought of the responsibilities of his job and knew that he could not say with any certainty that he had helped any of the hundreds of disturbed children who had passed through this institution's doors.

And Tess Byrne was no different. Looking through her file, he found it hard to believe that she could ever have hurt anyone. There had been a few small incidents in the early years which resulted in her being placed in a room on her own. Later, when her behaviour improved, none of the other children wanted to share with her, saying she was odd and stared at them. He had spent years trying to talk to the selective mute, with some success, yet in almost ten years he could count the number of times he had heard her speak at any length. Cosgrove exhaled loudly. Tess's family, who were farming in a remote part of County Wicklow, would collect her today and for all he knew she would spend the rest of her life cut off from people, but there was nothing he could do about it.

She was twenty-one years old and, apart from her detached personality and occasional loss of emotional control, she showed no signs of mental illness. He understood a little about her condition, autism, and knew that she had a younger brother with a more severe form of it, but he could never claim to have understood her. All of the children who passed through his office had behaviour problems, most of them due to mental illness, but he felt that Tess had never really belonged here. This saddened the weary psychiatrist and made him wish he could have done more for her over the years.

It worried him that he had never met Tess's siblings. This had spurred him to contact the local GP, who informed him that while Tess's older brother had a drink problem, her sister was a strong, capable woman who would take good care of Tess. Cosgrove wanted to talk to Tess's siblings in person so he phoned. He found Kate Byrne to be a soft-spoken woman whose voice gave the impression of a mildly depressed person and not the strong woman Dr Doyle described her to be and this concerned him a little. This was a big move for Tess and he had to be sure he was doing the best for her. Cosgrove decided to organise for the local community nurse to check in on Tess when she arrived home. That way he would have a pair of eyes within the house to be absolutely sure that she was okay.

When he had told Tess the news, the young woman had stared back at him, absorbing the information and fidgeting with her jumper. Tess had turned into a beautiful woman with porcelain skin framed by thick black hair, her expressionless face making her seem almost doll-like.

"Are you pleased, Tess?" he had asked, smiling at the girl, whose expression had not changed and who continued to stand staring as usual over his shoulder. She did not answer but simply nodded and walked away.

Cosgrove raised his body slowly from his chair and stood there, holding Tess's file tightly in both hands, lost in thought until awakened by the sharp shrill of the exercise yard's bell. He lowered the file slowly into the tall metal filing cabinet. He gently shut the drawer, picked up files on the two new children who had arrived today from his desk and prepared for his rounds.

Dermot Lynch was a serious man who at age thirty had found himself not only landless but also homeless following a dispute between him and his headstrong, domineering father. Despite being long past retirement, Dan Lynch had still been interfering in how his eldest son ran the farm and Dermot had finally had enough.

Dermot thought of going to London or New York or even as far as Sydney. He had family in all those places, but he knew he was not cut out for the building game and definitely not cut out to be cooped up in a factory.

Instead he had come here to Wicklow, where he worked in his aunt and uncle's pub and also worked part-time as a farmhand for the Byrne family. That farm would never be his but at least it kept him in the work he loved. Like his own family farm in Galway, it was a livestock farm. The climate was milder over here in the east with much less rain. He liked it, worked hard, and generally kept out of the way of his employers – not that they bothered him much. The brother, Seán, had a drink problem as far as he could see and rarely helped out. The sister Kate wasn't a bad-looking woman and ran the house, caring for a younger brother, Ben, who never spoke and rocked and hummed to imaginary music. The silence in the house was always palpable and Dermot usually kept his visits to a minimum, eating whatever meal was put in front of him and trying to ignore the boy's staring eyes before darting back out to his work. He couldn't actually say he minded the strange atmosphere at the farm. No one asked him any questions, which suited him fine. The last thing he needed was small-town gossip about how he lost his own farm to a younger brother. It may have been 1981 but things changed slowly in Ireland and he had no wish to be the focus of gossip in the small County Wicklow community that he now called home.

Dermot spent each day in the same way, tending to the livestock, cleaning out barns and going to marts with Seán Byrne whenever he was sober enough to go. This morning, however, was different. Dermot thought it strange that the family did not drive to Dublin themselves to pick up their sister who a little local gossip had informed him "was not all there". He felt uneasy about this task and uncharacteristically wished one of the Byrnes would accompany him. Why weren't they collecting her themselves? Why was she living in an institution? Would she be some kind of nutcase that might attack him on the way back to the farm?

All these questions clouded Dermot's usually calm mind until he arrived at the institution with a throbbing headache and sick stomach. His father would be laughing his head off if he knew what he was doing this morning and the thought of this made Dermot angry.

In the waiting area of the hospital, he shifted uneasily from foot to foot. Eventually a large official-looking man approached him with a smile that looked more nervous than happy.

"Hello, I'm Dr Cosgrove," the man said, shaking Dermot's hand a little too enthusiastically. "I'm a psychiatrist. You must be Seán, Tess's brother?"

Dermot could feel himself turning bright red. He was not used to speaking to educated men like this psychiatrist and the man seemed to be expecting his employer instead.

"Eh, no, I'm – I mean – I work for the Byrnes – they sent me to collect her – Tess, I mean." Dermot recognised the look of shock on the doctor's face and had no idea what else to say.

Eventually, after what seemed like hours, the doctor

spoke. "Are they ill, the family – is something wrong?"

"No," Dermot replied, not knowing what answer would cast his employers in a kind light when he himself thought it downright bad manners not to have come here themselves. "They just asked me to come. I'm Dermot Lynch, I work at the farm . . ." His voice trailed off as he could see the look of disbelief deepening on the doctor's face.

"She does know you though, she's seen you before?" the doctor asked.

"No, sir, eh, Doctor – I just started on the farm a few months back. Do ya want to call them? I mean, check who I am and all that?"

Dr Cosgrove stared incredulously at the young man. He could not believe that Tess's family, knowing her condition, would send a complete stranger to collect her. He suddenly had grave misgivings about releasing her into their care but knew that there was nothing he could do. She was, after all, an adult now and could no longer stay in this section of the institution. She was supposed to be moved into the adult wing once she turned eighteen and he had done everything in his power to prevent this, citing that her disability would make the adult ward unsuitable for her. There were times during her early years when he thought she would end up there and would remain in care for the rest of her life, but she had eventually settled in and he had seen no reason not to release her into the care of her family. Until now. He was aware that the family had not visited over the years and the fact disturbed him though he knew Tess's siblings were under pressure caring for their younger brother and running the farm and that their parents were dead. In reality, Tess could have been returned to her family some years back but they hadn't responded to his requests to attend progress meetings. The older sister sent Tess a present on each birthday and at Christmas but he had often wondered why they couldn't visit even a couple of times a year. But to do this! She needed to see a familiar face, not the face of a stranger he knew she would be afraid of. The doctor ran his fingers through his hair and turned slightly to look around the large foyer, as if an answer lay in one cold corner or another, and then he saw her, packed, waiting, watching.

"Tess! Em, this is Mr, em, I'm sorry, what did you say your name was?"

"Dermot, Dermot Lynch."

"Mr Lynch. He has come to take you home today. How did you get downstairs?"

This was an afterthought. He was always meeting Tess on stairs she shouldn't be on, in rooms she had no access to, staff never knowing how she got there. After many incidents he stopped investigating her whereabouts as she never once went outside the grounds and did not seem to be doing anything wrong. So everyone got used to seeing her anywhere she wasn't meant to be and not finding her where she was expected.

"I'm sorry, Tess. I was expecting your brother or

sister to come. I'm not sure what's happened but I will telephone immediately and ask that they come on another day to collect you."

Tess shook her head at the doctor and walked slowly towards the shy young man.

Dermot felt as though he was on one of those television programmes where a joke was pulled on you and everyone watched you look like a complete idiot.

Dr Cosgrove thought that she didn't understand. "Tess, this is not your brother but I will telephone him to sort this out. I'm sorry, Tess." He knew she had been looking forward to this day.

"I'll go," Tess said flatly.

Dr Cosgrove was taken aback but recovered quickly. "I'm sorry, Tess," he said again and knew that he was not apologising for this mix-up but for the years he had failed her. "Goodbye and keep in touch. If there's anything you need or . . ."

But she was already walking out of the building, sailing past nurses and orderlies who had been part of her life for so many years. She did not look right or left but carried on straight with her suitcase. With ease she climbed up into the truck, pausing only to look for her window from a different angle, from the outside. She had promised herself she would do that although she didn't know why and she pondered this as the truck started up and headed for home.

Árd Glen was a small farming community in the south

west of Wicklow county. Although a beautiful scenic place, surrounded by mountains and lakes, its population count of about three hundred people remained generally unchanged over the years. There was little to do here, most families having small livestock farms, the land too hilly for crops. Spring was busy with new lambs to tend to. Summer brought the usual snippets of tourists, mostly Americans looking for their great-grandfathers' or grandmothers' graves, but in autumn and winter a heavy grey sky descended on the village, confining all within to their memories, good or bad.

It was these memories that made Seán Byrne pace the kitchen floor of the modest house in which his family had lived since he was a baby. The house had a long dark T-shaped hallway. The room to the left of the hall, once a bedroom, was now a sitting room that they rarely used. To the right was Seán and Ben's room. Kate and Tess's room was around the corner to the right at the end of the hallway and faced the small bathroom which Seán had built on to the back of the house, his father being too mean to allow the family such "luxuries" in his lifetime. The kitchen was at the end of the hallway to the left. It was dominated by a large old-fashioned range that had blackened the once whitewashed walls. A small sink stood underneath the window that faced out onto the back yard and was flanked either side by two cupboards, their doors peeling and flaking. An old-fashioned wooden kitchen table and four worn upholstered chairs sat in the middle of the kitchen, using up the limited space.

Seán was proud of the changes he had made to the house and farm as a young man. Preferring farming to school work, he had left the books for the fields at thirteen. His family didn't have the best of reputations in the village and he had worked hard to change this during the late 1960s. But it had all been for nothing. He had spent his youth trying to develop a farm and a reputation that was destroyed faster than a fire spreads through a barn of hay. It was hard to imagine himself now – young, fit and full of hope – but he had been that man. Now he spent his days trying to hide his drinking from the nag his sister had turned into and from the farmhand who, although he said nothing, could see that his employer was an alcoholic. Over the past ten years they had managed to maintain some semblance of normality within the house: Seán working the farm as best he could, if only to keep some money coming in; Kate, resentfully running the house and caring for Ben who would never be a man and who would need to be cared for long after they were both gone. Somehow they had managed. Now, when they seemed to be getting on and putting the past behind them, it had reared its ugly head in the form of their younger sister. Old memories would be stirred up in the village and people would begin talking about it again. Seán could feel his face redden. If only they didn't have to have her back. If only the institution could have kept her there. If only she was fit enough to have lived out her life in Dublin on her own or in one of those residential homes. He had tried to put the nosy psychiatrist off, ignoring letters regarding her wellbeing, not visiting. You'd have thought they'd have got the message. But no. He couldn't very well have said "We don't want her back." It wouldn't have seemed right, would have got people talking just the same.

He could feel the blood rising in his face, not sure himself if it was in anger or shame, when Kate interrupted his thoughts.

"No point dwelling on it, we have to make the best of it. Maybe she'll have changed, mellowed a bit. She was just a child, remember. She might be a good help with the lad. God knows she might understand him better than me."

Kate always knew exactly what he was thinking and even feeling. Kate, always one step ahead of him, cool and calculating, smarter than her older brother by far. Seán looked at his sister who he felt was just like their mother had been, calm and beautiful. He was always conscious of how different he looked to his siblings and parents. He was the only redhead in a raven-haired family. He had green eyes and freckled skin whereas his siblings had blue eyes and clear white skin that neither burned nor tanned. He stared at Kate, envious of her composure. His sister had even more reason to resent Tess's return than he as she was engaged when the "accident", as they liked to refer to it, happened. Kate was a different woman then, popular and about to be married to the eldest Moore son who would eventually inherit a large farm and money with it. But it wasn't just that. She was in love with Noel Moore. His family hadn't been the happiest about it in the beginning but Kate soon won them over, even Noel's mother who had thought there would never be anyone good enough for her eldest son. Her future looked bright and happy but Tess had been waiting in the wings to destroy it all.

Dermot sat uneasily into the driver seat of the battered truck and shot a nervous smile in Tess's direction. She didn't look dangerous. She was small and like her older sister was not bad-looking. Dermot thought that she looked like a younger Kate, with long hair that was so black it made her white skin look even paler than it was. He noticed she did not look at him when he spoke and that her dark blue eyes looked neither happy nor sad. He hadn't realised that he had thought so much about how she would react both to leaving this place and going home but she didn't seem to care much one way or the other and spent the journey staring out of the truck's muddy window.

The silence was making Dermot uneasy.

"Shouldn't take us too long to get back at this time, not much traffic."

No reply.

"You must be looking forward to seeing your family again – it's been a long time."

Silence.

"Do ya not answer someone when they ask you a question?"

"Yes, I do."

"Well, why don't you answer my questions?"

"You didn't ask me a question. 'Shouldn't take us too long to get back at this time, not much traffic' and 'You must be looking forward to seeing your family again, it's been a long time' are not questions."

Dermot stared back at the strange girl, amazed that she had repeated word for word what he had just said and a little annoyed that she was right: he hadn't asked her a question.

"Sorry," he said. "You're right, they weren't questions."

"I know," Tess said coolly and turned her head towards the window.

She didn't want to talk to this man who she had never met before. She wanted to savour every minute of this drive, hoping to get through noisy Dublin city quickly and arrive at the edge of Wicklow with its cool mountains and lakes, hoping they would be as she remembered them. Dermot, sensing this, focused on driving as fast as the law allowed. He wasn't great with people at the best of times and this one was different, impossible to talk to. He couldn't wait to get this job done and get back to what he loved best, tending to animals.

Chapter 2

1970

Summer was always a beautiful time in Árd Glen when most families seemed willing to forget the miserable winter and the hard work of spring, and could relax and enjoy the fruits of their labour. However, the Byrne family was not like most families. For the Byrne family, nothing was ever normal. Maura Byrne had lain in her bed for just over one year, the birth of her last son causing severe depression which had never lifted. The doctors later diagnosed some rare disease where a person becomes old and confused before their time – pre-senile dementia they called it. In the beginning she would walk out of the house in the middle of the night, always looking for something she couldn't put words to. Later, there were no words and she mumbled constantly, sometimes roaring at invisible menaces and finally taking to the bed with Kate and Tess caring for her round the clock. Michael Byrne could always be found in the local pub when Maura needed a doctor. If he were sober enough he would drive his wife to the nearest town where the only doctor in a twenty-mile radius lived. It was a well-known joke among the townspeople that with the amount of vets in the area you would be luckier to be a cow than a human being if you got sick in Árd Glen.

When Maura passed away, only Kate cried. Her father, remorseful, head bowed, smelt of the whiskey he had consumed until the early hours. In her cheap wooden coffin, the one-time local beauty looked nothing like the radiant girl she had once been. Her hair, almost grey, was once raven-black, her dark-blue eyes once surrounded by the palest flawless skin. Now, her face was lined with the worry her married life had brought her, her skin slightly yellow, darkening as the coffin lid slammed shut.

Kate's tears, in truth, were more for herself than her mother. She had silently hoped that her mother would pull through this strange illness and return to her responsibilities around the house. With Maura gone and Tess's problems, what would happen to the baby? She knew that, as good as Noel was, he would not want her to take the child to live with them.

Seán stood erect, lost in his thoughts. His mother had always protected him from his father, protected them all. Now she was gone and he wondered if his father would lose the farm through drink, a farm his mother insisted was rightfully his and was his only chance of a future.

Tess looked around at the small crowd dressed in black. She had never seen some of the people before. She wanted to ask their names as she always liked to know people's names. She listened as the priest chanted prayers from a beautiful black book with gold writing. She wondered how her mother would get out of the large box in front of her when she felt better. She knew it was another question she should not ask and, at age ten, her head was full of such questions. She wondered when her mother would be back as she was the only one who could do her hair just right. No one thought to explain to her that her mother would never be back.

After the funeral, the Byrne children's days were mundane and predictable. Seán tended the farm while their father recovered from the latest hangover. Kate and Tess cared for the house and the baby between them, although Tess did not like looking after Ben and would put her fingers in her ears whenever he screamed. Tess knew that, like herself, the baby did not like to be touched and wondered if he was going to "have problems" like her when he grew up. She knew her family would not like this and that everybody thought she was troublesome. She never quite understood this. She knew she was different but wondered how she was a problem – she worked as hard as Kate, didn't she?

There were things other than the baby's crying that Tess didn't like. She didn't like the smell of whiskey or the way her father acted when he had been drinking. Tess liked things to be predictable but found herself hiding more and more in the barn and humming, which usually made her older sister very angry. Tess knew that Kate wanted to leave, to marry Noel and have her own family, but wasn't this her family? Tess didn't want to look after the baby and didn't want to be left on her own when their father had been drinking. Seán would be no help. He had to keep their father happy, as he had to get the farm when Daddy died. Tess had heard all these conversations going on around her – Kate needs to get married, Seán needs the farm and the baby needs to be lifted up – but nothing ever made much sense to her. She tried to remember all these important facts and behave normally but could not understand why they were important and wanted everything to stay the same. At age ten Tess knew that she did not understand as much as she should. Rare visitors to the house shook their heads at her and said things like "God help you, Kate, you have your hands full" to her sister. But Tess knew that the only one who was a problem was Daddy. He caused Mammy to get sick with a new baby, made Seán have to work hard because he went to the pub at night, and if Mammy hadn't got sick Kate could have got married and there would be no baby to make Tess put her fingers in her ears and get into even more trouble. If Tess could see this and she had "problems", why could no one else see it?

Tess decided it was a sensible question and made her

way to the kitchen where Noel was visiting with his mother and aunt who was a seamstress in Dublin and was going to make Kate's wedding dress.

Kate looked nervous when Tess entered the room as she always did when they had visitors. She never knew what her peculiar sister would say next. The child worked hard and according to the special school she attended she could be a lot more trouble than she was. Sometimes Kate felt sorry for this sister who would almost certainly end up in some home whenever Seán had a mind to marry. Kate couldn't very well take her to live with her. At the very least Kate hoped Seán's wife would care for the baby, but knew there would be no place for poor peculiar Tess. Kate had tried to teach Tess to run the house and care for Ben but had found her more often than not hiding under furniture with her fingers in her ears. All sorts of sounds bothered her – the tractor and even the radio if it wasn't tuned in right. Tess lived by rules she had made up herself – what time to go to bed, what time to sleep, what clothes were only for Sunday. Anyone who knew her well could get Tess to stay quiet for hours by saying it was a new rule. Kate, who found that she always had to tell Tess what to do and when to do it, sighed and softened as her sister stood awkwardly in the doorway, knowing Tess had one of her "questions".

"Yes, Tess, what's your question?"

"When will Daddy die, Kate? How much time longer before Seán gets the farm?"

Kate could feel herself redden. She had told Tess not to come into the kitchen while Mrs Moore was visiting but, even so, it was not like Tess to ask this sort of question. But how could she begin to tell her future mother-in-law and husband that?

"Tess, that's not a very nice thing for you to say. Daddy is still young and Seán would rather Daddy didn't die just so he could get the farm – you know that!"

"No, Kate, you said that we would have to put up with him even when he is drunk so that Seán would get the farm when he dies, remember?"

Kate was caught. One look at Tess's innocent face was worth a thousand words and she could think of nothing to say except to shout loudly "Tess, leave the room please!"

Tess left, her face showing her bewilderment. Kate sat down again and hoped her visitors didn't notice her hands shaking around the teacup. She felt that she had nothing to lose and said, "Poor Tess, she imagines all sorts of things, nightmares and all. I worry about her but it's her condition, the child can't help it."

"I hope it doesn't run in the family," her mother-in-law said all too quickly before settling back down to a strained conversation with her future daughter-in-law.

Kate wasn't to know that this would be the last time that either Mrs Moore or Noel would ever cross her doorstep.

Seán Byrne lay on in bed for the first time since he could

remember. As a child he was always up with the dawn, working on the farm before the dreaded school day began. He did poorly in school but was smart enough to focus on a job he knew he could do and do well. He had heard his father throwing up behind the shed in the early hours, having downed money they could ill afford to spend, but he was powerless to do anything to stop him. Even though the farm had been his mother's, it would not rightfully be his until the old man died. There was no way he would sign it over, retire early and let Seán make his mark. No, his father had somehow always resented him, never missing an opportunity to insult or embarrass him. Seán knew there had been talk in the town that Michael Byrne was not his real father but had married his pregnant mother quickly to avoid scandal, the offer of the farm too good a compensation to refuse. As a child, Seán would hear his father come home drunk, shouting at his mother about how he "wanted a son". His mother, having endured several miscarriages after Kate was born, would lock the bedroom door until he kicked it in. She would go quiet then. Seán had wanted to ask his mother about his conception many times but was too embarrassed to raise such a subject, aware that he had been born only six months after their marriage, the anniversaries of which were never celebrated. In reality he knew that some truths were better left alone. He sensed, even as a small child, that he was her favourite and was somehow more special to her than his siblings.

Seán now knew that at twenty-one he was man enough to run the farm and that the only thing standing between him and his future was the old man. As he lay in his bed he couldn't help but think that if his father had been the one to die and not his poor mother, who had always stood in his corner, life would have been better for everyone.

Jimmy Kelly sat quietly in the bar that he frequented with his son Liam, both lost in thought. Even though Liam was still a teenager, the men looked more like brothers, both tall and thin with black dishevelled hair and skin brown from labouring in all kinds of weather. Jimmy thought of his deceased sister, Maura, and of all the events that led up to her inheriting the farm that should have been his and now his son's, over twenty years ago. He and his sister had been close and were each other's allies in a strict Catholic home which saw them each receiving an almost daily beating for breaking a commandment or committing a sin, even before either of them had made their First Communion and understood such things. The family was unusual for its time in that there were just the two of them when most other families had nine or ten children, and this made them even closer. Jimmy, like a lot of people during the 1940s, had caught tuberculosis and was moved to a sanatorium in Dublin. By the time his ravaged body reached eight stone his father had all but given up on his only son ever recovering. And by the time he did recover, his birthright had been handed over to his sister and her husband.

Maura was dead now and her drunken husband was letting the farm rot. The boy turned out all right, trying, Jimmy supposed, to keep the farm going but a bitter knot twisted in his gut as he looked at his own son Liam beside him, who like himself was done out of his birthright.

Over the years Jimmy had mostly found work in Dublin, working hours too long to come home at night, leaving his wife alone to raise the boy. He blamed himself for the way Liam had turned out as he wasn't around to discipline him and a boy reared by a woman could not turn out right. There had been problems making friends at school and later bullying for which Liam had been expelled at fourteen. Liam was now well known for fighting outside pubs after he'd had more than enough to drink. Although the boy worked hard enough, there was a wild streak in the lad that worried Jimmy.

He gave Liam the nod to finish his pint and, as he finished the last of his, it occurred to him that if only Michael Byrne had died first, he might have convinced Maura to do the right thing and return the land to its rightful owner. He would have sorted her Seán out with some acres. He felt his sister would have seen the sense in it and could not help but feel that the only thing standing between himself and his farm was Michael Byrne.

Chapter 3

1948

During Jimmy's illness his parents remained in Dublin for most of the time, reluctantly leaving the seventeen-year-old Maura to tend the farm with the help of a lad from Dublin, Éamonn McCracken.

Éamonn's mother was born in Árd Glen and had moved to the North following her marriage to a Derry lad she had met in Dublin. When the family came south to finally settle in Dublin, rumour had it that they had to leave Derry in a hurry due to their involvement with the Republican movement.

Maura's father was not keen on Éamonn's family, but thought the lad seemed okay and knew farm work well enough. He would have preferred his neighbour's son, Michael Byrne, to help out but he was busy that summer reclaiming fields on his own father's farm. He would have to settle for Éamonn, who, with his sister

Brigid, spent most summers in Árd Glen with their mother's family and often spent time on the farm with Maura and Jimmy.

For the first few weeks after her father's departure, the rebellious Maura left Éamonn to do all the work himself, riding into town on her bicycle with Brigid, making the most of her new-found freedom. As the weeks passed, however, bored with wandering the one-horse town, she spent more time on the farm helping Éamonn, who despite being raised in Dublin, took to farm life easily. Maura loved to listen to his broad Dublin accent and was attracted to the confident young man. With his red hair and freckled skin, he was not a handsome youth but Maura found herself fascinated by the intensity of the young man, who having just turned eighteen, had earned a scholarship to UCD where he planned to study law, the work this summer helping to pay for his studies. He was going to be the first in his family to go to university. He could talk for hours, and often did, about proper education and housing for the poor and he was passionate about Irish history. When Maura tired of his ranting, she would tease him about being a rebel whereupon he would chase her through the fields as he had done throughout the summers of their childhood.

When Éamonn showed no physical interest in Maura, it was she who, free from her parents' ever-watchful eyes, followed him into the outer field, touched his sunburnt face and kissed him lightly before walking back towards the house. He did not follow. Several days passed with an air of tension between the two, Maura tending to her work near the house and Éamonn avoiding the beautiful young girl whom he had thought about each night since his return to Árd Glen this summer. Three nights later, he left his grandparents' cottage less than a mile away and walked in the midnight blue sky of the summer's night towards Maura's parents' farm.

Éamonn lowered his head as he walked in the door of the small stone cottage which was never locked and, as he opened the door of her bedroom, Maura seemed unperturbed and smiled as though she had been expecting him. He stood awkwardly in the tiny room, wondering how his legs had carried him there and wondering had he lost his mind. He knew old man Kelly well and if he found out about this he'd surely kill him.

Éamonn looked at her and, even in the shadows of the room, she was beautiful. His heart pounded loudly. Maura, still smiling, pulled back the covers and he eased himself into her single bed. His body tensed as it touched hers but not because he had never been with a woman before, even though this was true, but because he had to be sure Maura knew, knew that he always planned to leave.

"Maura, in autumn I have to go to Dublin, to college – it's my dream."

"I know," she said quietly, happy to have almost two more months with him and unconsciously shaking her black hair as if to shake off the doubts that rattled in her head.

"Maura, your father doesn't like me, you know."

"I know. Maybe that's why I do!" she laughed.

The knowledge that her father would definitely disapprove meant she would enjoy the next two months as if they were her last. In the weeks to come she often fantasised that Éamonn was her husband and that they were working this farm together and raising a family. At times she didn't recognise herself for she had never thought of herself in that role, a farmer's wife and mother, and had plans to move to Dublin or London after school, marrying when it suited her and by that she meant not marrying Mr Poor. She felt a little guilty about Jimmy, dying in Dublin while she was committing mortal sins, but those moments were fleeting. The doctors were doing everything they could for him. Maura was changing, the goals of a financially secure marriage no longer that important to her. She could marry Éamonn when his studies finished. She could wait. But some days the dread of him leaving caused her stomach to turn as she rushed for the outside toilet. Love, she thought as she busied herself with neglected household chores before her father's return. Brigid came by less and less, sensing her intrusion on the love-birds. She did not tell her grandparents, though she knew she should, the thrill of being part of such a secret being the most exciting thing that happened to the freckle-faced tomboy all summer. The weeks to October flew by as time does when you are happy,

Maura's father eventually returning to run the farm, leaving his wife in Dublin to hold vigil over Jimmy.

As Éamonn left for university, Maura promised to get to Dublin whenever she could, the excuse of visiting Jimmy perfectly acceptable to her parents. But she was still occasionally getting sick and, when this persisted, a trip to the doctor confirmed her suspicion. Maura was pregnant. Her thoughts twisted between running away to join Éamonn in Dublin or asking for her parents' help until he finished his studies. She didn't want to ruin his dream; getting married now would almost certainly put an end to college for him. She couldn't give the baby up, go into one of those girls' homes and never see the child. Her best option was to go to her parents and plead with them for help. "*Blessed are the merciful*," her father was always saying.

Maura waited until her father was saying his daily rosary to approach him. He was kneeling on a mat beside his bed, the old wooden beads swinging as he murmured continuous identical prayers to God. Maura waited until he began his prayers for the sick and dying in the village, offering up their suffering to the Lord, knowing this was the end of his daily ritual. She crept into his tiny room and stood behind him as he knelt on the stone floor. He was a small, thin man, who had married late in life and at fifty-eight looked much older than his years, his shock of thick white hair seeming at odds with his small physique. He knelt, his blue eyes tightly shut, as he offered up his own suffering to God.

Maura cleared her throat, her heart pounding loudly beneath her thin dress.

"Daddy," she whispered quietly.

"Not now, girl, can't you see I'm saying my prayers? *And forgive us our trespasses as we forgive those who trespass against us* –"

"Sorry, Daddy, I just wanted to talk to you."

He looked at her, his face full of irritation. "What could be important enough to interrupt my prayers, child?"

"I'm in trouble, Daddy."

His eyes seemed to bore right through her. "You mean . . .?"

"I'm . . . I'm going to have a baby."

There. It was out. There was no taking it back now. No running away. She was facing up to any judgement he would pass on her. She closed her eyes and waited for his response. Then she heard a loud noise and, hardly feeling the slap in her shock, fell backwards to the floor. She had not seen him removing the leather belt she and her brother had received so many beatings with and lunging at her.

"Who?" he shouted.

Another slap, then another, the leather making red blistering marks on her skin. Her father was beating her harder than he had done for a very long time.

"Who? By God, you'll tell me if it's the last thing you do!"

Lashed on the back, the legs, her bare arms, Maura

finally fell to the ground, her arms too tired to protect her body any longer. She did not plead or ask him to stop; she knew this would make him worse and it was best to stay quiet until it was over.

Finally, he collapsed beside her and started sobbing.

"What shame have you brought into this house, you filthy whore? Who was it? Who? By God, he'll pay for the shame he's brought on me!"

Maura reeled more from her father's language than from the beating she had endured. She had never heard him use profanity before. He rose from his knees, still sobbing. He tried to catch his breath and, upon standing, swung his belt one last time onto her crumpled body. He stepped over her, putting his belt back on. He walked out of the room and she saw him fixing his jacket and glancing quickly into the mirror that hung roughly on a rusty nail on the wall outside.

He smoothed his hair, put his hat on and left the house; he was almost late for evening Mass.

Maura, who continued to lie on the floor long after he was gone, curled up and whimpered quietly. She knew that her father had complete control over her now and that the only power she had was that she would never tell him who father of her child was.

When Michael Byrne was invited for lunch the following Sunday, Maura was told to stay in her room, her bruised face inappropriate for a visitor to see. She had not been allowed into town or anywhere else for that matter. The following Sunday, Michael called again and the silent Maura was encouraged to "walk out" with him after dinner. Michael never asked about her yellowed cheek and eye and spent time alone with her father in the parlour – "discussing business" he said when Maura asked.

Michael was ten years older than Maura, tall and thin with hair as black as hers. Despite his large, work-roughened hands, he had a soft, almost feminine face and was known to be fonder of a pint than company. Maura's father encouraged Michael to call often, despite Maura's sullen demeanour. She knew or at least suspected what her father was planning. One evening after dinner he stated that she was to marry Michael and give the bastard child a name. There was no discussion, no pleading, nowhere for her to run. She had no way of getting word to Éamonn who would surely come and rescue her. She looked to her mother for protection but found none.

Four weeks later Maura and Michael were married. There was no large reception such as one would have expected for an only daughter. Maura stood silently in her bedroom as her mother fastened the wedding dress and felt tears streaming down her face.

"Mam, I'm sorry. I don't want to –"

"Don't start. You've brought enough trouble on your father. Lucky to be getting married at all and no right whatsoever to be wearing my white dress."

Maura was wearing her mother's wedding dress,

purely because money would not be spent in giving her away.

"We trusted you and look how you've repaid us while your brother is dying in Dublin. What right have you to say you don't want to? It's for the best. You'll see that once you've settled down and the baby is born. Give it a father and a proper home. You don't know how lucky you are. When it's born your father and I will be the laughing stock of this village. If it wasn't for the farm, we would have sent you away!"

She ran from the room, slamming the door behind her, not in anger but because she could not let her only daughter see her tears. She stood for a moment in the hallway, wiping her eyes, and as she entered the kitchen her husband eyed her closely.

"The girl is lucky to have us to support her so I want no nonsense out of you," he said.

Seven people attended the wedding, which was held on a weekday so that people would be in work, children back at school and few people would see Maura entering and leaving the church. Michael's older brother stood as best man and Maura's mother as matron of honour. Maura's father almost ran down the aisle and squeezed her arm painfully as he handed her over to the waiting groom. Michael's parents smiled as she passed, not because they were pleased their son was marrying a pregnant girl, but because he would now have a farm of his own and would not have to leave home for his living.

The ceremony was short, no "Ave Maria", few flowers, no friends and not the groom she had hoped for. As the priest moved through the prayers, Maura could not look at Michael who she had no interest in. Instead she thought of Éamonn. She had protected him by not giving his name up. She would find a way to see him again. She had nothing to lose.

After the ceremony the wedding party went back to Maura's parents' house where they ate sandwiches and Michael and his brother drank too much whiskey and laughed constantly in the corner of the small cold kitchen. Maura looked out of the kitchen window at the approaching winter and felt a loneliness and desperation she had never before felt in her young life. Leaves were falling against the window, making a tapping noise, and Maura imagined it was Éamonn calling to her.

That night, she and Michael slept in her room. They would have to live with her parents until they could build a house of their own. Maura did not want her husband in the bed that she had shared with Éamonn. He did not touch her that night, for which she was grateful. She comforted herself by placing her hands on her stomach where the remnants of her time with Éamonn lay and listened as her husband snored loudly into the night.

Six months later the "premature" baby Seán was born and his large size and bright colouring was marvelled at by the suspicious villagers.

When the wedding was over, Maura's father, believing his son would never recover from his illness, signed the farm over to Maura and her husband for their living. When Jimmy eventually returned home, a weak but recovered man, his inheritance had already been given away. Jimmy had thought Maura's husband would do the right thing and perhaps share the farm but he had refused and Jimmy moved into town, unable to watch what was rightfully his being farmed by someone else. He never forgave Maura for not standing up to her husband and fighting for him, even though he understood she was lucky to have had anyone marry her at all under the circumstances. He took little satisfaction in knowing that his wild, rebellious sister was trapped and had to play happy families with a man who had married her for land.

Chapter 4

1981

Sam Moran sat on the barstool furthest away from the door, sipping his second Paddy of the day. He hated this job, a weekly report on the local cattle mart for the rag of a newspaper he worked for, and usually needed at least two stiff whiskeys to cope with the boredom. Moran was a well-groomed man who always made sure he was smartly dressed, his mousey brown hair always slicked back from his chiselled face, showing his intense deep-brown eyes. He had been a real journalist once, working in London for a large newspaper. There he met his wife, Mona. She was from Wicklow town, the daughter of the local doctor; he was born and bred in Dublin, the eldest son of two street traders. Looking back now he could not see what they had in common. She was pretty then and he guessed he was not bad-looking at that time either. He had plans to go all the way to the top in reporting, maybe even get his own decent column. It didn't matter in England who you were or where you came from. He knew that some Paddies got a hard time in London but he hadn't had much trouble and had settled into the city well. At night, he attended school, planning on finishing with a qualification in journalism. That was before Mona said she was expecting and he was quickly marched up the steps of the local registry office. Two years later, with another baby on the way, he found himself living in a two-room flat with no option but to go begging to her family for help. They moved to Wicklow where her father gave them a site to build the modest three-bedroom home he had now lived in for almost eight years. Like many people he knew, Sam spent hours wondering where it had all gone wrong.

The bar was unusually quiet for mart day. He knew a lot of the local farmers and even though he lived over thirty miles away many considered him a local.

"What's new, Mattie?" he asked the middle-aged publican who he had come to know well.

"Not much, Sam, you know this place. Except that the Byrne girl is supposed to be coming home today – my nephew was sent to collect her. He works part-time at the farm."

"Coming home from where? I mean, is she someone special, a celebrity or something?"

"Hah, a celebrity of sorts you might say. The girl is retarded or something. Smashed her father's head in some years ago at the lake. Been in some loony bin since. It must have been ten or eleven years ago."

"Who is she? Which Byrne family?" Sam could feel his blood pressure rising.

"You know Seán Byrne – he has a farm out on the Dublin road. Her brother. Bit too fond of the beer, you know. Have to send him out of here some nights."

"Yeah," replied Sam, "I know who you mean. Wouldn't say he'd like taking her back, what with the gossip and all."

"Expect not, but I'd say the sister would be in even less of a hurry. Do ya not remember any of this happening? It was all over the newspapers."

"No," Sam replied, remembering glumly the high life he had been living in London at the time. "I think I was still in London then."

Sensing a story coming his way, Sam quickly finished his drink and headed not in the direction of the cattle mart, but towards the Byrne house. He suddenly felt his luck was about to change.

Dermot Lynch thought the Dublin traffic had conspired to make him spend more time with Tess Byrne than he would have liked. He was a quiet man by nature and would rather listen than talk and was always happy to fade into the background. He felt uneasy in Tess's presence. Now that they were on the open road, the quiet inside the truck was disconcerting and he wished she would say something. He decided to ask her a question.

"Eh, you're called Tess, but it's Teresa, isn't it?"

Tess nodded.

"You look a lot like your sister Kate."

No answer. He was making the same mistake. Had to be an actual question.

"Did you make any friends at the hospital?"

"Yes."

Christ, she was hard work! "What were their names?" he asked hopefully

"Leroy Brennan," Tess stated solemnly.

"Leroy, that's unusual." Wrong, not a question – ask again. "Was he foreign – you know, from a different country?"

"He said he was American – his skin was brown," she replied flatly.

"I have family in America. New York. I'd like to go see them some day." Dermot was nervous and was talking more now to Tess than he ever had to any of her family who had employed him for several months.

"Did they send you away?" asked Tess.

"No," replied Dermot, thinking he might have opened a can of worms.

"My family sent me away," said Tess matter-of-factly although Dermot thought he sensed some sadness in her voice.

He stayed silent. He did not want to know his employer's business, did not want to get involved and did not say another word to Tess for the rest of the hour-long journey.

Chapter 5

1971

Summer was here and Árd Glen was transformed into the picture-perfect postcard village Americans dream about visiting upon retirement. A three-hundred-year-old castle ruin dominated the village, once belonging to the Protestant landlord family that owned the majority of the area during English occupation. The ancient stone church was still in use despite being freezing cold and needing constant makeshift repairs by the local men to a leaking roof and a sinking foundation. With such a small population, the building of a new church was not high up on the bishop's to-do list. Apart from three small shops, a post office and three pubs, Árd Glen had nothing to offer a visitor except its beautiful landscape. The village was nestled between large blue mountains and lakes that attracted fisherman from all over the world, many staying in larger towns in Wicklow as the village had no hotel. In summer, Saturday was spent lazily beside the lake by many, with children paddling or trying to catch small fish in improvised fishing nets made of their mothers' old stockings strung tightly over bits of wood and tied with string, only returning home at dinnertime starving and exhausted. In the evening, the men, with a week's work behind them, would sit in whichever pub was their preferred watering hole. Old men would reminisce while the young made great plans for the future, with talk of emigrating and making a new life in America or Australia.

Michael Byrne would sit and listen to the talk but rarely took part. He had no friends and was considered an odd sort. On the rare occasion that he spoke, it was usually to make some outlandish statement, causing those around to stare at him before going back to their pints. Michael did not seem to know how to talk to people and, when strangers entered the pub, Michael would spend the time staring at them until they left and was usually unaware of the effect he had on those around him. He never felt like he fitted in anywhere and the frustration he had felt all his life was dealt with in the usual way: a pint followed by several small ones, followed by more pints until he felt numb, which was the feeling he preferred by far. He was aware though that some locals sneered at him. They knew he had taken advantage of an unfortunate situation in the Kelly household and had married Maura Kelly quickly, inheriting Jimmy Kelly's farm and the man still alive.

Few believed that he was the lad's father. Some went further and doubted he had fathered any of the children for that matter, as Michael was born and reared in Árd Glen and was never known for his interest in the fairer sex.

It was one such Saturday night that found Michael sitting in his usual seat in Mattie Slattery's bar. In the corner he could see his brother-in-law Jimmy talking quietly with his boy, Liam. Jimmy looked up, stared resentfully at his brother-in-law before turning away. Michael did not fully understand Jimmy's look – he rarely knew what people meant unless they said it out straight – but felt uncomfortable enough to get up and find another seat. Maura was dead only nine months and he understood enough to know that people thought he should be at home with his children. His children! He almost laughed out loud at the thought as he settled down for a night's drinking in peace.

Back in the cottage, Kate Byrne was alone in the tiny kitchen. It was after midnight and there was no sign of her father who had being drinking since morning, her future sister-in-law Rose Moore making sure to stop by and let her know that her father had been in Slattery's all day and had been shouting at some tourists who had come in for a drink.

"He's going to ruin everything," Kate said aloud although she was alone in the tiny cottage.

She had put the baby to bed earlier and had not seen

Seán who would normally keep her company at night. Tess went to bed at exactly the same time every night, her need for rituals and rules never fading. Kate was tired; the responsibility of running the house and caring for Ben was taking its toll.

"Why couldn't he just behave until my wedding is over?" she said again to invisible company. She knew he resented her, had always given her and Seán a hard life, running them down no matter what they achieved. He was better with Tess when she was born but was less interested when her problems became noticeable, and she had never, not even once, seen him lift the baby up. Kate could feel the tears well up and wondered why she was feeling so low. She wasn't normally like this; perhaps it was all the worry of the wedding. She was missing her mother who should have been here to see her big day. Small, hot tears started to roll slowly down her pale face.

"Poor Mammy! You would have loved all of this. You would have loved to see me get married!" she cried as she ironed one of the bridesmaid's dresses.

She found herself sobbing louder now and was glad that she was alone in the house. She didn't want to be seen crying – everybody depended on her after all. Everything that had happened in her life seemed to tumble down on her tonight. She sat beside the range, a seat her mother had once occupied. She had cried for her mother at the funeral but somehow tonight her absence seemed more real, seemed much more final. She thought of the awful life they had endured. Her father had often beaten her mother and hit both herself and Seán when they tried to protect her. Just when Kate felt her tears subside a lump rose in her throat, almost choking her, until she felt the years of anger and frustration rise up in her like never before. She heard a loud sound that was neither a scream nor a moan rise from her throat, a sound that seemed to come from some crazed animal. She was angry for Seán, for Tess and for Ben, but mostly for her mother who would never see another day, who would never see Kate's day. Kate's eyes widened as she thought she heard her mother calling her, pleading with her as she had done during the final days of her illness.

"That bastard!" she said aloud. "He ruined her life, he robbed her of being here now, with her children, with me. He'll ruin all of our lives." She wished that her father was dead so that neither she nor her siblings would suffer any more at the hands of Michael Byrne.

With only the glimmer of the street-light to guide him, Michael Byrne made his way down the village's main street towards his farm, the two-mile walk feeling like twenty to his unsteady legs. It was almost four in the morning and he had woken in a ditch on the wrong side of the village. He wondered how he had got there and rose to find his shirt covered in vomit. He remembered that he had felt dizzy and had sat down until the feeling passed. He remembered being thrown out of Slattery's, having had words with his wife's nephew Liam. He had a vague memory of trying to get into Massey's then and having words with Massey himself. He didn't remember anything after that except sitting in this ditch for a rest and thought he must have dozed off. He set out to walk back through the village. He could see streaks of light forming in the sky, the sun trying to rise, still partly hidden by the tall dark-blue mountains that stood on almost every side of the tiny rural village. He had been drinking like this for days and could not see the blood in his vomit which spilled out onto the street outside the graveyard.

Michael walked slowly, stopping each time the pain in his stomach stabbed him. He thought about how he had not eaten all day and how he might get that bitch Kate up to fix something for him when he got home. He continued walking, his hand placed firmly over his stomach.

About a quarter of a mile further, Michael could hear footsteps behind him and turned but could see no one in the dark isolated road. He walked on a few yards but then could hear it again.

"Who's there?" he shouted nervously. He didn't think he believed in ghosts but now that his wife was dead, he briefly wondered if she could haunt him.

Clip clip!

There it was again although it somehow didn't seem as loud. Maybe it was someone going the other way. Had he passed someone in the dark without seeing them? He laughed at his stupidity and kept moving, his stomach having eased slightly.

"Ha! Ghosts! Must be going crazy!"

Michael walked further down the dark road and turned left onto a slip road that led to his farm. There were no houses here and the only lights he could see were the first rays of a new dawn.

He continued on, cursing his pain, with only the darkness of the silent road before him. He heard them again. Footsteps.

"Who the hell is there?"

The footsteps stopped.

Michael, who thought himself a man not easily frightened, quickened his steps, twice slipping on the cow dung that littered the country road.

He swung around again.

"Jesus, come out! God damn you, what do you want?" Michael's new-found bravery surprised him as he felt himself becoming angry. People were usually afraid of him, not the other way around. When no one spoke, Michael started to sprint, fear moving his weak legs, but the footsteps also quickened and became even louder. He decided to run off the road. He could hide in the long grass that surrounded the lakes not far from where he was.

But the footsteps followed him.

"What, for Christ sake, what do you want?" he begged, his bravery now sensibly abandoned.

Michael stood still and decided to throw the

contents of his trousers pockets into the darkness.

"Here, it's all I have!" he shouted.

He had stepped back, ready to run again, when he fell, tumbling down to what he knew was the lake's edge. He was surprised to find himself wondering how he had misjudged it – after all, he knew this place so well – and wondered simultaneously why this fact mattered at all when some lunatic was chasing him in the dark. A hard sharp object stopped his fall. He could hear the water lapping behind his ears and wetness drip down from the back of his head. He touched it and knew that he had hit a rock and that blood was pouring from his head. He felt no pain and lay there, glad that he had not fallen into the lake itself as he had always been afraid of water and could not swim. Michael put one arm out, feeling the water in his right hand and laughed quietly when he realised his luck. He could hear nothing except the water and had decided to move when he saw it, a figure to his left, the shape of a person standing above him.

"Wha' –"

With his word hanging in mid-air, Michael felt the full force of a fist in his face. He tried to move, hands raised, turning his face away from the blow. He felt another fist again at the side of his head and then another until the punches rained down on him. Blood poured down his face and he could not see his attacker. Michael grabbed on tightly to the figure's legs and tried to stand but felt the hard blunt force of a rock in his face. He felt the rock again and fell backwards onto the water's edge. He could hear his attacker panting near him and looked up, trying to wipe his eyes, his hands outstretched. The shadow stood and Michael cowered, thinking he was going to finish him off, but was relieved to hear him running away. He knew his nose was broken and could hear his own laboured, wheezing breathing. The dizziness he had felt earlier returned and he could feel himself losing consciousness as he drifted off beside the cold water's edge.

At half past six in the morning several fishermen had already cast their lines along the lakeshore. The sky was clear blue with hardly a cloud in sight. The lake was actually two separate lakes divided by a long narrow ridge. From the top of nearby hills it looked like a giant blue butterfly with wings outstretched towards the equally blue mountains that almost surrounded the water. The air was still chilly despite the early sunshine and small pockets of mist still hung around damp areas, giving the lake an almost eerie feel. The angling contest that would be held later that morning had already attracted a large group, with some having to move further along the lake toward Árd Glen for a quiet catch.

Tom Healy had moved even further down the lakeshore, the noise from the crowd irritating him. He had fished at the lake since he was a boy and knew all the good spots, and was hoping to win the competition for what would be the second year in a row.

"Wish me luck?" he had said to his wife during one of her "good-luck breakfasts" before setting off. This year he hoped to set a record, catching the biggest trout in the shortest time. As he cast his line, he noticed a young girl standing further along the shore. He hated children near his fishing area; they made too much noise and frightened fish away.

"Hey, go play somewhere else, girl!" he shouted at the child, who ignored him. He wondered what on earth she was doing out at this time of the morning.

Kids today, he thought as he marched toward her, angry that she had ignored him – no respect for elders, won't do anything they're told. He recalled his own grandchildren's weekly visits which irritated him.

As he drew nearer he saw that the girl was standing over something.

"Must be a dead animal," he said aloud when he noticed the swarm of flies around the area. He hoped no one would catch anything in his absence and glanced back to ensure his line was okay.

Peering closer as he approached the spot, he wished he had brought his glasses. Then he realised what she was looking at and fell backwards into the grass before vomiting what remained of his wife's cooking, the hope of catching the biggest fish now far from his mind.

The body of Michael Byrne, bloodied and beaten at the water's edge, was the last thing he had expected to see. Even more shocking was the girl, Tess, standing over her father, a large rock held firmly in her hands.

When Kate Byrne rose from her bed, she was not surprised to find her sister missing from the bedroom. Tess often got up before dawn and slipped out of the window of the room they shared. She would walk down to the lake and spend the entire morning there, only returning at the exact time that her next meal was due. Butterflies fascinated Kate's younger sister and she often spent hours drawing them by the water's edge. As a smaller child, she had convinced Seán to make her a wooden sign for the front gate which she painted butterflies on and named the farm *"Butterfly State"*. Tess had been studying the formation of the Republic of Ireland at school and was amazed that people could make their own country, which is how she saw it. Seán and Kate had laughed and explained to her that countries were always there, that only boundaries were changed, but she didn't believe this. When their father saw the sign, he ripped it off the gate saying it was ridiculous and that they'd be the laughing stock of the town. Since then Tess had slept with the sign beneath her pillow, informing anyone who listened that she would nail it back up when her father was dead.

Kate decided to sit in the kitchen until the rest of the family woke up. She had heard someone moving about in the night and then again in the early hours of the morning. She wasn't sure if it was her father or Seán, like herself, unable to sleep. From the window she could see Seán talking to someone in the distance. She wondered if it was the vet as they had a sick calf and she watched as the two men walked towards the house.

As Seán opened the door into the kitchen, Kate noticed his flushed face and worried expression.

"Kate, this is Sergeant Mullins," he said nervously. "He wants us to come to the station with him."

Before Kate got a chance to ask what was wrong, Seán beckoned for her to stay silent. She quickly dressed Ben and got her coat, leaving a brief note for her sister who would almost surely come to some outlandish conclusion when she arrived back to an empty house.

At the tiny rural station, Kate and Seán sat quietly as the sergeant explained how a fisherman had found their father's body, beaten to death by the lakeside, Tess standing over him with the murder weapon in her hands. He had taken statements from several fishermen at the lake but a team of detectives would now take over the case. He had tried questioning their sister but she had remained silent. He had warned her that her silence would be seen as guilt, to frighten her, but she didn't seem to understand.

Kate sat stunned, waiting for him to finish, her mind trying to grasp what had been said. Eventually she spoke.

"You hardly think Tess did it! No, that's not possible. She must have come upon him like that. She'd never do that, she's harmless. Why would she do it? There's no way. She doesn't understand what's going on around her."

Kate ranted for some minutes while Seán remained completely silent beside her, the baby sensing the anxiety and beginning to cry. She looked at Seán, amazed that he had nothing to say, and gave him a look he couldn't quite understand.

"I gave her every opportunity to tell me what happened but like I said, Miss Byrne, she wouldn't speak."

"She gets like that, you don't understand. She won't speak if she's frightened. It's part of her condition."

"Her condition?"

"She's autistic."

He didn't know what that meant so he wrote "retarded" on his notebook.

"Can I see her please?" Kate asked.

"Okay. Only a few minutes," Mullins replied.

In a small cold room off the main office, Kate sat hugging her sister who squirmed in her arms. She was not allowed to ask Tess about what had happened and a young policeman stood with them there. They would not permit her to take Tess home until the investigation was completed and she sobbed as she left Tess screaming after her and cried all the way home.

About an hour after they reached the cottage, a detective came and took statements from them both. Seán had asked Kate to say they were together all evening. He explained to her that he had sat in the barn with the sick calf into the early hours but that no one could verify this so it was best if they said they were together.

The following day, Kate's head spun when she heard that her Uncle Jimmy had told detectives that Seán had a good reason to have done it, that the old man was holding back on letting the lad run the farm. Kate couldn't understand why he would have said such a thing. Talk like that could have got Seán jailed for life.

The three detectives assigned to the case tried individually to interview Tess but she remained silent. When they mentioned the lake she would put her finger to her lips as if to say "shhh" but no sound came from her mouth. They interviewed four local men who were classed as suspects as they were known to have had a recent gripe with Byrne but they all had alibis. The area around the lake was cordoned off and examined thoroughly. There were so many different sets of smudged footprints that it was impossible to identify individual ones. It was a useless exercise, needle in a haystack, they had said. The post mortem results revealed that although the blows to the head and face contributed to Byrne's death, the actual cause of death was drowning. Detectives couldn't understand how a small child could overpower a grown man. Motive was also an issue. Although they had been informed that Byrne treated his children cruelly, no one felt that the younger daughter had been treated particularly badly.

The following day Tess was moved to Knockbeg station for further questioning and within hours had begun to injure herself, tearing pieces of flesh from her hands and face. The local doctor was called and sedated her. The investigating team was inundated with villagers' statements saying the child was never right. Mrs Moore gave a statement saying that Tess had asked how long before Michael Byrne would die only a week before the murder. Kate didn't need to ask Noel if the wedding was still on as he passed her by in the street, looking down to avoid her cutting eyes. After all, his family could not afford to be mixed up in such a scandal. The evidence against Tess was growing. Eventually the detectives brought in a psychiatrist who interviewed her and felt she had no memory of the crime, possibly because she didn't do it or because she had separated herself from her actions. With no other suspect, Tess was charged with her father's murder. The investigating team decided that they had enough evidence as she was found at the scene with the murder weapon in her hand.

As the Byrne household waited to know what would become of Tess, an invisible wall of suspicion grew between Kate and Seán. Except on rare occasions, they did not speak about it and never asked about each other's whereabouts that night. Neither of them believed Tess had done it and they tried and failed to have her returned to their care. Tess was transferred to a state mental institution in Dublin where she would stay until she was no longer a threat to society. There would be no trial as she was a minor and not accountable for her actions. Tess sat and heard the fat sweaty man say he was her friend and that he would speak for her to the man with the wig. She heard the words "murder", "retarded" and "unaccountable". She could not see Kate in the small room with large brown seats like a church but her sister was there, head bowed and crying in the back row, afraid that Tess would spot her and plead with her to take her home. The man who was wearing the wig said she could not go home, that she needed help, but it was Kate who needed help with the wedding coming up and who was going to look after Ben? She wanted to ask the fat sweaty man if her father was all right but could not speak without feeling tears welling up in her eyes. As she was ushered from the building, Kate ran from the crowd and hugged her tightly, and they stood, both crying, hanging onto each other until gently separated by police.

Tess was driven to a huge building with four levels. She had never seen such a big building before. A large woman in a uniform accompanied them but did not speak or tell Tess her name. A blond man with huge glasses met her at the door. *"Dr Cosgrove"* was written on his name-tag.

"Hello, Teresa. I'm Doctor Cosgrove. The nurse will show you to your room and I'll talk with you a little later, okay?" was all he said.

He tried to pat her on the head but Tess pulled back. She didn't like people touching her and didn't like strange people or places. Kate always said that everywhere is strange "till you get used to it" but this never made Tess any happier. She followed the nurse with frown marks on her face even though she did not look old. She could hear other children shouting, some crying, as she walked gingerly along the long, shiny corridor. She did not like this floor as it looked like you could fall so she started walking on her tiptoes.

The nurse, sensing Tess's tardiness, looked around and shouted loudly, "Come on, you! I haven't got all day!"

Tess placed her fingers in her ears and began to cry as the door of the dormitory closed firmly behind her.

Chapter 6

1981

Dermot Lynch drove the old truck up the gravel driveway towards the Byrne house. His shoulders ached as though he had wrestled a sick cow for half the day and the headache that he had earlier was returning. He thought he would feel relief when he got to the farm but somehow he felt that the worst was yet to come. The back door of the farmhouse did not open, as you would expect when a car pulled up. Instead it remained closed as he walked towards it, carrying Tess's bag which did not seem to have very much in it. Tess stood nervously behind him as he knocked loudly and opened the latch leading into the cottage's small, old-fashioned kitchen. To his surprise, both Kate and Seán Byrne were sitting there, silent, the lad nowhere to be seen.

Dermot stood without speaking until Kate got up and walked towards them. He could feel Tess breathing so heavily on his shirt that she must have been standing right behind him.

"You'll be hungry after that drive," Kate said as if her sister had just gone out for the afternoon. "I'll get you some food."

Tess stared directly at her sister and said nothing, moving her gaze to her brother who pretended to read the newspaper, not looking up at his newly returned sister even once.

It was not the first time that day that Dermot Lynch felt as though someone was having a joke on him.

"Where is the baby?" Tess asked simply.

"He's not a baby any more, Tess," Kate replied flatly. "Ben is nearly thirteen now. He's at school. The bus brings him home every day at four."

Tess was glad Ben was not there when she got home and she hoped he didn't scream any more.

"Come on, Tess, I'll show you where you're sleeping. Same as before –" Kate did not want to discuss the past. In her heart, though, the heart she'd had when her father was killed, she did not believe that Tess could have done it. Now she had lost her faith in most people and tried not to think about what had happened. It was best to let sleeping dogs lie.

Tess followed her sister down the hall and noticed that almost everything was the same except the room where Daddy used to sleep was occupied by two single beds. Kate walked on to the last bedroom which also had two single beds, one at each end of the room, placed underneath two small windows. A small room Tess had never seen before jutted out awkwardly from the right of the long dark hallway – an indoor bathroom with a toilet and bath. Tess covered her eyes as she passed the new room, anxious about the change, but simultaneously glad that she didn't have to go to an outside toilet at night as she had become accustomed to indoor bathrooms in the institution. Dermot Lynch, who was still standing in the Byrne's kitchen, was unsure if he should leave. He normally ate with the Byrnes but felt that he would be intruding tonight. He wanted to ask Seán Byrne if he had gone to the mart that day but knew by his employer's bloodshot eyes that he hadn't.

It doesn't really matter, Dermot thought to himself. Let him do whatever the hell he likes with it, it's his farm. He felt angry although he wasn't sure why. He opened the back door and walked out. Despite the bright sunshine, it was a cold February day and an icy wind had started to whip up brambles that lay around the yard. Dermot pulled his collar up around his ears and headed off towards the shed where he had work to do and thought that if he was a drinking man, he would have had a few tonight.

Sam Moran had just enough time to drive to the newspaper office in Wicklow town before it closed. He had driven by the Byrne place and seen no sign of life. He thought the place looked rundown and old-fashioned, like time had stood still at the farm. Poetry, he thought. He could really make this story like poetry and began practising his headline on the way to meet his boss: *Murderess Returns to Rundown Farm.* Maybe he could have a spooky theme to it. Mattie had told him back at the pub that the girl wasn't right in the head. Nothing much ever happened around here and, now that it had, he was going to make the most of it. All he had to do now was convince his boss that he had a story and that was going to be his biggest challenge. He had worked for Robert Talbot since he returned to Ireland and couldn't say that they had struck up any kind of friendship. Talbot had been talked into giving him a job by Sam's father-in-law, anxious to keep his only daughter where he could keep an eye on her, and more importantly, an eye on Sam.

Talbot found Sam conceited and obnoxious and had a hundred reasons to sack Moran over the years, least of all being his exaggeration of stories. He had built up the small local newspaper on truth and sincerity and Moran had done nothing to uphold this reputation. Talbot, who had planned on retiring this year, found he spent more hours at the office now than ever before, keeping a tight rein on Moran and worrying a little about the decrease in sales. Everywhere in Ireland jobs were being lost and many were leaving for America, Australia and London. A recession was on its way, the papers claimed. Talbot was a little worried, as his newspaper would be passed down to his son, Robert Junior, when he returned home from New York with his young family and Talbot had to make sure there was a newspaper for his son to return home for.

Back in Árd Glen, Dermot Lynch made his way to his aunt's pub where he worked part-time. It was his night on and, although he didn't feel like it, he needed every penny. Inside Slattery's pub, Mattie Slattery was jovial as usual, laughing with customers who were spending hard-earned cash on drink, money that should be going home to wives and countless children. It sickened Dermot. His father had been the same, putting drink before food and as a result he himself had never taken a drink and was saving to buy a small farm of his own some day. He never told anyone this. He knew they'd think he'd never make it, laugh at him. He thought about Tess and how strange she was and he was expecting there to be talk in the pub that night. He couldn't help but be interested in the woman who caused both Seán Byrne and the usually cool Kate to look so nervous, as if they were afraid of her.

At the back of the pub, Jimmy Kelly sat quietly in the snug, out of the way of the talk that would surely be focused on his niece's return. He had told Liam to stay out of the pub that evening, fearing his headstrong son would say something stupid. At the end of the evening he beckoned the young bartender to him. He had a question he wanted answered quietly.

"Dermot, you picked up the young Byrne girl today, didn't you?" he asked.

"Yeah," Dermot replied. He was still relatively new in town and was unaware that Kelly was related to his employers.

"Did she say anything, like . . . does she talk?" he quizzed further.

"Yeah," Dermot replied, "she talks." Then he snatched the two empty glasses off the table and walked abruptly away. It seemed to him that no one was happy to see the poor girl home.

When the pub closed that night and he began to clean up with Mattie, the publican told him the whole story about how Tess had clobbered her father with a rock all those years ago, about how he was a drunk and that no one missed him. Mattie went on to say how Kate Byrne's wedding went down the plug as a result and that Seán Byrne took to the drink. Dermot stayed silent throughout the publican's chatter. He thought of Kate's cancelled wedding and felt he understood her harsh ways a little better. Although she rarely had conversations with him, Dermot liked Kate and thought she was an attractive woman. Dermot also thought of Tess and realised that in the short time he had spent with the girl that day, she didn't seem capable of killing anyone. If she had done it, why?

"Why would she have killed him, Mattie?" It was a sensible question.

"I don't know, son. Funny, never thought about it really, just assumed she did it, being a little strange and all."

The publican went quiet and as he finished counting the day's takings could not stop thinking about that very obvious question that no one seemed to ask. Why?

Sam Moran was in luck as his boss was still at the office, sitting quietly in the back room of the small newspaper business. Robert Talbot, who had been lost in thought, looked up to find Moran grinning, obviously pleased with whatever seedy story he had come across.

"What's up, Moran?"

Sam sat without being asked, his employer's social graces always lost on the Dublin man who had been reared on Dublin's streets with the arse out of his trousers.

"I have a great story, one that will send sales through the roof."

"Hmm," replied Talbot who was not impressed easily and was fully aware of what Moran classed as a good story.

Sam just grinned at him.

"Well, don't just sit there, tell me what it is!" said Talbot impatiently.

By the time Sam finished his act on his boss, Talbot knew that although the story was a little immoral, people would be genuinely interested in the girl. Moran might even be able to interview her or the family. On one side of Talbot's expensive oak desk sat a picture of his son, flanked by his daughter-in-law and grandsons, taken in the tiny New York apartment they rented with no garden for growing boys. He inhaled deeply.

"Okay Moran. You've got the story, only no dirty tricks and the truth, do you hear me?"

Sam was already on his way to the door.

"And I mean it!" Talbot shouted as Sam left the room.

As Sam drove away, it occurred to him that he had no idea what the truth of this story was and would have to play his cards right to get an interview with the girl. He felt excited at this opportunity and also felt sad that here he was panting like a hungry, begging dog to cover a story that would have been routine to him ten years ago. He shook himself, loosening the tension that had built up in his neck on the way to see Talbot. He wondered what would have made the girl kill her father. How could a father mistreat his child enough to make her do that? Sam, who had been heading to his usual local, pulled in and turned the car around, heading towards home, realising that he hadn't seen his children all day.

Chapter 7

1949

After the birth of her first child, Maura Kelly, now Maura Byrne, used to go to Dublin each Saturday to see her brother. With the child on her lap, the young mother endured the rocky two-hour journey to Dublin, the bus stopping off in many small towns and villages along the way. Her weekend was always the same. She would drop Seán off to her friend Brigid McCracken before crossing town to see Jimmy, the fear of her treasured child catching TB too great to take him with her. She would sit with her brother and talk about home, being careful not to mention the fact that her father had signed the farm over to her husband. Maura's parents felt there was no point in upsetting their son who probably wouldn't see Christmas. Maura would then return to Brigid's house where she would spend the night with her old friend.

What Maura did not tell her parents or, for that matter, her husband, was that Brigid shared the two-bedroom house with her brother Éamonn. Not that it would have mattered one bit to Michael Byrne, who spent his Saturdays drinking any money the young couple made.

Each Saturday evening, Brigid would make herself scarce and Maura and Éamonn would make believe they were a family, Maura cooking the evening meal while Éamonn played with his son. They would sit and chat, pretending that they were always together, before making love in Éamonn's bedroom, their child sleeping soundly in the corner in a makeshift cot. In the morning they would walk around St Stephen's Green where Éamonn would talk about his week. They did not attend Mass as Éamonn believed the Church was as responsible as the British government in keeping the Irish Catholics poor and being poor meant other people always had control over you. Maura rarely spoke about her life. There was nothing to tell, at least nothing Éamonn would want to hear but she could listen to him for hours. He was doing well at college and had a part-time job in a solicitor's office on Aaran Quay, hoping to work there full-time after he qualified. He spent any free time he had canvassing for the local Republican Party, sometimes writing articles for their monthly newsletter. Brigid earned an average salary in her job as a secretary and didn't mind supporting her brother, who was surely going to improve support for the Republican movement in Southern Ireland. Though less enthusiastic about the cause than her brother, Brigid helped out whenever she could, collecting donations and attending political meetings and rallies. Sometimes Éamonn would look like he had been beaten up and although Maura worried about this, he would always laugh it off, telling her that the police had done it during a protest.

She also noticed a change in Éamonn's personality. Some weekends he seemed on edge and when pressed would become annoyed with her and show signs of a temper that she had not noticed during their romance in Árd Glen. She tried to put these worries to the back of her mind. Éamonn was her only happiness and they had little time enough together for her to raise her concerns. Each Sunday he would walk her to the bus station in time for the last bus to Wicklow, all the while promising her that some day they would be together. Some day he would make a home for them, to be a family in Dublin. Maura wanted to believe that. She couldn't bear to live out her life with Michael Byrne, whose only redeeming feature was that, despite the fact that they were married almost one year, he had never tried to obtain his marital rights. Maura always lifted Baby Seán's hand and waved as she left behind the life she really wanted, the bus heading towards the life she dreamt of leaving behind.

Chapter 8

1971

Tess Byrne sat uncomfortably in Dr Cosgrove's office. It was cramped with too much furniture and papers hung off the desk at awkward angles that annoyed her. She wanted to move them, to tidy them up but was aware of the doctor's eyes on her.

"You see something interesting on the desk?" he asked.

No response.

Dr Cosgrove had read as much literature as he could on the child's condition but hadn't found any of it particularly useful. He knew that some people with this condition could have bouts of rage and in the weeks she had been at the hospital, she had exhibited some aggressive behaviour but her history to date showed no sign of any serious psychiatric disturbance. Apart from her alleged crime.

"Tess," he said gently, "if you don't talk to me and

explain why you – why you did what you did to your father, I cannot help you to get better and return to your family."

Tess stared at the doctor. He was using too many words, losing her as she was still focusing on the first part of his sentence. What does he want, what's the question?, she asked herself.

Martin Cosgrove sighed. He had brought this child to his office almost every day for three weeks and still had not heard her speak. He was tired and frustrated and had no idea how to get through to her. He leant forward, towards the seated child, anxious not to get too close, aware that this made her uncomfortable.

"Okay, Tess. I'll make a deal with you. I'm going to have to be direct with you because I know you'll understand that better. I want to help you. I need to know why you killed your father, to help you get better. I only want to know why you did it, nothing else. So, Tess, why did you kill your father?"

Silence.

Dr Cosgrove let out a long disappointed sigh and leaned back in the worn leather chair that had been his predecessor's.

"You can go now, Tess. The nurse will take you back to your room."

As Tess walked back to her room, only four words that Dr Cosgrove said stuck in her head.

"*You killed your father.*"

When the door of the large dormitory closed, Tess

crawled under her bed and hunched there, arms wrapped around herself, humming loudly to drown out the sound of the other children and more importantly Dr Cosgrove's words. She couldn't understand why Dr Cosgrove and the police thought she had hurt her father.

When she finally fell asleep she had the same dream that she had on several nights since that morning at the lake. She could see herself walking through the back door of her home. Seán and Kate looked older and were sitting in the kitchen, the hiss of a boiling kettle the only sound to be heard. Neither looked up as she passed through the house. She could not see or hear the baby. Two large coffins rested on her mother's bed. She did not know who was in them and walked slowly towards them. But before she could look into the coffins, a hand grabbed her shoulder and spun her around, to face a man she had seen before, someone who had scared her. The dream always ended there. Tess would wake up, frightened, unable or unwilling to go back asleep. She knew that she had seen this man's face before but did not know where. She knew she was terrified of him but did not know why.

In the morning, Tess dressed slowly and methodically as the other children stared at her ritualistic behaviour. Tess would carefully unfold each item of clothing, all of which had been placed in the exact same order. Her cardigan would always be at the bottom of the pile, being the last item of clothing to go on. Underwear and socks always sat on top, followed by her shirt, then her skirt or a dress in summer. Shoes were always placed neatly under the bed, facing inwards. Sometimes, when the older children were sure she was asleep, they would climb out of bed and move her shoes so that the heels were facing the side of the bed, or turn her clothes pile upside down so that her cardigan was on top instead of her underwear. When Tess would wake to find her clothes disturbed a deep rage would rise from within her. If the culprits were lucky, Tess would tear and claw at herself, removing skin from her lips or fingers as they watched. Occasionally, Tess would attack children in her room, regardless of their size, scratching faces and pulling hair but the damage to herself was always worse. Eventually Tess was placed in a room on her own. She understood that it was punishment for hurting the other girls – the nurse had explained this to her but she didn't care. At home, Kate never touched her clothes or other belongings. Kate knew how upset it made her but no one knew her here. If she couldn't have Kate here in the room with her, she was happy to be on her own.

Kate Byrne rose early and sat nervously in the kitchen, sipping a cup of tea and staring out into the awful weather. The weeks had passed since Tess had been taken away. A doctor named Cosgrove had written to them, initially asking herself and Seán to give Tess a couple of weeks to settle in before visiting and for this Kate was grateful. She had thought about Tess every waking moment since they had taken her away and dreamt that she was crying, pleading with Kate to take her home. The image broke her heart and she decided that, as hard as it was going to be, she would travel to Dublin today to see her sister. Seán had refused to come with her, saying he couldn't cope with it and would mind Ben until she returned.

Despite the late July warmth, it rained heavily and she was soaked by the time she finished the two-mile walk into the village. The early morning bus was not due for fifteen minutes and the village was deserted. Kate stood in a doorway for shelter. Rain had curled her thick black hair and her face glistened. She was worried about how today would go, praying silently that Tess would be all right, would be happy in her new home, but she knew that wouldn't be the case, she knew Tess would cling to her. Silent tears rolled down her face as she waited in the still pouring rain, glad that there was no one else waiting.

As the bus pulled up Kate's heart pounded. There was no going back now. It was empty except for one or two people from neighbouring villages and she chose a seat at the back where the heater was, shivering slightly from the drenching. As the bus rocked and swayed down the narrow country roads towards Dublin she could not get the image of Michael Byrne out of her mind. She did not see him in the morgue, Seán had identified him, but she had built up an image of him in her mind, bloodied and battered by the lake, and could feel herself begin to shake slightly. She couldn't accept that Tess had done such a thing – but if she did, why? A wave of nausea hit her. She had a slight headache and she was feeling weary. Her shoulders ached as she sat and stared out at the misty grey sky, the equally grey road spinning out before her.

When the bus finally arrived in Dublin, Kate had a throbbing headache and the nausea had not improved. The rain had stopped and the sun was desperately trying to shine through heavy grey clouds. From the bus station she walked down Abbey Street, stopping off for a cup of tea on O'Connell Street before walking the rest of the way to the hospital, using the time to ease her mind and decide what to say to Tess if she was upset.

By the time she arrived at the front door of the hospital it had started to rain again. She stood and looked up at the four-story redbrick building whose front entrance was adorned with four large round pillars. She walked up the six stone steps and stood inside the narrow glass door. Dark wooden benches lined the entrance's long corridor which was covered in large shiny black and white tiles. They looked wet and Kate instantly knew that Tess would be afraid to walk on them. A gulp rose from her throat out of nowhere. She held it back and pretended to look at a list of wards on the left-hand side. A porter stood watching her from a distance, as if he knew it was her first time. A family brushed by her carrying a child of about nine who kicked and screamed. He had a strange helmet on his head, like ones hurlers wear. The porter rushed to their aid.

"Tried to get away again, Paul, eh?" he laughed jovially as the child's family members smiled.

"Oh, on a daily basis," a female relative replied nonchalantly.

Kate looked on horrified as the child continued to kick out, nursing staff finally carrying the boy off as the family members slipped quietly out the front door. Kate could hear him scream "Mammy, Mammy!" long after he was out of view. She felt dizzy, the nausea she had felt earlier that morning increasing tenfold. She sat on one of the benches and leant forward, as though she was in pain. Rainwater dripped from her hair and onto her lap. Tears sprang up in her eyes and she lowered her head, hoping no one would notice in the busy foyer. The porter, who had continued to watch her, smiled sympathetically and walked slowly over to her. He had a kind face and looked at her as though he knew exactly what she was thinking, even before she did.

"Need some air, Miss?"

Kate straightened her spine, wiping her face roughly and trying to raise a smile. "Yes, thank you. I think I'll just go outside for a moment. I'll be right back."

"Grand, so, Miss. When you feel better. We're always open."

Kate looked at him quizzically, unsure what he meant, before walking down the steps and out into the fresh air, breathing it in in huge, hungry gulps. She walked down to the long low wall that ran either side of the hospital's front entrance, the walls on the other sides being over twelve feet high. She leant her hand on the moss-covered wall as though to sit but it was wet so she remained in this position for a few moments, unaware of how odd she looked in the busy street. She took another deep breath and straightened herself up. She noticed a small park across the road from the hospital. She crossed the road and sat on a wet bench with her back to the hospital, trying to collect her thoughts as the noise of passing traffic blurred into the distance. She put her head in her hands and sobbed quietly into her handkerchief in the deserted park. She had not expected it to be this hard. After what she felt was about an hour, she stood and turned slowly to look back towards the hospital's entrance. Her sister was somewhere in there, alone and frightened, but she could not bring herself to go back in. She began to slowly walk in the opposite direction. She was glad that she had not told Tess she was coming. She would come back another day when she felt better, she reasoned to herself as she quickened her steps back towards the bus station.

Dr Cosgrove had thought long into the night about his next session with Tess Byrne and as he approached her he felt energised at the prospect of delving into the mind of this autistic girl.

"Good morning, Tess. Do you like your new room?"

Tess nodded, which pleased the psychiatrist. At least it was communication of a sort.

"Tess, I was thinking today that we could talk in the

garden. You must be fed up sitting in my boring office. A change will do us both good."

Tess did not answer but followed the doctor through a maze of identical corridors and out into a courtyard, the door to which he opened with a key from a large bunch.

He had noticed that every few steps she took she moved closer to the wall, hitting her shoulder off it twice before moving into the centre of the corridor again. She repeated this ritual for the entire walk. She also skipped over the black lines of the floor tiles, never once making contact with them. Even though Cosgrove was fascinated by the girl's ritualistic behaviour, he found her silence put him on edge; many of the children he dealt with had a little too much to say. He looked closely at the girl whose eyes did not give anything away. She looked neither frightened by this change nor excited to be outdoors. Her sister had written to him, telling him of her likes and dislikes, but Tess was in a completely new environment now. He had asked Kate Byrne to visit, the brother too, but as yet they had not responded to his invitation. Maybe it was too soon for them, with the father's death and caring for their younger brother. He also guessed that they would be feeling angry with Tess at the loss of their father. Dr Cosgrove had no idea just how wrong he was.

Later that day, Tess stood at the nurses' station with two young nurses, her punishment for biting another child during dinnertime. She watched as they wrote their reports, occasionally glancing at her through narrow slit eyes and eyeing each other. Tess knew the nurses were a little afraid of her although she didn't understand why. She would not have bitten the child if he hadn't torn her drawing and she was being doubly punished because she would not say that she was sorry.

"Apologise, Tess, and you can go back to your room."

Tess scribbled a short note: *No.*

"Go on, Tess, you don't want to sit here with us all evening, do you?"

Another note: *No.*

"Then apologise to Colm, there's a good girl!"

Note: *No.*

"You're missing the movie, Tess."

Note: *I don't care.*

Both nurses sighed and looked at each other, trying to come up with a different tactic. They couldn't stand the girl's staring eyes on them for their entire shift.

"Tess, do you know what apologise means?"

Scribble: *Yes.*

"Tell me what it means."

Scribble: *It means sorry but I didn't do any sorry.*

The nurses sniggered quietly. The child was unusual but she was entertaining at times.

"Do you think Colm should apologise to you, Tess?"

Note: *Yes.*

"How would you like him to apologise?"

Scribble: *Stick my drawing back together.*

"Well now, Tess, you know that's not possible. The drawing is in a thousand pieces. Sometimes people just say that they are sorry."

Sorry is not enough of apologise, Tess wrote quickly. *You have to do something right to make the person better. You have to fix it.*

The younger nurse sighed. She felt sorry for this child but she was extremely stubborn and hard to coax.

"Tess, sometimes people do things that they cannot fix. Do you understand?"

Note: *Yes.*

"Then will you apologise?"

Note: *No.*

The nurses, knowing they were wasting their time, returned to their reports. It would be a very long evening.

Chapter 9

1951

Saturday finally came around again after another week of wishing her life away: Saturday was the day Maura lived for, the day she saw Éamonn and lived her dream of being his wife, mother of his child. This weekend though would be different. Maura quietly dressed Seán for the journey, anxious not to wake her sleeping husband who had been drinking late into the night. She found Michael more aggressive lately, flying off the handle when the child cried and she found herself more regularly shielding the crying infant with her own body when her husband's hangover found Seán's crying too much to cope with. Maura knew that she had to get out of this situation, to take Seán to safety. She had bravely raised the subject with Éamonn in the last few weeks but found him less enthusiastic. He was now in his final year of his degree and he said it would be a shame to waste it by giving it up and going out to a menial job. Maura could see the sense in that. Sure, what would another couple of years matter?

This week though she found out she was pregnant, expecting Éamonn's second child. She had worried about this happening. She'd thought she would panic but her mind was calmer than she'd expected. Éamonn would have to take her to live with him now. She could get a job – mind other children or something after the baby was born. She thought that maybe this was the best thing that could have happened – it would force Éamonn's hand in a way. They would manage; they had each other and what else mattered? Maura packed as many clothes as she could carry as she did not plan on returning. She opened the door and quietly slipped out. As she passed the bedroom window she could hear her husband snoring loudly.

She made her escape, carrying her two-year-old son and her suitcase the entire two-mile-long journey to the village where she could catch the early bus to Dublin.

Éamonn smiled as he met her off the bus and carried her case as they walked arm in arm down the quays. They bought bread in a bakery and laughed when Seán squealed as they fed seagulls that flew low over the Liffey. She waited until they reached the Ha'penny Bridge to tell him that she was pregnant. They both loved the bridge and Maura felt it was their romantic spot, often daydreaming about them both standing there, the sun shining on their happy, smiling faces.

Éamonn stared at her as she broke the news, a look of shock registering on his face.

"No, Maura, you couldn't be!"

His expression frightened the young woman who had come here seeking comfort and reassurance.

"I'm sure," Maura replied wearily, Seán weighing heavily in her arms.

Éamonn stood beside her speechless, staring at her before darting his eyes rapidly from left to right.

"Are you sure it's mine?" he asked a little too quickly.

"Of course, Éamonn, he's never touched me. Not once. I have to leave. He'll kill me."

Maura was reeling from Éamonn's implication that he didn't believe Michael had never had sex with her but decided to say nothing.

"Maura, I can't . . . I can't take you and Seán on . . ."

"Take us on! You make it sound like you'd be doing us a favour! Seán is your son. You promised you'd see us right, take care of us. We can't go back there."

"You have to, at least for now. You'll have to – make him think it's his . . . you know . . ."

Maura's mouth dropped open. He wanted her to have sex with Michael! She felt her knees weaken and tightened her hold onto Seán who was starting to cry at the sound of the raised voices. She looked at Éamonn as if he were a stranger to her.

"Please, Éamonn, you don't know him."

"I'm sorry, Maura. It's too soon, I have my studies, you know and –"

"Éamonn!" she said, her voice raised even louder, the sound of desperation audible. "Listen, Éamonn – he'll kill me, please let me stay!"

Éamonn stood there, silent.

Maura stared back at the man she thought she knew. She waited, hoping he would say something, but he stood there, motionless, his eyes now on the ground. When he eventually looked up at her he had a strange expression on his face, an expression Maura had never seen before, one she did not understand.

"Éamonn," she began, "it'll be all right. I can work. We could live with Brigid until we get a place of our own. I know we can't get married –"

"No! I can't take you. I never could. Don't you get it?" His eyes looked wild, his face red. "This is as much as there'll ever be – this, weekends, that's all I have to offer, Maura. Do you understand?"

Maura took a step back and stared at Éamonn. She put her hand to her mouth, which was moving without speaking, as she tried to make sense of what he was saying. She reached forward and touched his face with her free hand while Seán squirmed and struggled to be set free and allowed to run on the bridge. Her eyes implored him.

"Éamonn! We could –"

"No!" he shouted as he pushed her away, her body knocking off the bridge railings. People were beginning to look at them but neither noticed. "No, Maura, go back, go back to your husband. I have nothing for you!"

He put her case down and took one final look at her, then turned and disappeared into the bustling crowd. She chased after him, shouting his name, pleading, but she could not find him. She climbed onto the railings to get a view of the crowd, awkwardly holding Seán in her arms, but he was nowhere to be seen. He was gone.

She took one last look into the throng, then lifted her case and turned, losing herself in the Saturday shopping crowd. She walked along the quays, carrying Seán. Happy shoppers pushed by her as she made her way toward the bus station in a daze, sweat running down her face and back. Seán screamed with hunger but she did not notice. She crossed the Liffey and gazed down the river to the spot where they had stood only moments before, hoping to see him standing there, looking for her. At Aston Quay she stood and stared into the filthy Liffey water and felt its slow melodious current calling her in, offering to cool her and bring peace to her troubled mind. She had nowhere to go. Michael would surely kill her. Her parents would not protect her. Maura stepped closer to the Liffey wall which was not high on this quay and could be easily climbed. She could no longer hear the traffic, the people, the noise of Dublin around her. Silence enveloped her and she felt a peace she had not felt since before she met Éamonn McCracken. Closer now, her worn black shoes touching the wall. She longed to sleep now, sleep forever where Michael's hands could not find her or Seán, where the baby she carried would float inside her forever, never knowing the pain life brought. Maura raised her left foot onto the wall and stopped, the dream of peace being almost better than the peace that was to come. Tears streamed down her face which was ghostly white beneath her black hair. She imagined herself, rows of colourful flowers floating beside her, her body limp and peaceful. Seán, tranquil, sleeping beside her. Maura lifted her right foot. She thought she heard a voice praying in the distance. She touched her mouth to find the voice was her own. She had not prayed in a long time.

"Hail, Mary, full of grace, the Lord is with thee . . . blessed are thou amongst women and blessed is the fruit of thy womb . . ."

Maura moved her gaze to Seán who had started to cry again. Everything seemed to move more slowly, like it does in a dream. Seán's screams were inaudible at first and she could only see the child's face contorting, his body rocking to and fro in her arms. Slowly his screams pushed their way in front of the peaceful place that beckoned her, becoming louder now, pleading, imploring her. Maura shifted her gaze from her raised foot to the child's face and back to her feet again before collapsing onto the quayside, the screaming child still held tightly in her arms.

When Maura came to, she found two nurses standing over her, one calling for a doctor. Her confused eyes looked around the hospital ward.

"What happened? Where's my baby?"

"Don't worry, love. Your baby's fine. He's down in the nursery being fed. You fainted on the street and bumped your head – a taxi driver brought you in."

"How long have I been here"?

"About four hours. What's your name?"

"Maura Byrne."

"Where are you from?"

"Wicklow, Árd Glen."

"You had no identification on you so we couldn't call your husband. We'll do that for you now."

"No! I mean, it's fine. It's too far and we don't have a phone in the house. If I can just go home, I'll be fine."

"Home! Oh no, love, you'll surely be with us overnight and anyway the doctor wants to speak to your husband. We'll send the local police to tell him you're here."

"No, please, please, just let me go. You don't understand!"

The nurse smiled sympathetically at Maura, nodding all the while but not listening to the poor woman's protests, thinking to herself that the concussion must be worse than the doctor thought. Maura tried to stand but the room spun around her. She could feel something sticky on her forehead and in touching it found she had a large dressing above her right eye.

"The fall – it was a nasty gash but it'll heal fine, don't worry," the nurse said kindly.

Maura was caught. As she lay back onto the stiff

white pillowcase she wished she had done it, had jumped and finished it.

At seven thirty that evening Michael Byrne appeared in the hospital ward, red-faced with anger. He could not get the truck started and had to ask a neighbour to drive him the whole journey. Dr Smith walked Michael over to Maura's bedside, mistaking Maura's frightened look for confusion.

"Well, Mrs Byrne, your husband has finally arrived. You can go home if you wish but you must take it easy. I've explained to your husband that a lot of rest is vital if you are to hold on to the pregnancy. Good luck now and take care."

Maura turned away from Michael, her face red with shame – and fear. She did not need to see her husband's face to know that when they returned to Árd Glen she was in for the beating of her life.

Maura raised her bruised body slowly from her bed. Seán was screaming and she had better get to him before Michael did. As she put on her worn housecoat she caught sight of herself in the mirror that Michael had broken in one of his rages and sobbed quietly as she placed her fingers over her split lip. Both eyes blackened, she looked nothing like the girl she had been less than two years ago. Maura lifted Seán from his cot and pain gripped her as she held him against her ribs which were badly bruised from Michael's punches, each breath bringing a fresh gasp of pain. She carried the screaming toddler into the kitchen and spoon-fed him cold porridge as she stared listlessly into thin air. She could not grasp Éamonn's rejection of her. He loved her, didn't he? He loved their son. So why would he abandon her now? He had promised her they would be a family, together in Dublin. Her mind refused to search further, to see Éamonn differently. She could not bear to reach any conclusions, could not bear to think that she had been a fool and that he had used her. She wasn't ready to face the cold hard facts of her situation. She knew she could do nothing now that Michael knew about the baby. Secretly she had hoped the beating she received last night would cause her to miscarry. After he had beaten her, he stood over her and said "This will be our little secret so don't go telling a soul. Your trips to Dublin are over. You don't leave this house and you don't have anyone in the house unless I say so and you don't have anyone in at all until your face looks better."

At first Maura used to wonder why he would keep her secret, why he would not leave, abandon her. But she knew there was always the farm: land, land, land. That's why he would stay. And by now she had realised that there was another reason. In the time since they had been married he had never touched her and always slept in the other bedroom. Maura felt that Michael had a secret of his own, a secret that meant he would never try to touch her, or any woman. It suited him to remain quiet about her behaviour. He had nothing to gain and everything to lose if he made her conduct public.

They were trapped together with their secrets and shame and Maura felt, for once, that maybe that was all she deserved.

Chapter 10

1981

Kate had risen early and busied herself about the house while she waited for Tess to wake up. Seán had risen even earlier and had left the house without breakfast, which was unusual these days. This was a relief as her brother had truly replaced their father in the house, communication now taking the form of grunting and slamming doors. She found herself frightened of him now where they had once been close, his temper flaring often at Ben who could not help the way he was.

She was nervous and wanted to get her first day with her sister over with as soon as possible. She thought about how shocked she had been to see that Tess had turned into a woman in the ten short years that she was away. She wondered what she had expected her to look like – surely not still a child? But somehow that is exactly what she was expecting, as if her sister's life was somehow frozen just as Kate's had been on the day Michael Byrne died. She had been trapped here on the farm since Tess's departure and she sometimes wondered which of them had been incarcerated, for her life seemed like a sentence of never-ending work and worry.

She thought again of the day she had received the letter from Dr Cosgrove saying that, due to Tess's age, he was no longer able to keep her at the hospital and because he'd had no contact from the family regarding her wellbeing, he would assume that they were not able to offer her a home. He would shortly be contacting the local GP to organise alternative accommodation for her in her home town.

Kate had been horrified. The idea was unthinkable. To have her sister live somewhere in town would be embarrassing and would start tongues wagging but, more importantly, this was Tess's home. She had a right to be here. Besides, Kate had always wanted Tess home but Seán had stood in her way. But now she no longer cared what her brother thought. She would not allow him to dictate to her any longer. She had written immediately to Dr Cosgrove and said that Tess could come home.

Kate, lost in thought, did not hear Tess creep into the room.

"Kate, why did you not come to see me?"

The startled Kate reddened, embarrassed and ashamed. She did not want to tell her sister that she had taken the bus twice to see her but had not been able to go through with it, that she simply did not have the strength to cope with Tess pleading with her to take her home. Kate stood upright and tensed her jaw as though under attack. She looked at her sister who was staring at her, her vacant eyes seeming to look through her.

"I was busy, Tess. There's a lot of work to do here, remember?"

Kate watched as Tess digested this and knew her sister was not satisfied with the response.

"You could have come during the summer when there are no lambs or at Christmas before they come," Tess said innocently although Kate thought she could see something in her sister's usually calm face, an expression she couldn't name.

Kate tensed up even more, her shoulders rising up, her jaw firm, her lower teeth showing slightly.

"I – I found it hard, Tess. I don't expect you to understand, you're too young. It was hard – it –"

"I'm twenty-one," Tess said angrily, frightening Kate slightly and making her move away.

"Yes, Tess, I know you are a woman now. But . . . what are you saying, Tess?"

Tess looked steadily at her sister and did not answer, making Kate more nervous than before.

"Why did you not marry Noel?"

Kate drew a sharp breath. She was not used to being asked such direct questions – at least, not since Tess went into care.

"Didn't they teach you any manners at that place, Tess? You ought to know better now."

Tess, not satisfied with this answer, persisted. "Why did you not marry him?"

Kate turned to face out the window that overlooked the farm's yard, placing dishes in the sink as she thought of what answer she could give her sister.

"He didn't want to. After Daddy died, he never called here again," she replied simply.

Tess stood still, watching her sister's mind stumbling over memories that were, to this day, painful.

"Where is Noel?"

God, the child never gave up. Kate had not expected Tess to have remained so simplistic.

"He's still in Árd Glen, Tess. He married Marion Hynes but she left him a few years ago. Took their two boys to live in England."

Kate was disappointed that she did not feel any fleeting pleasure from Noel Moore's problems. She hated herself for feeling sorry for him. She heard that he had buried himself in his work on the farm, rarely coming to town unless for supplies. She saw him once in a while at Mass with his mother and was always careful to leave before him. After all these years she did not want to see a repeat of the look he had given her the day of her father's funeral. Kate saw pity in Noel's face and she didn't want pity from anyone. Noel had been spineless in the end, sacrificing their happiness for his family's reputation and they had both ended up alone.

Kate turned to look at Tess, trying to figure out what she was thinking but her sister stared back with a blank expression, her head nodding.

"Were you sad, Kate?"

"Yes," Kate replied simply, unwelcome tears springing in her eyes.

Tess stood in the kitchen nodding thoughtfully, digesting her sister's answers before returning to her room to draw.

Sam Moran stood a few yards away from the Byrne house and watched Dermot Lynch drive the battered truck out of the driveway towards town. He had seen Seán Byrne drinking in Slattery's earlier and knew he would not be home until after dark. As Sam approached the farmhouse he could hear a humming noise coming from inside the house and glanced quickly through the kitchen window. He could see a boy sitting on the kitchen floor, rocking and laughing as he repeatedly waved his fingers in front of his eyes.

Sam knocked loudly until a nervous Kate Byrne answered.

"Yes?"

He threw Kate Byrne his handsome smile which usually got him inside places but he could tell at a glance that his charms would not get him anywhere with this woman.

"Hello, Miss, I'm Sam Moran from the *Weekly News*. I heard your sister had come home and –"

Before he got a chance to finish his sentence, the door slammed firmly in his face. This job was going to be harder than he'd thought.

Sam stood alone at the counter of Slattery's pub. It was still quiet, with a few hard drinkers sitting in the snug out of view. He beckoned to Dermot who had just started his usual Saturday night shift at the pub.

"Dermot, you work for the Byrnes, yeah?"

"Yes."

Sam sighed. Another great orator, he thought sarcastically. "What's it like there – I mean, the family?"

"It's fine."

Groan. "The girl, the one that's come home, how's that going?" Sam was smiling as enthusiastically as he could at the sour-faced bartender.

"It's fine." Dermot stood and stared at Moran. He did not want to be rude to his aunt's customers but there was no way he was getting involved in local gossip.

"Is she, is she – you know, mad?"

"No, she is not mad and even if she were it would be none of your business, or mine for that matter – now do ya want a drink or not?"

"Same again then," Sam sighed.

He was used to people blanking him and he would have to find another way of getting his story.

Kate was tired. Having Tess back was exhausting as she

followed her around the house all day, asking questions, trying to fill in the gaps of the past ten years. Kate had found Tess standing over Seán twice that week, staring at him as he slept in a drunken stupor and for some reason it had made her blood turn cold. The questions would start as soon as Tess rose. When did Seán start drinking? Why did Seán start drinking? All perfectly normal questions but Kate hated it. Tess's questions somehow made Kate aware of everything that was wrong with her life and it depressed her. She had questions of her own. She longed to ask Tess about the day their father died but couldn't find the words. A part of her didn't want to know what happened that day yet somehow she felt that knowing the truth would free her, but free her of what she wasn't sure.

When Ben finally fell asleep Kate went into the room that she and Tess now shared. As she put clothes away, she glanced briefly at Tess's paintings which were much darker than before and difficult to understand. As she lifted Tess's most recent painting a small notebook fell from behind it. It was open and Kate read the first page.

<u>Apologise</u>

Seán

Kate

Ben

Kate stood and read the list. She was unsure of what it meant but she felt frightened by it. She walked to the kitchen where Tess sat silently by the range.

"Tess, what is this list for?"

Tess stood quickly and grabbed the notebook from Kate's hand.

"That's my property, Kate! You shouldn't touch it!"

"I know, Tess, but it fell out. What does it mean?"

"You need to apologise, Kate."

"Okay, Tess, I'm sorry for touching your belongings. Will you tell me what it means?"

"No, Kate. It's my secret. It's my job."

"Job? What do you mean, Tess?"

Tess would not answer and Kate felt herself becoming nervous.

"Tess," she said crossly and somewhat loudly, "please tell me what this is about!"

Tess looked toward the floor and started flicking her fingers together. Kate knew their confrontation would not end well and tried to decide whether or not to pursue it.

"Tess, stay calm. Is this something bad, Tess?"

"*It's for apologise!*" she screamed.

"But who? Who has to apologise, Tess?"

"*It's my secret!*" she screamed louder.

Kate looked at Tess in horror. It had been a long time since she witnessed one of these meltdowns and they usually took longer than this to brew. Tess started to bite her hands. Kate ran to the airing cupboard, grabbed a warm sheet and wrapped it around her sister, shushing her and smoothing her hair as Tess's hands flew about hitting herself on the head and body. Kate dragged them both to the floor where they sat until Tess quietened.

"Shhh, it's okay, Tess. I won't ask you any questions. But you can tell me anything that's upsetting you, okay?"

When Tess went to bed Kate sat there alone, thinking about Tess's list. At first she had thought the list referred to Tess trying to make up for what she did to the family but now she wondered if somehow Tess blamed them for what had happened and for her being taken away? If this was true, was she intent on revenge? An image of her father beaten and bloodied flashed into her head. But no, she didn't believe Tess was a violent person, at least not unless someone had done something to her first. But maybe she thought they had betrayed her?

All of these questions whirred around in Kate's head until she was exhausted. She dragged herself to bed with a splitting headache. There was no point in talking to Seán about it; he had barely spoken to Tess since she returned home except to shout at her.

Kate fell asleep and dreamt of Tess, her list, and Dermot Lynch.

Chapter 11

1971

When their father had been buried a few weeks, Seán Byrne ventured into town for much-needed supplies. It was a moment he dreaded. He knew it took a long time for the dust to settle in small towns but in a place like Árd Glen, it could take a lifetime. He drove his father's truck by the church and took a left past the rows of tiny houses to the shop. He wished there was another way to get there but the only road drove right past the people he was trying to avoid. Seán did not want to thank people for their condolences. He couldn't care less that the old man was dead. People knew there was no love lost between them but said their piece anyway and Seán had to suffer their sympathy in two of the town's shops as he picked up shopping for Kate. People looked up from their work as he passed, some tipping their hats and nodding. Women were the worst, holding his hand and crying for his loss. And what loss was he to them? Michael Byrne had terrorised him and his siblings all his life but especially his poor mother. The only real loss in his death, as far as Seán could see, was that Kate's engagement was off. Noel Moore didn't even have the decency to break it to her himself and had not called to the house since the funeral. Coward. Kate had said nothing, dignified to the last, but he had heard her crying late into the night. As he drove back to the farm, he wondered about Tess. He wondered how she was coping, knowing how frightened she'd be in unfamiliar surroundings. He had never had a close relationship with his youngest sister but he did pity her. A lump swelled in his throat. He wanted to go and see her but couldn't bear to see her eyes, accusing, staring and pleading. He would wait for a while, wait until she had settled in a bit.

At home, Kate was also thinking of Tess as she put Ben down for a nap. She normally made Tess's lunch at this time, too early for the rest of the family but her sister had to have lunch at the same time each day. The same lunch too: sliced cheese on two slices of homemade brown bread, no butter, with a cup of tea, no milk.

Kate was missing her unusual sister so much. Tess had been the only female company she had. Many of her friends had fallen by the wayside when her mother became ill and she had little free time to spend with them. She thought about their father, now rotting in his grave. She was glad he was gone.

Kate sat down and hugged a hot cup of tea in her hands. It was still summer but the house felt cold. She had not ventured out since the funeral. She couldn't bear people asking her if she thought Tess did it, if she saw it coming. Two newspapers sent people from Dublin and she had to ask the police to remove them from the front yard. Thankfully the local newspaper respected their privacy and did not write about the murder – but they didn't need to, everybody was talking about it. She shook her head, trying not to think of Tess, alone and frightened in a strange place. She spent every night crying alone in the room they had shared, wondering if her sister was okay. If Tess did do it, Kate wondered, what would have made her do such a thing? Did she think it would make life better for them all? Kate shook her head again. No, she did not believe Tess did something so evil. Someone had murdered their father but who and why? She felt guilty that she had fleeting suspicions about Seán. She didn't like lying to the police that they were together and wondered why Seán wouldn't just say he was with the sick calf, but she had done as he asked and she wondered if she would regret this. It was all so hard to understand.

Kate was surprised that she did not think more about Noel Moore. He had abandoned her when she needed him so she set about hardening her heart towards him. She knew that it would always be just her and Seán now, caring for Ben, and that neither of them would marry. The thought of this neither saddened nor depressed Kate; it was just the way things had turned out. She also knew that it was smarter to accept her fate than fight it, as either way there was nothing she could do.

Tess had been at the hospital for quite a while and neither her sister nor brother had come to see her. Tess thought it must be because they were dead but Dr Cosgrove kept telling her that they were fine, that they just had too much to do on the farm to visit right now. Tess was sure this couldn't be true because Kate had promised to visit her and Kate always kept her promises.

As she sat at her desk in the hospital school, Tess watched closely as a new girl was brought in and put at the next desk which was usually empty as none of the other children would sit beside her. She noticed that the girl had an unusual colour hair, deep red that didn't look like it was real. She had an earring in her nose which was something Tess had never seen before. She wanted to touch it to see how it went into her nose and she wondered if it hurt. She noticed that the new girl had a cough and sniffed every few seconds and found herself copying this after each sniff.

Within seconds, the girl looked up and stared crossly at Tess.

"What's your problem?"

Tess did not answer.

"I said, what's your problem?"

"She doesn't talk!" a voice from the other side of the class shouted. "She's retarded! She just bites!"

The teacher looked up from her book and shouted "Silence!" before returning to her novel, promising herself to give the class more silent work to do when they were finished.

"Are you a retard?" the girl asked, not wanting to pick a fight with a dummy.

Tess did not write the girl a note. She did not know what the word "retard" meant so could not answer the question.

The new girl realised that some of the others were taking an interest in this and she wanted to make an impression; she had to make sure they knew she was tough.

"Well, you better not bite me, or I'll give you something to worry about," she whispered.

This made no sense to Tess who got out of her seat and came closer to the new girl who shrunk back a little.

Tess leant forward, closely inspecting the nose-ring before placing her finger lightly over it, feeling for its entry point.

"What – what are you doing?" the girl asked nervously.

"Just bite her!" a voice said from the other side. "Give her a taste of her own medicine!"

The new girl's lip trembled slightly. "Get away from me!" she demanded but Tess, mesmerised by the ring, could not hear her and leant in closer, trying to pull the nose-ring out.

"*Aahhggh!*" the new girl screamed.

The others moved from their desks and gathered round.

"*Fight, fight, fight!*" they chanted.

The teacher automatically shouted "Silence!" once more from her seat at the top of the large class, unperturbed by the din.

The new girl reached her hand forward and slapped a shocked Tess into reality.

Tess had not heard any of the conversation in the room since she moved from her seat and had no idea why the girl had hit her. She lashed out and held the girl's offending hand firmly before biting down hard and then retreating under her desk for safety. The girl screamed and stood at her desk, screaming for help, while other children tried to drag Tess from her hiding place. The teacher, knowing her reading time was over, moved quickly down the room and grabbed Tess who kicked out and scratched the hands that touched her, including those of two nurses who had come to investigate the noise. Eventually she had to be sedated and carried away by an orderly to her solitary room.

Chapter 12

1981

Kate Byrne heard another knock at the door and opened it swiftly, shouting, "Leave us alone!", only to find a small, fair-haired woman standing white-faced on the doorstep.

"Are you from the newspaper?" Kate asked accusingly.

"No, I'm Nurse O'Connell, from the Health Centre at Knockbeg. I'm here to see Teresa."

"What for?" Kate asked gruffly, not sure if she was any happier with this visitor than she was with the newspaperman.

"Dr Cosgrove asked me to check on her, see how she's settling in," the nurse replied, undaunted by the unwelcome reception she was receiving.

"She's fine, tell him she's fine," Kate said nervously. She hadn't expected the hospital to send people and didn't want this type of attention. It was mostly because of Seán. He hated people visiting the farm and discouraged Kate from inviting neighbours in.

Deirdre O'Connell placed her small foot inside the door that Kate was trying to close.

"Em, if it's all the same to you, I'd like to see her myself, for my report, you know, Mrs –?"

"Miss – eh – Kate. I'm Tess's sister."

Sensing that this woman could cause trouble, Kate swung back the door and, standing to one side, let the diminutive community nurse in.

"Wait here, I'll go get her, she's in her room," she said gruffly, suddenly aware of how Tess's presence was going to disrupt the predictable existence that she and Seán had lived.

Deirdre O'Connell remained standing just inside the front door, in a hall which led into the tiny, old-fashioned kitchen. She looked around and saw that the house was not kept as clean as it could be. She knew there was another autistic child in the family and wondered if the responsibility was wearing on the older sister who had reluctantly let her in. She was used to the half-hearted welcome she got from people. Most people were suspicious of help from the Health Board, especially because it was free.

Deirdre turned to find Tess had come into the room and was standing there, staring at her.

"Hello, Teresa. I'm Nurse O'Connell. Dr Cosgrove asked me to look in on you."

"Look in on me?" Tess asked flatly, turning her head

to one side as she always did when she didn't understand what was said.

"She doesn't understand expressions like that," Kate offered quickly, embarrassed now that she had been so rude to the nurse who was, after all, only doing her job.

"Of course! Sorry. Can I call you Tess?" Deirdre asked

Tess nodded, waiting to hear what "Look in on you" meant.

"What I mean is, I wanted to see how you are," Deirdre went on quickly.

Tess wondered why people had to say things so strangely when there were easier ways to speak.

"Tess, I'm the community nurse for this area and I wonder if it would be all right to visit you from time to time? I have a lot of experience working with people who have –" Deirdre paused, unsure if Tess was aware of her condition and looked to Kate who nodded to her, "– who have autism. Maybe I could call in to see if I can help you in any way . . ."

Tess nodded and walked out of the room, back to her drawing which was nearly finished. On a large piece of paper, placed squarely on the chest of drawers, Tess had drawn Kate standing at the kitchen sink, her eyes looking out into the field. Seán was sitting in a chair beside the range, his back turned to the artist while Ben had no mouth and sat in the corner, staring into space. Through the kitchen window a miniature Dermot was walking towards the house, his face blurred in the distance.

Kate offered the woman a cup of tea, hoping Seán would not come in until she had left.

Deirdre accepted. Kate made the tea and joined her at the table.

"I know it's my first time to meet you but you seem to have your hands full. Is there anything I can do for you?" the nurse asked dutifully.

"No, no, I mean, it's hard sometimes but I'm used to it," said Kate, her head lowering slightly. She was not used to people asking her how she was coping and unexpectedly felt tears welling in her eyes.

"What about your younger brother – he attends school?" the nurse asked, pretending not to notice the woman's tears. She felt she understood her and if Kate Byrne was to fall apart on their first meeting, she knew her pride would get in the way of Deirdre visiting on a regular basis.

"Yes," Kate replied, quickly brushing away the tears before looking straight at the nurse. "He goes every day, a bus picks him up. He turns thirteen in June. He can't do much for himself and now with Tess here . . ." Damn. More tears. What was happening to her? She used to be stronger than this.

"What does Tess do all day?" Deirdre asked.

"She helps me a bit but mostly she wanders around the farm. She likes animals and follows Dermot around – you know, asking questions and that. He works here. She's – she's acting a little strange. I found her trying to open my older brother's mouth when he was sleeping the other day. He roared at her and she ran off. When I asked her about it later she said she wanted to check his teeth! Oh, I don't know. She's so hard to understand sometimes because she can't tell you what she's thinking."

"I could get some help for you, organise someone to come in –"

"No!" Kate said loudly, before lowering her voice, embarrassed. "My brother doesn't like people in the house. He hasn't been the same since our father died."

Deirdre, undaunted, persevered. "I can see if there is any day placement for Tess in the area. If not, perhaps you'd let me visit, give you a hand while I'm passing. I think I can help Tess and perhaps there is some work I can do with Ben. You know, help him become more independent?"

Kate smiled at the nurse. The school had worked with Ben for years and had worked with Tess before that and neither of them seemed to make much progress. Ben, of course, had a more severe form of autism than Tess and Kate did not hold much hope for him as he seemed so much more helpless than Tess ever did. Despite her misgivings she found herself saying yes and thanking the nurse for her interest and as she closed the door she found herself looking forward to her company. Kate had not realised just how lonely she was until now.

Chapter 13

1951

Maura screamed while the local midwife tried to pull thc almost blue baby from her. She had been in labour for over nine hours and the pain had been unbearable, much worse, she was sure, than when she gave birth to Seán. Michael was nowhere to be seen. Once he had fetched the midwife and dropped Seán off to Maura's mother, he had disappcarcd. With one last push, a baby girl gushed out and to the midwife's relief started to cry.

"There you are, Mrs Byrne, a lovely baby girl! I'll go find your husband after I clean you up."

When Maura held the baby in her arms, she felt pangs of guilt as she thought of the early days when she had hoped she would miscarry this beautiful baby.

"She's beautiful! Another redhead! Have ye a name picked for her?" asked the middle-aged midwife who had also delivered Seán.

"Kate," Maura replied quietly, "I'd like to call her Kate. I always liked that name." She stared at her daughter's beautiful face and caressed her dark-red hair as one solitary tear moved slowly down her cheek and onto the sleeping baby's face. "I was that colour too when I was born. I think she'll be as dark as me when she's older," she said more to herself than to the midwife. "Seán's hair was a much brighter red."

When the midwife left and she was alone in the house Maura kissed the sleeping baby, squeezing her lightly for fear that she would vanish.

"You'll never know the pain I've felt being a woman in this world, Kate. I'll teach you all you have to know to survive. You'll be nobody's fool, Kate, and no man will ever lay a hand on you. I'll make you strong if it's the last thing I do in this life." Maura leaned back upon the pillow and fell into a deep sleep, the baby still sleeping soundly in her arms.

When Maura woke it was dark. She got up and placed the baby in the crib that Seán had now outgrown, then went back to bed. An hour later, Michael came home and Maura heard him noisily making tea in the kitchen before coming into the room, banging drawers and wardrobe doors, the smell of whiskey saturating the tiny, stuffy bedroom. Maura sat up and stared into the darkened room, frightened that he would hurt the child. She didn't know what he was looking for and was afraid to speak. After a few seconds, he walked out, banging the door and waking the sleeping baby. Maura rose to pick up the startled baby and heard him bang his bedroom door to settle down to sleep.

Relieved, she dragged her aching body to the kitchen and made herself some tea. As she sat by the cold range, she realised that she had not thought of Éamonn at all this day. She felt numb as she sipped her tea and stared out of the kitchen window into the darkness. Her thoughts of escape were now gone. She had made her mistakes and had to pay the price. Her mother would bring Seán back tomorrow and she would devote her life to bringing up her two children and protecting them as best she could from the husband to whom she was now tied. Michael had married her for her land and was using her indiscretions as currency to protect his own secret, imprisoning and binding them together for better or worse.

Michael Byrne sat in a quiet corner of Slattery's pub, wanting to stay out of sight tonight in particular. The baby had been christened today and it had gone off okay, his naïve father cooing over the little girl as though she really was his grandchild. Michael realised his mother knew better as she eyed him over ham sandwiches and pots of tea in Maura's tiny kitchen. He also noticed how Maura's father would not look him in the eye. Old Man Kelly was no fool and knew that marriage had not tamed his wild daughter. Poor fool, Michael thought. He had got what he wanted, a farm, and if Maura's father thought it was ever going to be a real marriage he was wrong. Even Maura's brother Jimmy, recently returned from the sanatorium in Dublin, knew that he was not the child's father and the polite, strained conversation that took place irritated him. He felt trapped. In any case he found these family get-togethers intolerable and was happiest when roaming the farm alone or in the pub where he was still alone despite the crowd, watching other people live the life that he never quite understood.

Michael had accepted that he would have to take the boy on and play family with the slut his wife had turned out to be but he hadn't counted on more children arriving. He had hoped to settle into a quiet life, Maura happy to hide her illegitimate son in marriage and he happy to have a farm of his own, but now here was another bastard child.

Michael ordered a pint and settled in for the night. He could see Maura's brother Jimmy looking at him, still sore over Michael inheriting the farm that should have been his, had he not got TB. Too bad, thought Michael, no going back on the deal now. He put the creamy head of Guinness to his lips.

At the bar sat Frank Ryan, the local gossip, who was always in the know about what was going on in town and not shy of stirring trouble when an opportunity presented itself.

"Evening, Michael, I see your child got christened today," he said as he elbowed his drinking partner.

"Yes," Michael replied sourly, aware that Ryan was

poking fun at him. Ryan had been to school with Michael. He had sat in the same class with him from age five and knew him well.

"Oh now, you don't sound too excited! Lovely little girl that she is and another redhead! Queer that, with you and Maura both being as dark as can be."

Michael stared at Ryan and said nothing. A few old timers laughed quietly in dark corners and Michael could feel their eyes on him. He didn't like being the centre of attention. He was even less happy when he was the butt of jokes. Weighing up the situation, he finished his drink and headed off to another pub. As he slammed the door behind him, he could hear raucous laughter rise up as though the whole bar was laughing at him.

Inside, the laughter settled and died when Jimmy Kelly came from behind the snug to the counter, customers eyeing his thin, consumption-ravaged body. Everyone fell silent, feeling guilty for mocking Jimmy's sister when the poor man had lost everything.

Jimmy, sensing this, raised his glass and laughed loudly. "To my new niece, may her hair never darken!"

The laughter rose again. Only a slight tinge of guilt rose in Maura's brother's heart. His health was gone, his farm taken from him. His only enjoyment was having a few drinks with the people here in this bar, people he had known all his life and he wasn't going to lose that by standing up for his sister's honour.

Michael Byrne found Massey's pub at the bottom of

the town more welcoming and sat quietly at the bar chasing each pint with a short one, trying unsuccessfully to drown out the laughter of the men in Slattery's. By closing time, he was imagining that they were sitting beside him, taunting him, laughing right into his face.

"What kind of a man are you that you let her off with other men?"

"Who is in charge in your house?"

"Sissy boy, guess who's afraid of girls?"

Taunts from his childhood tormented him as his head whirled from too much whiskey. He found himself mouthing responses, sometimes saying them aloud. People stared at him as he waved his arms at imaginary attackers until the publican finally asked him to leave.

On the road home, the voices became worse than even those he had suffered as a child.

"Idiot!"

"Who's in charge?"

"Show her who the boss is!"

"Yes!" shouted Michael, answering the voices that only he could hear.

"She's lucky you took her. Slut!"

"Damn right, I'll show the bitch who's the man in the house!" Michael spat into the darkness.

When he arrived at the farm, Maura was still awake, sitting on the side of the bed with Kate to her breast. She heard him crash into the pram in the hallway and curse loudly.

"Christ, bitch, I'll teach you!"

Fear gripped her, as she knew his pattern by now.

Michael opened the door and stared at Maura, his eyes seeming to bulge from their sockets. He opened his belt and moved towards her as she cowered on the edge of the bed. Maura thought he was going to beat her and stood quickly, the baby clutched to her. She watched, terrified and confused as he took his clothes off and stood naked in front of her, a sight she had not ever seen in the time they had been married.

"I'll teach you to make a show of me, you whore!"

Maura's mouth opened but no words came out, her mind disbelieving what she realised was about to happen.

"Put that child down," was all he said.

When she did, he moved toward her and dragged her by the hair onto the cold stone floor.

Maura Byrne had not known that a man could do what Michael Byrne had done to her that night. He had not beaten her, there were no bruises to see but he had done something far worse, something she didn't understand. She had thought he wasn't interested in her that way, wasn't interested in any woman. When he finally left the room she sat up. She wet a towel under the kitchen sink and returned to her room, trying painfully to wash away the shame, the humiliation, but it was useless. When morning came she went about her daily routine, fighting back tears while caring for Seán who had become quite demanding since Kate's birth. She could not tell her mother, who would surely say: "You made your bed, now lie in it." She could never imagine saying that to her sleeping daughter. Twice, when she was in town shopping, she took Éamonn's work phone number from her handbag and stood halfway inside the phone box but hung up when the secretary answered. She had hoped he would have contacted her, worked out that she must have had the baby by now. Sometimes she dreamt of him, always dreaming the same dream. He would knock at her door, the sun shining in rays around him as though he were a saint. He wore a white uniform and drove a large car, which was waiting, engine running. She always had make-up on in the dream, hair neatly done, suitcase sitting on the table, packed. But the dream always ended the same. When she looked in the car, expecting to see her children smiling, Michael would be sitting in the back seat, laughing, his head rolling backwards and Éamonn would disappear. On the mornings after the dream she always felt angry, angry that even now she hoped that Éamonn McCracken would come and save her.

The rape she had endured was the first of many such incidents; each attack more vicious than the last until it eventually became a normal part of her life. She wondered about the change in her husband's behaviour and why he did what he did to her but she knew deep down that he had figured out a way to hurt her more than bruises hurt. She didn't cry or wish for someone to save her. She simply drifted off to someplace else and stayed there until he climbed off her and left the room. Then she would repeat the ritual she began on that first night, washing herself as roughly as she could stand it. Maura would then lift her two sleeping children and wrapping her arms about them would simply look at them as she faced another sleepless night.

Chapter 14

1971

Seán Byrne ran his hands through his red mane in exasperation. He had searched everywhere, pulling out drawers and emptying boxes of old papers onto the kitchen floor while a silent Kate stood by, watching. His red face contorted as he tore open envelopes that he was sure would hold his father's will. He did not want to approach Brown & Son, the solicitors in the next town that his family used. He felt it would seem greedy to want to know what was coming to him so soon after his father's death, but he needed to know now. There was little money coming in and he needed to sell some of the livestock and the herd was not officially his yet even though he had represented his drunken father on many occasions at the mart over the years. People knew the farm would automatically be his but rules were rules and proof was what they wanted to see. He would have to visit the solicitors now, ask them to draft a letter to his suppliers until the official reading had taken place.

When every box was upturned Seán sat on the floor and stared at the mess he had made. Even now his father was complicating his life and making him beg for what was rightfully his.

Dr Cosgrove was trying again. Things were not going well for Tess at the institution. She was now confined to a bedroom on her own which, however, did not seem to bother the strange girl one bit. She was no longer permitted to eat her meals in the large canteen but ate with a small heavily supervised group of the institution's most difficult children. Tess still went to the yard each day but was shadowed closely by an orderly and never left alone with other children.

Cosgrove knew that none of these sanctions bothered Tess and that she was in fact relieved to be left alone. The previous session with her in the garden had not gone well and he was beginning to run out of ideas. Noises seemed to worry her and he spent his time trying and failing to reassure her that they were simply birds flying overhead or leaves blowing about in the wind. He decided that for the time being he would not ask her about her father or any of her family for that matter as this upset her greatly. He hoped to get her to speak today and had spent a lot of time researching her condition. He learnt that any questions he did ask her had to be short with no idioms used.

"Hello, Tess. Today we are going to walk wherever you want to walk to in the hospital. You can tell me whatever you like about yourself and you can ask me anything you like also. Okay?"

"Yes."

Cosgrove was shocked but tried not to show it. This was the first time he had heard her speak and he needed to keep her talking.

"What's your favourite colour, Tess?"

"Green."

"Why is green your favourite colour?"

"Because fields are green. I like green fields."

"Do you miss your home, Tess?"

"Yes. Is it my turn to ask you a question?"

"Of course."

"Do butterflies ever turn back into caterpillars?"

"No, Tess, they never do."

"Can you be sure, one hundred per cent sure, of that fact?" she asked in her flat monotone.

"Yes," Cosgrove answered. "It's not possible."

Cosgrove was pleased with himself. To the best of his knowledge, he was the first person Tess had spoken to at the hospital and he felt he was finally getting somewhere. Even if her questions were a little odd, they were communicating. He looked at her face and realised she was not convinced about the butterflies.

"Do you like butterflies, Tess?"

"Yes, more than anything else. The Peacock is my favourite but I also like Small Coppers and Purple

Hairstreaks. I have a book that tells you all about them. I don't like caterpillars. They might hurt me."

Cosgrove was astonished at her vocabulary and fluency but was careful not to show it.

"No, Tess, caterpillars cannot hurt you. I promise."

"I watch butterflies at Butterfly Lake," she said without looking at him.

"I've never heard of Butterfly Lake," he said, hoping for the conversation to flow. "Where is it?"

"It's at the back of our farm, Butterfly State, but I'm not allowed to call it that. My daddy doesn't like that name."

Cosgrove found it interesting that Tess referred to her father in the present tense, as if she didn't accept that he was dead.

"Kate said the lake is not called Butterfly Lake but I've seen butterflies there so I don't think she is correct."

"Well, if you want to call it Butterfly Lake, that's okay, Tess."

She smiled and seemed happy with his response.

"What does Butterfly State mean, Tess?"

"It means my country. I made it."

"You made it?"

"Yes, I have my own Proclamation."

Cosgrove smiled, amazed at all this. "Tell me about your proclamation – how does it go?"

Tess opened her eyes wide, surprised that anyone wanted to hear about it, her brother and sister having often told her that they had heard it before and were sick of listening to it.

"In my Butterfly State, no one is stupid or troublesome. Everyone is pretty, as pretty as Kate is. No one shakes their head at you, even if you are a caterpillar because caterpillars turn into beautiful butterflies some day."

Cosgrove looked at this vulnerable child and smiled sadly at her. Did she see herself as a caterpillar?

"Tess, are you a caterpillar?"

She turned towards him, frowning, her eyes as usual not looking directly at him but over his shoulder. Her tongue seemed to be moving in her mouth as though mouthing an answer that she decided not to give.

"How many questions am I allowed to ask?" she said, changing the subject. Cosgrove's questions had obviously made her feel uncomfortable.

"Why don't we take turns?" he suggested.

Tess nodded. "Why did they bring me here?"

"Because you need help, Tess."

"I can wash and dress myself. I can make tea and look after Ben even when he is crying. I don't need help."

"Not that kind of help, Tess. You need the help a doctor like me can give you by talking to you about the things you've done and finding out why you did them. Then we need to make sure you would never do those things again before you can go home."

"What things?"

"Well, Tess, like what you did to your father."

Tess thought about this for a while, a confused expression spreading across her pale face.

"Dr Cosgrove, if my daddy is dead, how can he be dead again?"

Dr Cosgrove took a deep breath. "Tess, I mean hurting other people when you are discharged from here. Can you tell me if you've ever hurt anyone badly?"

"Yes," Tess breathed quietly. "I pinched Ben because I wanted him to stop screaming."

"Tess. I mean hurt someone more seriously than pinching your brother. Like hurting them so bad that they die. Have you ever hurt anyone like that, Tess?"

"I did. I made a caterpillar die in the garden. He was eating Kate's cabbages."

Dr Cosgrove sighed one of many sighs to come. He realised that either the child had completely separated herself from her violent behaviour, or she simply didn't do it. What he also realised that day was that he was probably never going to know which answer was the right one. Tess Byrne did not have the understanding to answer his questions, her cognitive ability being that of a child much younger.

Cosgrove found himself becoming attached to the child. Her innocence and simplicity saddened him at times; at other times her rigidity frustrated him, but he liked her and deep down he knew he didn't want to know, didn't want to believe that this child could kill.

Seán climbed the steps to the solicitor's offices in Knockbeg and sat patiently on an old wooden chair in the small reception area. A young man opened the door to what had been Mr Brown's office and shook hands with Seán, his face beaming enthusiastically.

"Mr Byrne, I'm Ciaran Brown, Terence Brown's son. My father retired last year. Hope you don't mind dealing with me?"

"No, not at all," the nervous and slightly embarrassed Seán replied.

"What can I do for you?"

Seán looked awkwardly at the polished young solicitor who had obviously had a privileged background and could not help but feel a little resentful of the fresh-faced, university-educated man in front of him.

"My father, Michael Byrne, died recently and I am enquiring about his will," Seán said quietly, blushing as he finished the sentence.

"Yes, I heard about it. I'm sorry for your loss, Mr Byrne but your father took his legal business from us. He moved all of the deeds etc to a Dublin firm. He didn't inform you of this?"

"What? Why, why would he do that?"

"I couldn't say, sorry. I checked the file and he did write a will with us in 1961 but it's void now as he wrote a new one in Dublin and asked us to send on the file to the new solicitor. It's on the quays as I remember. I'll just tell Claire to get the address for you."

"When did he do that?" Seán asked, his head spinning.

"Some months back now," Brown replied matter-of-factly.

Seán's mind went blank as the solicitor spoke to his secretary though a machine on his desk. Within minutes, the young woman who had met him at the door appeared and handed a slip of paper to the waiting lawyer.

"There you are, Mr Byrne. Again, I offer my condolences. If there is anything my firm can do for you, please let me know. We would be happy to handle your legal needs in the future."

Seán did not listen as the young man chattered about how their families had done business for years, how his father knew his grandfather, the late Tom Kelly. Seán heard Ciaran Brown mention his mother – "Lovely woman, I remember her well" – but did not listen to the rest.

Instead he stared down at the piece of paper in his hand and read it aloud.

Roberts and Holford – Attorneys at Law

Aaran Quay – Dublin 1

Seán looked up from the piece of paper, a knot rising in his stomach. He did not have to ask these solicitors to find out why his father had moved firms. There could be no other explanation. His father had done him out of the farm.

When Seán arrived at the Dublin solicitor's office with no appointment, the snooty secretary looked him up and down and sighed heavily as she murmured something down the phone to one of her bosses. Seán looked down at his shoes to see that he was not exactly dressed for such a meeting. His trousers were splattered with mud from the farm. His hair was untidy and he badly needed a shave. But he didn't care. He needed to know what was written in Michael Byrne's will. The offices were well furnished and smelt of strong wood polish. Two large offices stood on either side of the main reception area and were divided by a long narrow corridor. Seán looked down the corridor which seemed to be lined with smaller offices. Phones rang constantly and people buzzed around him.

After some time, a tall grey-haired man looked out of one of the large offices at Seán but seemed to be talking to someone in the room with him. Eventually he came out and offered Seán his large, roughened hands that seemed to have seen plenty of work.

"Hello, Mr Byrne. I'm Paul Roberts, a partner with the firm. Sorry for keeping you waiting. I understand you wanted to know something about your father's will."

While Roberts introduced himself, the man with whom he had been talking came quietly from the room. Seán caught a glimpse of him as he passed – a middle-aged, red-haired man who glanced his way. He was sure he had seen him before but could not place him. He stared after the man who was now hurrying along the brightly lit corridor.

Seán interrupted the solicitor who was still talking.

"Sorry, Mr Roberts. That man, there, I know him from somewhere. Is he from Wicklow?"

"No, Mr Byrne. That's Mr McCracken. He's a Dub through and through. He's one of the solicitors here."

Seán shrugged his shoulders and walked with the solicitor towards his open office. He didn't know any McCrackens.

He sat down uncomfortably in the chair facing the solicitor's desk, his father's death certificate folded roughly in his hand. He cleared his throat nervously and waited until the solicitor, who was leafing through documents, finally spoke.

"Seán, your father first came to this firm a couple of months back. He arranged for all his papers to be sent here from a local solicitor in Wicklow. He wanted to write a new will. I remember him well. At first he was convinced his wife had been in here. He said she was recently deceased and that he had found our business card in her handbag and thought she was 'pulling' something on him. We checked our files but had no record of a Mrs Maura Byrne and told him so."

Seán was amazed to hear his mother had the name of a Dublin solicitor's office in her bag and could think of no reason for her to come all the way to the city to see a solicitor. Maybe she didn't trust Brown & Son but he didn't think that was it.

Roberts was watching Seán carefully.

"The strange thing was, Mr Byrne, that the business card she had was at least fifteen, maybe even twenty years old. We had changed the logo on it twice in that time. She must have had it for a long time. I didn't mention that to Mr Byrne. He was agitated enough as it was."

"Can I ask about the contents of his will?" Seán asked as calmly as he could while his heart pounded loudly in his chest.

"Yes. I can tell you now that he's deceased. You could get this information anyway if you wanted to. I'll read it to you. But I must first tell you that a complication has arisen."

"A complication?" Seán could hardly speak.

"Yes. But let me read this first." Clearing his throat the solicitor began: "*This is the last will dated June 17th, 1971 of me Michael Byrne of Dublin Road, Árd Glen, Co Wicklow HEREBY REVOKING all former wills and Testamentary Dispositions made by me.*

"I give, devise and bequeath all of my estate to my only son, Benedict Byrne, for his own benefit absolutely. I appoint Mr Seán Byrne as the estates manager until Ben is twenty-one years of age. If Benedict does not survive me, I give, devise and bequeath all of my estate to my daughter Teresa Mary Byrne for her own benefit absolutely with Seán Byrne appointed as estate manager until Teresa comes of age."

Roberts watched the colour drain out of the young man's face.

"Mr Byrne, are you okay?"

Seán sat there motionless as though he was paralysed. His mind seemed to be going in slow motion, going over things that had little or nothing to do with what had just been said. Memories of Michael Byrne beating them flashed across his mind. It was clear to Seán now why their father had been so hard on him. He cleared his throat.

"What did his previous will say?"

"Let me see . . . yes, here it is. He wrote it at Brown & Son in 1961. It's pretty much the same except it leaves everything to his only daughter, Teresa."

Seán's eyes opened wide in surprise, the realisation that Kate was not Michael Byrne's daughter shocking him to the core. He had reluctantly suspected that Byrne was not his natural father but was stunned that his mother had borne two children for someone else.

Roberts was not embarrassed at informing Seán that Michael Byrne was not his real father. He had dealt with similar family situations over the years and the lad did not look too shocked by the news so must have had some idea beforehand. He looked sympathetically at the young man whose entire fortune had vanished in one short afternoon and proceeded to tell him the rest of the story.

"Your, em – father seems to have been a rather unsavoury character. I had handled his affairs up until that point but was away when the will was drafted. I asked Mr McCracken to see him when he came in to sign it but he never returned. From the death certificate it looks like he came to a bad end only days later. That explains why he never returned but leaves us with the question of what to do next. An unsigned will is not legal so the previous will is still valid, making your sister

Teresa the legal owner." He paused. "Are the police involved?"

"Yes," he replied flushing. "They think my sister Tess did it. She was – em – found over the body." Seán cringed at discussing such personal family details with this stranger.

"What do you think?" the solicitor asked cautiously. He didn't want his company caught up in a situation like this and had to tread carefully.

"Tess couldn't have known about the will. Anyway, it would have meant nothing to her. She's only eleven and . . . oh, I don't know . . ."

"Didn't the police ask about motive?"

"Yes, but the farm wouldn't have come into it. It was just accepted by all that it would come to me being the eldest son and all . . ."

"And you're sure you knew nothing of your – of Mr Byrne's intentions?"

"No, well, not like that. I knew he resented me but didn't really know why. Now that he has done this I'm not surprised, but I didn't know, that's the truth." Seán decided he had said enough and stood up.

"We'll have to inform the police, you know, of the will," Roberts said cautiously.

"I know," Seán replied as he walked out of the office.

"Thank you, Mr Byrne, and good luck," said the solicitor.

"Byrne? It's not really my name, is it?"

As Seán left the building, from his office window

Éamonn McCracken watched the shy young man as he walked down the steps, his head bent, shoulders hung forward. He did not feel as he thought he should upon seeing his son again. There was no rush of love, no urge to hug him. Instead McCracken felt a deep shame and guilt. He wondered if Seán's life would have been any better if he had done the right thing by Maura all those years ago. He stood and watched his son walk down the quays, the Ha'penny Bridge symbolically visible in the distance.

Chapter 15

1981

Sam Moran found himself yet again at Mattie Slattery's bar, too early in the day for a drink this time but there was information that he knew Mattie would be only too happy to give him. Mattie remembered the case well; it was rare for a murder to happen in the area back then. He remembered the sergeant on duty. Pete Mullins was retired now but still came into Slattery's sometimes. Also, Tom Healy, the man who found the child standing over the body, still lived locally. Mattie said that Healy, who was very old now and deaf as a post, might be willing to talk to Moran. He told Sam about Maura's brother, Jimmy Kelly, informing him that Jimmy was still bitter about losing his farm. He didn't think he'd talk to Sam but he suggested he try to talk to Jimmy's son Liam who was known to be a bit loose-lipped with a few drinks in him.

"What about the girl, Mattie? Do you think she'd talk to me, tell me her side of the story?"

"Ha! You're taking yourself a little too seriously there, Sam. It's worth a try, I suppose, but don't forget I warned you that she's odd. She's never on her own anyway. You'll have to get by the sister to talk to that one!" Mattie laughed as he walked away. Shaking his head at the small-time newspaperman who liked to call himself a journalist.

Dermot Lynch was becoming used to the strange woman he had picked up in Dublin only a few weeks before. Today as he worked in the barn he saw her coming towards him, a quizzical look on her face, and he knew he was in for more of her questions.

"Dermot, where are you from?"

"Galway."

"What is it like?"

"Like here, except it rains more," Dermot replied matter-of-factly. He was already learning to keep his sentences short when talking to Tess. Not that she wasn't smart – she was certainly bright – but he knew that too many words confused her.

"Do you have a girlfriend there?"

"What?"

"A girlfriend, someone you're going to marry?"

"Tess, that's a personal question!" Dermot replied embarrassed.

"You apologise," Tess said quickly. She did not want Dermot to be angry with her.

"Tess, you should say '*I apologise*', not '*you* apologise'."

"I apologise, Dermot," Tess replied, her head bowed.

Dermot, seeing the look of distress on her face, decided to answer her question.

"Tess, some people don't like answering personal questions but I'll answer you. No, I don't have a girlfriend in Galway."

"Do you have one here, in Wicklow?" she asked, her head suddenly rising with interest.

"No, Tess, I have no girlfriend anywhere. Now are you satisfied?"

"Yes," Tess replied as she ran back into the house, leaving Dermot laughing and shaking his head as he got back to his work.

Kate Byrne was busy. Since Seán's health had deteriorated and they'd had to take Dermot Lynch on to manage the farm part-time Kate found herself having to do more and more work on the farm as well as running the house. As she bottle-fed three lambs, Tess hovered around, her head bowed, preparing for yet another round of questions.

"Kate?"

"Yes, Tess?"

"Dermot Lynch doesn't have a girlfriend anywhere."

"Does he not, Tess? Well now, that's very interesting," Kate replied even though she knew that sarcasm would go over Tess's head.

"Do you think he's nice, Kate?"

Kate frowned, feeling suddenly worried. She had not thought of Tess maturing in this way.

"Yes, Tess. I think he's a nice man but he's more suited to a woman my age, you know?"

"Yes." Tess nodded in agreement as she wandered off.

Kate watched her sister as she walked slowly back to the outer field and thought that Tess must be lonely here all day. She felt angry that Seán continued to shout at Tess whenever she tried to talk to him. Kate tried to talk to him about it but all she could get out of him was that he hated Tess's staring eyes. Kate felt it had more to do with Tess owning the farm than her habit of staring. Perhaps Deirdre could suggest something for Tess to do besides hanging around the farm all day. It might even take her mind off Dermot Lynch.

Sam Moran climbed over the broken gate that led into Tom Healy's land. He rarely phoned ahead to ask for an appointment, knowing from experience that most people did not like talking to reporters and that catching them off guard was a much better way to get a story than asking politely if you could visit. A dog barked loudly in the distance, which made Sam nervous, and it became louder as he approached an old stone cottage about a hundred yards back from the gate. Sam hated dogs but he really didn't know why; there were always dogs on the street where he grew up. A psychologist he met in a bar once told him he could have got bitten as a small child and couldn't remember it. Sam didn't really think this was likely – it sounded too alternative to him.

He hoped to talk to Sergeant Mullins as soon as he had spoken with Healy. He needed to know exactly what the girl said when she was detained. By the time Sam arrived at the cottage his good leather shoes were covered in cow dung. To his relief the dog was tied up with just enough rope to enable visitors to knock at the door safely. An old man appeared after what felt like hours, the dog continuing to bark and pull at the rope that prevented him from getting to Moran who stood sweating at the back door.

The door creaked as Tom Healy finally opened it, peering out through bloodshot eyes.

He was now eighty-two years old and had given up fishing years before. His eyesight was bad and had not improved despite two cataract operations in Dublin. His wife had died suddenly eight years previously. He went fishing early one morning, leaving her asleep in the bed they had shared for over fifty years. When he came home he was surprised to find her still in bed. There was a faint smile on her ice-cold lips and as he kissed her for the last time he hoped she had been thinking of him. It had been a good marriage and they'd had nine children together, losing two in infancy. Tom never drank and never raised his hand to his wife or children and he believed that was why their life had been so happy. Tom's sons and daughters lived all over the world now with only one daughter living locally. They wrote often and sent pictures of their families from Melbourne, Auckland and Toronto. He had never visited because he didn't like the idea of flying and had only been to London once by boat for his older brother's wedding over fifty years ago. He had lived a simple life. The small farm he had inherited from a bachelor uncle did not bring in enough to feed his large family so Tom often worked in Dublin on the building sites when his eldest son was big enough to look after the livestock. He had missed Doreen so much in those days and could still remember the loneliness of being away from her, how it had a smell of its own. He felt that way now, since Doreen went, and even felt that way in a crowd of people. All people seemed to say was "You'll get over it in time, Tom." He didn't want to get over Doreen and had come to prefer to be left alone, to be left to go over the memories they shared. He could remember her better that way.

"Yes?" he asked Sam.

Sam thought the old man looked as if he'd been crying.

"Hello. I'm Sam Moran. I work for the –"

"You're not from the police, are you? My daughter told me the Byrne girl was home. Why can't you just leave well enough alone?"

"No, Mr Healy. I'm a reporter actually. I'm doing a story on the murder and I'm trying to find out what happened back then. I heard you were a witness to the scene. I thought you might remember something."

"Remember? What the hell does that mean? You think because I'm old that I've lost my wits! I remember all right but I still say leave well enough alone. I gave my statement to the police at the time. Girl paid the price, didn't she, so why don't you leave well enough alone?"

Sam stood at the door silently. He hadn't expected the old man to be so firm and didn't want to have to argue his case.

"Sir, I just want to tell the girl's side of it. See that her story gets heard, you know?"

"Well then, son, go ask her," the old man said as he slammed the door with full force into the reporter's face.

Sam walked away, his self-esteem only slightly damaged. If he hurried, he would make it to Mullins' house before lunch.

Sam walked confidently to the front door of the retired sergeant's home and knocked loudly.

"Come in!" a voice shouted loudly from within the tiny house, which was situated on a small side road to the left of the town's main street.

Sam turned the key, which was tied to a piece of old twine and left permanently in the front door. He was surprised that the ex-sergeant took such risks. Árd Glen was still a relatively safe place but Moran wouldn't go as far as to leave the key in the door. His wife was always telling him it was his Dublin upbringing but he denied this. He was simply a cautious man who admitted to seeing the worst in the human race.

Sergeant Peter Mullins sat slumped in a worn armchair in the kitchen. The walls were blackened from the range and an old oilcloth covered the kitchen table, still dirty from whatever meagre lunch he had prepared for himself. A white plastic television sat on a small table in the corner but was not plugged in and there was no radio to be seen. The small dog that sat by the old man's feet watched Moran carefully and snarled occasionally.

Great, thought Sam – another bloody dog to contend with.

"Does he bite?" he asked nervously.

"Not unless I tell him to," the retired sergeant answered, so straight-faced that Sam wasn't sure if he was joking or not.

From the sergeant's slumped figure and the smell of whiskey from his breath, Sam could see he had wasted his money buying the sweetener of a bottle of Jameson on his way over. Slattery had told him that Mullins was an alcoholic, often drinking alone in the house and in the daytime too. Sam could see that this information was right as Mullins was well oiled. This should be an easy interview, he thought to himself shamelessly.

"Sergeant Mullins, I'm Sam Moran from the *Weekly News*. I'm doing a story on the Byrne girl. She was released recently and I wanted to –"

"For a start, son, I'm retired now so call me Pete. Also, you cannot say released as she was admitted to a hospital, not a prison. She was only eleven years old, remember. You ever hear of a child going to jail?"

"Well, no, I didn't, but she was guilty, yes?"

"Who knows? She was found there, just standing and staring the witness said. At the time Healy said she seemed more interested in the piece of granite in her hands than the body she stood over. Infatuated with shiny things, I believe. You know she's retarded?"

"Yes. Some form of autism?"

"Yeah, something like that. My sister was teaching at the school the girl went to at the time and said she couldn't believe it, said she was a lovely child, smart too, working on normal books and all. Dymphna, which is my sister's name, said the girl was like locked inside herself or something like that. But she said she was harmless, more interested in collecting the strangest of things – like, one week it would be feathers from the farm, another week it could be coloured stones from the field – nearly drove that sister of hers crazy."

"But who else would have wanted to kill Michael Byrne?" Sam asked, hating the way the story was taking a different twist, preferring to think that he had it all sewn up.

Mullins sat up in his chair and leant forward. "This is confidential, right?" He was not quite drunk enough to make a fool of himself. He hated retirement and had not adjusted to the boredom it brought. People used to respect him and he had been an important man in the town. He had never married. He had never met anyone he felt that strongly about so the job became his life. He had worked every Christmas since he came to this part of Wicklow, letting the younger policeman off to his family. Not that much ever happened around here, mostly drunk and disorderly charges and the odd theft. He had a sister who had married locally but he had never got along with her husband so did not visit her often. Now that he was retired, his two nephews dropped in from time to time but it was too late to form any kind of a bond with them and he spent most of his time alone.

"Oh, absolutely!" Sam replied, knowing that if he did print anything Mullins said, he could claim the old man was drunk and never asked him to keep it confidential.

"Well, I'd say there were a lot of people who weren't sorry to hear about Byrne. There was Jimmy Kelly for a start. He was due to get that farm but Byrne pulled it out from under him, Jimmy's son too, for that matter. Byrne's own son Seán was a suspect but he had an alibi – he was with the sister Kate around the time of the murder. Seán and the old man never got along, chalk and cheese as they say."

"Would anyone else have done it, I mean, apart from the family?"

"He wasn't liked, that's for sure, but I can't think of anyone who would have wanted to murder him. He was always starting rows in the pub. I was called in a few times over the years, had to caution him, but he never seemed to care what people thought of him. He was a strange sort of man. I guess that's why the kids had the problems they did – must have got it from him."

Pete Mullins went quiet for a while as though he was trying to decide whether or not to go any further. Moran, sensing this, topped up the sergeant's glass, declining one for himself. He needed to remember all he was told today. He might not get anyone else so willing.

"You know, I've never been one for gossip but there was talk over the years that his wife, Maura, was a little bit on the wild side if you know what I mean."

Sam pretended he didn't. He needed to hear it straight from the horse's mouth.

"Well," Mullins went on, looking around the room as though someone might hear him, "it was said that she was pregnant when Byrne married her. I wasn't stationed here then, didn't come to Árd Glen until '51. People said it wasn't his. That would have been Seán, the eldest, which I suppose is why he resented the lad. Anyway, as I said, it's all gossip."

"Why would he have married her then, if the child wasn't his?" Moran asked as innocently as he could.

"Why? Ah lad, easy knowing you're a city boy! Land, of course. Not a bad farm they have there. I'm from a farming background myself. The lad has let it run down now over the years, turned into a drunk. Hate to see that in a young man."

Sam smiled to himself, the irony not lost on him. "Whose was it then, if not Byrne's? Why didn't the father marry her?"

"Nobody local, that's for sure. If you had known her old man you'd understand why. A right tyrant. I heard that he used to beat herself and her brother black and blue and then show up for Mass, rosary beads and all."

Moran was intrigued. A pregnancy outside marriage would have been a scandal back then.

"Anything else you can think of, Pete?"

"No, just that it never felt right, the girl being accused of it and all. Of course the investigation was out of our hands. A homicide team handled it – three of them there were, caused a real upset in the village. I understood their conclusion, even if I didn't agree with it. After all she was found standing over the body, the rock in her hand and blood on her dress – but it was all too convenient if you ask me. I told them so at the time. I mean, what murderer stands around admiring a rock when they should be miles away from the scene of the crime?"

"Can you remember the names of the investigating crew?"

"Em . . . oh, they'd mostly be retired by now, if not dead from working in Dublin. It was dangerous even back then!"

Sam didn't take the insult to his native city to heart.

"The youngest chap," Mullins went on, "Flynn I think his name was – sorry, can't remember his first name – I'd say he's still working. They were all stationed in Beech Street."

"What do *you* think, Pete, what really happened?"

Pete sighed heavily and looked over at the blackened

wall. "What I really think, and not that it made much difference to the Dublin crew, was that she just happened upon him. I interviewed her first and she was the calmest murderer I ever saw. Okay, admittedly I didn't see many in my years but she didn't understand a word I said. She even wrote me a note asking me if she could have the rock back – she liked the shiny bits in it. Can you believe that?"

Mullins sat still, his head lowering gradually. Sam thought the old man was thinking and waited for him to continue before realising he had fallen asleep, the half bottle of whiskey obviously taking its toll. Before he left, he took the bottle he had brought with him and put it into the inside pocket of his jacket. Opening the door slowly he slipped out and wondered if the old man would even remember talking to him.

Chapter 16

1971

Tess Byrne sat at her desk in the institution's school trying to write an essay titled "If I had three wishes". She did not enjoy these exercises as she did not believe that tooth fairies or leprechauns existed but she knew she would be in trouble if she didn't do her work. She told the teacher that she could not write stories but she didn't believe her and once smacked Tess across the hand with a ruler for defiant behaviour. It occurred to Tess to bite the teacher but Dr Cosgrove had told her that every time she did this, she moved six steps away from going home. She had worked out that she had stopped herself from biting people approximately sixteen times in the past few weeks which must mean that she was ninety-six steps closer to home. She did not know how many steps it would take to get home but ninety-six seemed like it would take her a good way there. Even though Tess could not write essays, she could paint well which she believed was like a story and she wondered why she wasn't allowed to draw her stories. The words would never come to her mind, no matter how much she begged them to. She even slapped her own face twice at her desk which was at the back of the room hoping the words would come but they hadn't. She sighed and put pen to paper, the teacher eyeing her, ready for trouble.

My Three Wishes
To go home
A happy face for Seán and Kate
A voice for Ben

When the teacher came around to read Tess's work she didn't ask her why she didn't write complete sentences but sighed heavily. "Another list, Tess?" was all she said as she walked away from her most troublesome pupil.

Seán drove slowly back to Árd Glen with only one thing on his mind, telling Kate that Michael Byrne was not their father. In a way he realised that he always knew but he couldn't face up to the fact that his mother was unfaithful in her marriage, regardless of what Michael Byrne had been like. His mother always seemed so respectable and he found it hard to think of her carrying on in that way. Seán had worked out that Michael had married Maura when she was pregnant with him but somehow she had become pregnant again. But to whom? Who was his and Kate's father? Why hadn't he married their mother and saved her from the life of torment Byrne had subjected her to? How had his mother access to another man? In Seán's memory his mother rarely went out. She went to the village for shopping and sometimes to Mass on Sunday but otherwise it was unusual for her to venture out alone. None of this made any sense. His grandparents were dead now so he couldn't ask them about it and he certainly wasn't going to approach his Uncle Jimmy who had tried to make out to the police that Seán was involved in Michael Byrne's death. He remembered a woman at his mother's funeral whom he had never seen before. She was crying and some local people seemed to know her but he had never asked her name. He had caught her staring at him a few times but had not approached her. Maybe someone in the village knew who she was; he could get away with asking about her without raising any suspicion. There was also the matter of the will. If the last will wasn't legal, Tess was the rightful owner of the farm with Seán only permitted an income from its management. He had to talk to Kate. She would know what to do.

Dr Cosgrove stood with Tess on the top floor of the institution looking out towards the city skyline. It seemed he got her to say more when the session was less formal. They sat down at the end of the corridor and began to draw, or at least Cosgrove pretended to draw.

The girl had real talent, he thought, as he watched her producing yet another picture of her "Butterfly Lake" which always included a little figure standing at the lake's edge, obviously herself, and some grotesque-looking insects with human heads. The effect was always surreal, fascinating – and alarming. Cosgrove knew that the lake pictures were connected with her father's death and that if he could get her to talk about them he might make a vital break-through. But Tess would not utter one word about her lake pictures and paintings.

"What are those insects, Tess? Caterpillars, I think? Are they?"

Nothing.

Cosgrove stifled a sigh and changed direction.

"Tess, the staff tell me you are writing lists almost every day. Can you tell me what they are about?"

"Secrets."

"Oh, secrets. Right. Do you trust me, Tess?"

"Yes."

"Could you tell me what the lists mean? I promise I won't tell anyone. Doctors have to keep secrets that their patients tell them."

Cosgrove spoke slowly and methodically, making sure to stop at the end of each sentence to allow Tess to absorb his words.

Tess turned her head sideways, looking away from Cosgrove, thinking.

"It's about apologise."

"Oh. Are there people who need to apologise to you?"

No answer.

"Tess, are the people on your list people who did things to you, bad things?"

Tess flicked her fingers, the snapping sound echoing around the bare corridor.

"You have to say you're sorry," she replied simply.

"Who, Tess, who has to say they are sorry?"

"Did you know that there are over one hundred thousand different butterflies and moths in the world?"

Cosgrove sighed. He was getting to know Tess better and she always made a statement like this when he was getting nearer to the truth. He was also learning that it was useless to probe when she did this as it set their trust back weeks.

"No, Tess, I didn't know that. Come on and I'll bring you back to your classes."

He was going to have to try another day.

Seán waited until Kate had put Ben to bed before he told her about the will. It occurred to him that if Michael wasn't his father then neither Tess nor Ben were his full sister and brother. It didn't really matter, he supposed, they were his mother's children. When Kate came back into the kitchen she looked at him and waited. His sister could always read him like a book.

"I went to Brown & Son," he said "but the will was not there."

"What? Where would it be?"

"In Dublin."

Seán told Kate about his day, leaving the bit about their true parentage to last. When he finished he found Kate silent. He had expected her to be calm. She always was. But there was something in her expression, something else.

"You knew!" he spat.

Kate lowered her head.

"I didn't know about me. I thought he was my father all right – she never told me that part."

"But you knew all along that Michael Byrne was not my father and you never told me."

"I couldn't, Seán. Mam made me promise. She said that you knowing wouldn't solve anything. She didn't want you to think badly of her."

"Think badly of her? I'm a bastard, you're a bastard. I now have no way of making a living. Tess owns the farm! Why on earth would I think badly of her?"

"She wouldn't have known about his will. How could she? She stayed with him all these years so you and I could have a future. She loved us. She sacrificed her happiness for us, Seán."

Seán thought his day could not get any worse but the realisation that his sister knew all these years and said nothing was a betrayal he could not bear. He stared angrily at her, the veins in his neck bulging as he clenched his fists, banging them loudly on the old kitchen table, startling Kate.

He took a deep breath and tried to calm himself.

"Who was our father, Kate? Please tell me."

"I only know his first namc. Éamonn. He let her down. That's all I know, Seán, I swear."

"Where did he live, Kate? How did she meet him?"

"I don't know, Seán, honestly I don't. She never said. It upset her to talk about it. She didn't want me to make the same mistakes. That's why she told me. That's all I know, Seán."

Seán needed some air so took his coat and strode out the kitchen door. He set off down the dark pathway that led out onto the Dublin road.

Kate followed him. "Seán, where are you going?"

"Go back inside and leave me alone. I have to think this through. Everything has changed, Kate, everything."

Seán Byrne walked the whole way to town in the darkness. When he reached the main street he walked into Slattery's bar where his "father" had drunk.

"Seán!" Mattie Slattery exclaimed. "I thought you weren't a drinking man?"

"I am tonight," was all the tormented man replied.

Seán sat as casually as he could at the bar and ordered another pint, amazed at how his life had changed in a matter of hours. Up until today he thought he owned a farm and thought his father was Michael Byrne. Until today his sister Kate was the person he was closest to in the world and now he found out that all the time she was lying to him, or at least not telling him the truth, which to his mind was the same thing. He also thought the world of his mother but she was not the saint he believed her to be. She was a whore as far as he was concerned. And also until today he was a pioneer, pledging never to drink alcohol, a pledge that had made his mother very happy.

Seán looked around him and saw his uncle and cousin whispering in the corner, watching him, but decided to ignore them even though it bothered him that he had all these questions that he knew his Uncle Jimmy could, but wouldn't, answer.

Seán beckoned for Mattie Slattery to come over.

"Mattie, I was just thinking about my mother's funeral," he said quietly, trying to sound as casual as possible. "There was a woman there that I didn't know. Short, chubby type with brown hair. You don't happen to know who she was by any chance?"

"Mmm, no, Seán. Doesn't ring a bell with me."

Before Seán got a chance to shrug his shoulders as part of his act, Mattie started talking loudly to another customer who was drinking at the other end of the bar.

"Frank, you were at Maura Byrne's funeral, yeah?"

"I was," the middle-aged man replied. "I knew your mother well, lad. Lord Rest Her. Is there something you want to know?"

Seán squirmed in his seat and could feel his uncle's eyes boring into the back of his neck. He wasn't too happy either to be talking to Frank Ryan who was the village's most notorious gossip. So much for his quiet, casual enquiry, he thought to himself while Ryan eyed him carefully.

"Oh, it's nothing much. I was just thinking about the funeral on my way to town and remembered a woman I didn't recognise there. I thought Mattie here might know who she was, that's all. It's not important." He swallowed hard.

A few other men in the bar had started to listen to the conversation and were leaning over in preparation to give their two bobs' worth.

"Small, you say, fat?" a voice said from the side snug. "Well now, who would that have been?"

"Sure, wasn't that Dan Whelan's wife from Knockbeg?" said another voice. "Sounds like her."

"No," Ryan replied. He didn't want to lose his audience so soon and wanted to drag this out for what it was worth. "Sounds to me like that girl Maura used to pal with. I'm sure I saw her at the funeral. She wasn't from around here. Her mother was though and she came here for holidays – now what was her name?" Ryan replaced the pipe in his mouth and chewed on it, hoping no one else came up with the answer first.

Jimmy Kelly shifted uneasily in his seat and knew that there was more to his nephew's query than idle conversation.

After what seemed like an insufferable silence, Frank Ryan removed the pipe from his mouth. No one else had spoken, aware that Frank wouldn't be too pleased with them stealing his limelight.

"Brigid, that's what it was. Lives in Dublin. Ah, Christ, I can't remember her people's name. It's on the tip of my tongue but it's an odd name, northern I think. Blast it anyway!" Ryan hated to fail.

"Are her family still around?" Seán asked, still trying not to come across as too keen.

"No. The youngest son tried to run it for a while but gave up, went to London. Was it Doyle? No. The land was terrible. The house is derelict now. There hasn't been anyone there for years. The old couple died many years back as I remember."

"Is it important?" Ryan asked hopefully.

"Ah no, just couldn't make out who she was," Seán said, his face lowered towards the pint of Guinness in front of him. As he put the black liquid to his mouth he shivered slightly. It tasted awful. He didn't think he'd ever get used to it and as he took his second sup he was aware that his uncle and cousin had left the pub, closing the door quietly behind them.

Seán was no better off really. If it was this Brigid, no one knew her last name and even if they did, she was probably married now. He'd never find her.

When Seán staggered home a few hours later Kate stayed in bed, listening to her brother fumble and smash against furniture in the darkness. She did not get up; it would only lead to an argument. She lay awake that night, long after Seán had fallen into a drunken slumber and wondered why Maura had not told her that Michael Byrne was not her father. Kate decided that tomorrow she would try to talk some sense into Seán. There was just the two of them now and they only had each other to rely on.

Chapter 17

1981

Deirdre O'Connell sat in Kate Byrne's kitchen for the second time in a week. Luckily for Kate, Seán was never around when the community nurse called. Deirdre was proving to be great with Tess and had come up with good ideas for Ben. Kate was already beginning to understand him better and found her younger brother calmer than he had been in a long time. As Deirdre put her coat on to leave Kate felt a rush of emotion towards her new acquaintance.

"You know, no one has helped me for a long time. Thanks."

Kate could feel the tears welling in her eyes. It was true that no one helped her but she hadn't needed anyone in a long time either – she felt more vulnerable that way and generally felt that it was best to stand on her own two feet. Even Seán had let her down over the last few years, drinking whatever meagre money the farm made and having to hire help to get the work done while he ruined his health through drink.

"You're welcome, Kate," the nurse replied, smiling warmly. "I'll be back Tuesday to see how things are going."

As they stood together at the back door, they watched Tess talking to Dermot who was teaching her how to ride the old farm horse.

"Hey, Kate, have you noticed that your man's not bad looking?" The nurse laughed and laughed even more when she noticed Kate blushing.

Kate stood by the door and waved as Deirdre drove off. Then she stood watching Tess ride the horse that looked like it had seen better days. Dermot, who was tall and had hair as dark as her own, wasn't bad looking and, yes, she had noticed him. She felt her face redden as she saw Dermot place his hands on Tess's waist and lift her from the horse. She would have to talk to him to make sure he was not getting any ideas about her younger sister.

Later that afternoon, Tess found Dermot under the ancient tractor, which had broken down yet again.

"Tess, hand me the large wrench there. No, not that one, the one beside your feet."

"I like helping you, Dermot."

"Well, I like when you help."

Dermot found himself a much more pleasant person around this girl. Her honesty amazed and pleased him, as he was a little like Tess himself. He didn't understand why people didn't tell the truth and hated to be lied to.

"Dermot, can I ask you a personal question?"

Here we go, Dermot thought to himself. "Yes."

"Do you think Kate is pretty?"

Dermot looked up in surprise. He was expecting a question about the population of Galway or something statistical like that.

"Em – yes, of course she's pretty." He wasn't going to lie to the only truly honest person he knew.

"Well," Tess replied happily, "Kate thinks it's very interesting that you don't have a girlfriend."

Dermot did not answer. He wanted to know more about the conversation that Tess and Kate had obviously had about him but couldn't bring himself to ask. It was true, he liked Kate Byrne. When he first met Kate he thought that although she was an attractive woman, there was something very sad about her. He felt sorry for her, not only caring for her younger brother but also her older one who became weaker by the month and was drinking even more heavily these days. In time, Dermot saw what a strong person she was and he started to think of her differently. He admired her.

He doubted if Kate put the girl up to saying this but if she did, he had to send the right message back.

"Well, Tess, I think it's a shame that your pretty sister doesn't have a boyfriend," he replied, cringing slightly as he could never be described as the romantic type.

Well, now he had said it and by morning Kate might be happy to know that he admired her or else Seán would sack him for making unwelcome advances to his sister.

Dermot finished his makeshift repairs to the tractor and stood up, dusted his overalls down and mounted the prehistoric machine. Tess, happy with his answer, jumped up beside him, anxious to see if the repairs had worked.

Kate Byrne saw Dermot through the kitchen window and knew she had to talk to him about Tess. Deirdre was coming today and she would mention the problem to her also.

"Dermot, have ya a minute?"

Dermot came into the tiny kitchen, carefully wiping his feet on the mat. He often saw Seán just walk in when Kate had just finished mopping without a thought for his sister.

"Yes, Kate, what can I help ya with?"

Dermot couldn't help but think about the conversation he had with Tess and found himself imagining himself kissing Kate. His face blushed lightly, hoping she didn't know what he was thinking.

"Dermot, it's about Tess."

"Oh, yes, I know, Kate." He was trying to make this easy for Kate who he noticed was almost as shy as himself.

"You do?"

"Yeah, I've had a lot of conversations with her lately. You know how she is for questions. I have to say I've grown very fond of her."

Kate felt herself reddening. She hadn't expected Dermot to be so forthright about his feelings for Tess and could feel herself becoming both angry and protective towards her younger sister.

"Dermot, Tess has problems as I am sure you are aware. She is years behind herself. She's like a young teenager really if you know what I mean."

"Yeah, I know that but I enjoy talking to her. She's so honest – there are not many people like her these days. You seem upset, Kate. Do you not want me to talk to her?"

"I don't want you giving her ideas if that's what you mean. She's very – vulnerable. She gets the wrong idea." She had not wanted this to turn into a row but could see that Dermot wasn't going to give in easily.

Dermot realised that Kate thought that he was attracted to Tess and smiled inside. She's jealous, he thought, pleased with himself.

"Ideas? Oh, no, Kate, you've got it wrong. It's em, it's you – I –" It was no good; he couldn't come out and say it, couldn't put himself on the line. He had to think of another way around it. "Kate, Tess gave me the impression that you liked me. I thought you had said something to her."

Kate looked shocked. "Well, I most certainly did not! As I said, she gets the wrong impression."

The two of them stood silently in the kitchen, two red faces pointed toward the floor.

Kate, unable to bear the silence, spoke first, her voice calmer than before. "So, you're not attracted to Tess then?"

"No, Kate, not Tess," Dermot said quietly as he turned and walked out of the house, embarrassed. It was as much as he could say.

He walked quickly to the side of the house and out of view. He thought he could hear Kate crying and stood there for a while, unsure what to do, before quickening his step across the yard and into the welcoming fields.

Back at the house Kate Byrne sat alone in the kitchen, her body bent forward as though she was in pain. Dermot cared for her, she knew that now and instead of feeling happy or revisiting that girlish giddy feeling when you find out someone likes you, she felt sad. No one had cared for her like that in a long time and it caused memories of Noel to flood back, memories best left alone. Wiping her tears she stood up and looked around the room. Ben would be home in less than an hour and she still had work to do.

Chapter 18

1952

Maura Byrne knew she was pregnant before any visit to the local doctor, her stomach heaving each time she tried to cook a meal. Morning sickness they called it but Maura had it all the time. She was never sick when she was expecting Kate but was sick all though Seán's pregnancy so she wondered if the baby would be a boy. This time though it was different because the baby was Michael's. Maura wondered how he would react and hoped he'd be interested in the child. Then a dark cloud descended upon her as she realised that Michael would surely disinherit Seán in favour of his own child. Once she married, the land was no longer her property but belonged to her husband. He could do whatever he liked with it. Maura's heart quickened as she thought of everything she put up with so that Seán would at least have a future. Kate would be all right, would hopefully marry well but Maura feared for her son who, although not quite three years old, was a shy, withdrawn child who would need every opportunity in life. She couldn't bring herself to pray she'd lose the child but unconsciously set about working as hard as she could in the house and about the farm.

One afternoon while Maura was on her hands and knees, scrubbing the rough, wooden kitchen floor, Michael walked in and while stepping over her, kicked the basin of water over and pushed her onto the soaking wet floor. Maura groaned as silently as she could, unwilling to let him know he had hurt her and scrubbed even harder. By Monday, she had started to bleed heavily and a few days later the sickness began to subside. She had killed this little human and yet she felt nothing. Michael had destroyed all the good that was once in her. Even her face, once beautiful, now showed hard lines about the mouth and frown lines on her forehead. Maura had only one ambition in life now, to see her two children grown and happy, Seán running the family farm and Kate married to a man who loved her and until then she was prepared to put up with whatever cruelty Michael inflicted upon her.

Chapter 19

1981

Kate tried to keep herself busy as Ben screamed in the bath. Deirdre was teaching him to wash himself and was holding his hand, showing him how to use the soap, and he hated anyone touching him. Kate wondered was it worth it, upsetting him like that. Several times she wanted to rush to his aid and tell Deirdre to leave it, that she'd manage, but something stopped her. Ben had a right to some dignity and it certainly wasn't very dignified having your sister wash you when you were almost a grown man. When she heard Ben quieten she was even more worried by his silence.

"It's hard, isn't it?" Deirdre had snuck up behind her.

"Yes. I know it's for his own good but he doesn't understand. He'll be wondering where I am and I can't stand that, Deirdre."

"Change is very hard when you have Ben's level of autism. Simple things like learning to bathe or in fact anything new will frighten him but he needs to be able to do things for himself." Deirdre was aware that Kate already knew all these things. She just wanted to reassure her that she was doing the right thing. "Sometimes, Kate, it takes a stranger to help them progress. It's not good for him to rely on you totally. What if you got sick or went on holiday, got married? It's better for Ben to get used to as many faces as possible, yeah?"

"Yes, you're right," Kate replied doubtfully. It was possible for her to get sick all right. But to get married or go on holiday? Nothing like that was ever going to happen to her now.

"All right then. I'll pop in on Friday and go through it with him again. You'll see, Kate, in no time Ben will be bathing himself and that's just the beginning. He just needs time. I've been looking into some work or a training course for Tess, get her out and about. We should be hearing any day soon. See you Friday."

As Kate waved the nurse off it occurred to her that if Ben was independent and Tess was working, what was *she* going to do?

Tess stood and stared at Kate in the dark hallway of the cottage. She tilted her head to one side which she always did when she was confused as Kate handed her a small white envelope with her name and address written on it in large, printed letters.

"What is it?"

"It's a letter, Tess. For you."

Tess stared back at her sister who stood and waited for her to open the envelope.

Tess tore the envelope and pulled the letter out. "It's from the training centre!" she cried. "I got a place on the course!"

Kate had never seen Tess get this excited about anything before and felt a surge of emotion, her eyes filling up with silly tears from a mixture of happiness and sadness.

"Kate, why are you crying?" Tess asked.

"I'm not crying, Tess. Read your letter," Kate replied as she opened the kitchen door and walked into the yard, straight into Dermot who was just coming in.

"Oh, em – sorry," Kate said quickly. She had tried to avoid Dermot since their conversation about his feelings for her almost two weeks back, leaving his meals in the range, always finding work in some other room when he came in to eat.

"Is everything all right, Kate?" The sound of Dermot's concerned voice made her feel weak, vulnerable.

"Yes, I'm fine," Kate replied, looking down at her shoes, embarrassed to have been caught crying. "It's just, well, Tess. She just got word that she has a place on that training course. She's so excited – she is actually happy. I just got a bit upset for her, that's all. You wouldn't understand."

"I think I do, Kate. She's lost out on a lot. She seems to have settled back in well though. I wouldn't worry about her, Kate."

"I know, but you see, my mother wanted more for her. She wanted her to get a job. She's smart, you know. She just doesn't know how to behave at times, that's all, but she never got a chance, spent half her life in that place in Dublin."

Kate noticed that Dermot was listening intently, his eyes fixed on her, dark blue like her own, listening as though anything she had to say was important. She could almost feel herself fall towards him as though he would catch her and in saving her fall take away all her problems and worries. Kate couldn't believe she was actually telling him this. She was afraid she might be going too far and shook herself slightly as though she had been daydreaming.

"It's all ancient history now, I suppose," she said, straightening herself up and wiping her tears. "Sorry." She brushed by him and walked quickly back into the kitchen, leaving him standing alone in the doorway, staring after her.

Tess brought her letter to the room she shared with Kate and sat quietly on her bed. She was tempted to sit on the floor and to lodge herself between the bed and the dressing table which always made her feel safe but she understood that this looked odd and that Deirdre said she was safe anyway. Tess looked slowly about the room, wanting to savour holding her letter before starting to read it again. The training centre wanted her to start the course in September, a typing and office skills course in Knockbeg. Tess knew that within a few days she would start to worry about the change to her daily life but for now, somebody wanted her and she was happy.

Sam Moran drove to Beech Street police station, about forty miles from Árd Glen, and hoped his journey wasn't going to be a waste of his time. His employer was growing tired of his excuses for not having come up with a story yet. And time was running out.

When he arrived Flynn was waiting for him in his large office with views over Dublin city centre.

Maurice Flynn was not the young, green detective he had been ten years ago when he was part of the investigative team in Árd Glen. He was only out of uniform a few years then and had been brought down to learn the ropes. He remembered the case well because it had been the first dead body he had ever seen. His uncle, an inspector, had got him into the force and shielded Flynn a lot, ensuring he worked only in the quietest parts of Dublin. When he passed his detective's exam and moved to Beech Street Station, the senior Flynn had little say in where his nephew went and Maurice had been relieved. He was ambitious, hoping to go even further than his uncle in the force and knew that he couldn't achieve that by hiding behind his apron strings. Since the Árd Glen murder, Flynn had worked his way through homicide, married and had three kids. When the late-night calls began to affect his marriage he asked for a transfer to the drug unit, monitoring drug dealers who were now bringing a whole new problem to Ireland, heroin. His success was noted and he received several commendations from the commissioner. He had become a sort of celebrity on the force with young recruits glad to shake his hand and claim they had met him.

"Pretty impressive view!" Moran said, as much to himself as to Flynn.

"Yeah," Flynn said coolly. "What can I do for you, Mr Moran?"

"Call me Sam, please."

Flynn did not answer. He dealt with shifty characters on a daily basis, some of them colleagues, and he wasn't fooled by the neatly dressed reporter who was now smiling at him.

"I'm writing about a murder that happened ten years ago in Wicklow. I believe you were on the case and I was hoping you could help me with some background information."

"Who was murdered?" Flynn pretended he was actually going to help this slime ball. He saw Moran visibly relax.

"Michael Byrne. A local farmer. His daughter was charged with the murder."

"Oh yeah . . ." Flynn breathed slowly, looking straight at Moran.

"Well, can you tell me anything about it?" Sam asked, starting to feel that he had misjudged the detective's ego slightly. "I mean, you were one of a skilled team sent to investigate, weren't you?"

Flynn smiled broadly. "No, Moran, I was a gofer, only a wet day out of uniform. I mostly made tea and went for chocolate biscuits." Flynn was enjoying the deflated look that was starting to show on Moran's face and guessed that he hadn't had anyone else to help him with his story. Flynn was no fool. He remembered the case well and he was the only one who had charged that girl with murder left on the force. Being a minor meant she went to some loony bin and he had thought about her often over the years. The two other detectives he went to Árd Glen with were about to retire when the murder occurred and were both dead now but he remembered the elation they felt when they charged her. "A cut and dried case," Burke, the senior detective, had called it and they were thrilled to get out of the tiny hick town so quickly and back to where the real action was. He had tried to ignore the niggles he felt on the way back. Something wasn't right about it but he was anxious to prove to his buddies on the force that he was more than his uncle's sissy boy so said nothing. In the years to come, especially when he came up against real murderers, he often thought of her and felt that the girl was innocent but he had too much to lose by then to say anything. Anyway, there was so much evidence against her what could he have said? I have a hunch, an inkling? He would have been a laughing stock. It wasn't the only dishonest thing he had done during his time on the force but you couldn't count harassing drug dealers as a crime against humanity.

Sam brought Flynn back from his reminiscing.

"So you didn't have anything to do with her arrest?"

"No. As I said, I was only learning the ropes. The other two detectives who were in charge are both dead now so I'm sorry this journey was a waste of your time." Flynn looked deliberately at his watch.

Sam knew he was being dismissed but didn't want to go without irking Flynn at least a little bit. He stood up.

"Yeah, funny that, you know. The local garda, he remembered you well, said you seemed to have some responsibility there. He said you were somebody's nephew or something like that. Still, I guess you wouldn't want to be the only one left to have put an innocent girl into an institution for the best years of her life, would you?" He watched Flynn's face go bright red, then he walked to the door. He knew he had hit a nerve. Flynn had known all along that the girl didn't do it but had done nothing.

Sam was tired. He had never worked on a story that shifted direction as much as this one did. At first he felt sorry for the murdered man, his life stolen from him in his prime. Then he felt sorry for the son, disinherited and facing ruin, all because the old man had resented the chap's true parentage. Now, he felt sorry for the girl. Someone had framed her or at the very least left her to take the blame for their crime and had said nothing.

"Thanks for your time," he said and slammed the

office door behind him, startling several policemen sitting outside at their desks. Smiling broadly at them, he said, "Sorry, folks, don't know my own strength, have a nice day!" Coming from a family of street traders, he was not a fan of the police.

Seán awoke from a fitful sleep to find his younger sister standing over him yet again.

"What – what the fuck do ya want, ya mad bitch?" he yelled.

Tess, startled by Seán's sudden shouting, ran from the room and hid beneath her bed. He lay back and decided he would have to get a lock for his bedroom door. He had caught her trying to hang her "Butterfly State" sign at the front gate the day before and he had ripped it down, telling her that it was stupid. She picked up the sign and stood staring at him with her huge blue eyes. The bitch gave him the creeps. He realised weeks back that he was afraid of her although exactly what he thought she was going to do, he didn't know. He thought she was harmless enough as a child but now, well, he wasn't so sure. He could hear the nurse visiting and decided not to get up until she was gone.

Deirdre O'Connell was making progress with Ben's independent living skills and Kate was relieved that her brother no longer screamed when Deirdre touched him. He was even learning to dress himself, shoving Kate away when she tried to hurry him each morning.

When she was finished, Deirdre followed Kate to the kitchen where she was busy making tea.

"Ah, you're finished, Deirdre. I was just making a fresh pot. Will ya have a cup?"

"Yeah, thanks. That was good news about Tess's course. Had you heard of ANCO before?"

"Yes, the new training place. But I'm surprised they accepted her because, well, it's not for girls like Tess, is it?"

"I think Tess will do very well there, Kate. You know it's in Knockbeg. The local bus goes there a few times a day so she'll have no trouble getting there and back."

Kate remained silent for what seemed to Deirdre a long time. Although she already knew what was worrying Kate, she decided not to speak but to wait until Kate came out and said what was on her mind.

"Tess has never gone to anything like that before. She went to a special school and then to the hospital where people understood her. If there's going to be normal people there, Deirdre, won't they laugh at her?"

"We prefer not to use the word 'normal'. Tess is intelligent, Kate, and she deserves this chance. She'll have to go out into the world sooner or later. You can't always be at her side."

"I know, but she's so innocent, Deirdre. What if I got Dermot to drive her there and collect her? She's not used to dealing with money or anything like that."

"I'll work on all of that before she starts. We have the whole summer to sort it out. If she's too nervous, we'll take a step back and go with the flow until she is more settled. You need to be in full support of this, Kate. It won't work otherwise. She values your opinion so much. Okay?"

"Okay," Kate replied quietly, already visualising all the horrible things that could happen to Tess out in the real world.

Chapter 20

1971

Tess Byrne sat upright when the door of her classroom swung open, a tall black boy entering loudly and accidentally slamming the door behind him. She had never seen this boy before, nor had she ever seen a black person before and stared hard at him as he sat in the seat opposite her. Other pupils looked around at the boy, some jeering as he passed, one pupil kicking him hard in the shin. Tess noticed that he did not flinch although it must have hurt. She also noticed that he did not hit back or bite as she would have done.

"Right, class, that's enough noise. Leroy, welcome back. I hope you kept your studies up while you were in hospital."

"Yes, ma'am, I sure did," the coloured child replied in a strong American drawl, much to the amusement of the other children who laughed loudly.

"That's enough!" the teacher shouted, silencing the small group.

At lunch-time, the pupils moved slowly out of the class to the small room where they ate their meals. Tess could feel her mouth working on sentences, things she really wanted to ask this boy. She never spoke to the other children, only to Dr Cosgrove and occasionally the blonde nurse whose foreign name Tess could never pronounce. She sat facing the boy and continued to stare at him, oblivious to her behaviour. Leroy grinned at Tess, revealing the whitest teeth she had ever seen. She reached out her hand to touch his skin but pulled back, anxious not to lose six more steps towards home and not wanting to be slapped.

"You never see a coloured boy before, Miss?"

"No," Tess replied much to the amazement of her fellow pupils who had never heard her speak. "You talk strange."

Leroy seemed to be enjoying the attention and didn't appear remotely offended. "Tha's 'cos I'm American," he replied proudly causing the other pupils to spit their food out with laughter.

Tess looked around at the others, unsure what they were laughing at.

"Why were you in hospital, Leroy?" she asked.

"I had to get my appendix out," Leroy replied, his American accent strengthening with every sentence.

"Ya should have got your brain ou' while ya were there with tha' stupa accent, Leroy!" one of the rougher boys shouted. "Anyway, retard," he said to Tess, "tha's not his real name. It's Declan – Declan Brennan and he's a fuckin' nutter – isn't that righ', Declan?"

Before Tess had a chance to ask Leroy if this was true, he jumped from his bench and grabbed the boy, holding him in a strong headlock and punching him in the head until they were separated by two orderlies. Tess, afraid of the noise, hid under one of the benches while the other children shouted with excitement.

"Jaysus, Declan," one of the orderlies said as they hauled Leroy off, "you're only back one day and you're in trouble."

Tess watched as Leroy was taken away. He looked back and smiled at her, waving to the group until he disappeared out of sight. Tess sat down and finished her lunch. She was interested in this boy and hoped that she would see him again.

Kate heard Seán vomiting early in the morning again but had not roused to help him, hoping once more the experience would prevent him from drinking again. By mid-afternoon he got up and Kate silently placed some food in front of him.

"What's that face for, Kate? Have I not got the right to go for a pint when I fancy one?"

"You have no right to drink the little bit of cash we have, Seán, no. And I thought you would have seen enough drunkenness to last you a lifetime."

Seán remained silent for a time, head bowed like a

naughty child. His head hurt and his stomach was sick. He couldn't understand how people did this to themselves regularly.

"I'm sorry, Kate, you're right. I . . . well, I just don't know where to turn. What are we going to do, Kate? The police are investigating the will. I told the solicitor I knew nothing about it. We can't sell any of the livestock, there's no money coming in. We're ruined, Kate."

Kate listened, her face calm, giving away nothing of the anger that was rising inside her.

"It's all about you, Seán, isn't it? Poor Seán! Nothing is going your way. Well, I've lost too you know. Has it occurred to you that I was due to be married this weekend? Did you think of that while you were out drowning your sorrows? It hasn't gone quite the way either of us planned, I know, but you wallowing in self-pity won't get us anywhere."

Seán quietened. Kate was right. He hadn't thought of her at all in all of this and suddenly felt a pang of guilt, not because Kate's marriage was off but because he was glad he still had her. He needed her. She was the strength behind him; she was also a lot smarter than he was. He couldn't let her know what a weak, selfish and shallow person he was though and he knew he had to think of the right words to calm her down.

"I'm sorry, Kate. I'm just worried for all of us. We need to stick together. No more fighting, eh? We have Ben to consider. I won't touch another drop. I'll go to

Brown & Son and see what we can do about the farm." He looked squarely at his sister to see if his words had any effect. He knew the mention of Ben would calm her.

She did look more composed. Women, he though smugly to himself, always a sucker for the child.

Seán braved yet another savage hangover and drove to Brown & Son's offices to speak to the young solicitor. Kate was still annoyed with him about his visit to the pub and the icy atmosphere in the house was enough to make him drive anywhere to get away from her. Admittedly, he had drunk more of their dwindling savings but even though he still hated the taste of alcohol, he felt happy and a little numb after he'd had a few and worries of Tess disappeared from his mind. He had still not been to see her. He just couldn't face it and the longer he left it, the harder it was becoming. His biggest concern, being being his age and owning nothing, seemed almost like a bad dream when he was under the influence. When he woke each morning, he longed for that feeling again, the peace of intoxication. It was not how he had planned his life though. He'd had great plans for the farm and before Michael had died he had already reclaimed two small fields which his grandfather and "father" had never bothered to do.

At the solicitor's office, Ciaran Brown greeted Seán like a long-lost friend.

"Seán! Welcome. How are things?"

Seán still didn't like the young, upbeat man and

found himself enviously eyeing up his clean-shaved, handsome face and expensive suit. He felt that the solicitor probably hadn't a worry in the world. He also hated that he had to come here and discuss such private problems with this man who surely mustn't have a clue what hardship was.

Seán eventually spoke. "Well, no change. I found out the will my em – father wrote here in '61 is still valid. He left everything to my youngest sister. I am to run the farm until she comes of age. There was a second will but it was never signed, leaving everything to my brother who is just a baby." Seán couldn't look up at the solicitor when he said that part but continued. "I understand that this will is void because it was never signed but the first will isn't really much better. Tess is retarded, she'll never run the farm herself but I have to look after it for her until she turns twenty-one. It's a joke."

Ciaran Brown sat still for some time before he spoke.

"You could challenge the will but you know how that would look locally," Brown advised.

Sean knew what he meant. Everyone would know about his true parentage then and he couldn't risk that getting out.

"I suggest you organise a doctor to sign an affidavit, stating she couldn't possibly run the farm and arrange for you to become her guardian. How old is she?"

"Eleven. She's in – an institution." Seán felt himself redden mentioning the institution and couldn't understand why. After all, she belonged there, didn't she?

Brown made no comment. "Right then. Well, after you become her legal guardian you will be in a position to run the farm for her. Will she live permanently away from home?"

"No. They're trying to sort out a few problems with her. She'll be back whenever they say she's ready."

"Right then, Seán. Well, I'd organise to get those letters as soon as possible. Will she understand she's been left the farm?"

"No," Seán lied. "Does she have to know? I mean, it's too upsetting to visit her."

"Well, if you say she wouldn't understand and you become her guardian, I see no reason why she has to be told but you'll need a doctor to state her level of incapacity. The papers will then have to go to your father's solicitor. But then you'll be able to manage the farm the same as though you owned it. I'm sure you'll look after your sister's interests." Ciaran rose from his seat and offered Seán his hand. "Let me know if there is anything else I can do for you. The deeds of the farm will remain at Roberts & Holford as well as any other legal business your father had but I anticipate that Brown & Co will have the opportunity to handle your own legal affairs?"

"Yes, of course," Seán replied quietly.

He wasn't sure what "anticipate" meant but he wasn't going to let Brown know that. As Seán walked back to his truck, the words "manage the farm as though you owned it" grated on him. Large veins began to bulge on his forehead and neck as his temper flared.

When he reached the battered truck he noticed he had parked right outside the local pub. He'd just have the one before heading home . . .

Chapter 21

1981

Sam Moran sat quietly at the dinner party organised for his father-in-law's birthday. He hated these uppity evenings and felt like a fish out of water. He never felt comfortable in the company of "middle-class" people and now that they were settled back into life in Ireland, he often looked at Mona as though she were a stranger. She had been wild when they met in England, carefree and down to earth, and they'd had great times together, out on the town in London. Those days seemed like million miles away as he watched her walk confidently around the room, mixing with people that he felt intimidated by.

He was just about to get himself another stiff whiskey when he noticed his boss, Talbot, walking towards him, his face grim.

"Moran, I thought I'd catch up with you here," he

said in a voice a little too loud. "Where the hell is that story?"

"I'm having trouble getting people to talk. You know how it is in this place." Sam cringed. Wrong thing to say!

"I don't know what you mean by 'this place', Moran, but I'll tell you this much: you haven't shown up to do your regular stories for weeks now. I've had to send my youngest son to cover the mart. These stories are the bread and butter of this paper. Sales are slipping, Moran. I need to have something to leave my son in my will so don't you disappoint me. You have two more weeks and then forget it."

Sam smiled as his angry boss strode back across the room. He noticed Mona staring at him crossly.

People were all the same around here. It was all about wills and inheritance. Sam's own parents had left him nothing more than an out-of-date street traders' licence and two hefty funeral bills. Neither of them would even have known what a will was, never mind worrying about what to leave their children.

That was it. The will. He needed to read Byrne's will. If he had that, he would surely know who had a motive to kill him.

Tess stood still as Kate inspected her face and hands. The training programme was starting on Monday and she had torn the skin off her lips and fingers because of the worry of the change to her routine.

"Tess, you'll have to stop doing this to yourself," Kate said as calmly as she could. It upset her to see her sister like this.

"I know, Kate. I apologise," Tess replied, knowing that she would do the same thing tonight as she lay in bed. Kate had phoned the centre several times to find out what time lunch was and what the timetable was going to be but no one had returned her calls and Tess had become more and more frantic with questions.

"Will they let me eat whatever I want?"

"Yes, Tess."

"Will they let me have my lunch at my usual time?"

"I don't know, Tess. There may be different rules there. You'll get used to them," was all Kate could reply.

By Monday, Kate was exhausted. Seán had called her twice during the night, claiming that his skin was itchy. He seemed a little confused, muttering that Tess had been in his room tormenting him again, which worried Kate until she found an empty bottle of whiskey under his bed. She put calamine lotion on his skin even though she told him that he had no rash and to go to sleep. When she returned to her room she wondered what had become of her brother. Scratch marks were appearing on his face and hands and he sat in his room all day, never venturing out to see if Dermot needed a hand. She wondered how on earth she would cope without Dermot's help. Her cheeks reddened as she thought of the silly girlish dream she had about Dermot the previous night in which he rode an old, tired horse in the dark and as he passed her he saluted and offered her his hand, lifting her clean off the ground and riding off with her into the night. By morning, the dream made no sense to her.

She decided to ask Dermot to drive Seán to see the doctor and was tempted to get him to drop Tess off at her training centre, especially as this was her first day, but she resisted. Deirdre had put a lot of work into training Tess to go Knockbeg on the bus independently so Kate wouldn't interfere now, no matter how frightened she was for her younger sister. Besides, Deirdre had promised to phone her after she met Tess off the bus and had walked her to the centre.

By eleven Kate and Seán were sitting in Doctor Doyle's office with Seán constantly grumbling about how there was nothing wrong with him. Kate went into the doctor's room with him, knowing that Seán would not mention the drinking or the itchy skin, or most worrying of all, his claim that Tess was tormenting him in private, something Kate was sure was untrue.

Doyle had been their doctor when their mother was ill and seemed concerned.

"Seán, how much would you drink a day?" he asked.

"About five pints," Seán replied

"About ten," Kate corrected him, "if not more."

"What about spirits, Seán?"

"No, don't touch them," Seán lied.

"At least a bottle a day," Kate corrected.

"Seán, have you noticed your skin colour?" Doyle asked.

"No," Seán replied.

Kate knew he was telling the truth. She had noticed his yellow complexion for weeks now but she knew her brother never bothered to look at himself in the mirror, his unshaved face and growing hair evidence of this.

Kate watched the doctor examine Seán and knew from his demeanour that there was something wrong.

"I'm going to send you to Dublin for tests, Seán. I don't want you to worry but I do want you to lay off the drink completely. That means no pints, no whiskey, nothing but tea, understand?"

"Why, what's wrong?" Seán asked, suddenly becoming aware that the doctor was concerned.

"I can't say without blood tests but I think your liver is in trouble – so no drink, okay?"

"Okay."

Doctor Doyle looked sympathetically at Kate. "How have you been, Kate?"

"I'm all right, doctor. Tess started a training programme today."

"That's great. Your mother would be proud. But I asked how *you* were?"

"I manage." Kate looked at the floor.

"You seem to have your hands full," the doctor stated simply as he placed his hand on her arm. "Call me if I can help in any way. The hospital will post out the test date. When I get the results I'll phone you."

Kate walked back to the truck where Dermot was parked and waiting. He looked at her and nodded. A look that said "Don't worry, it'll be all right." She nodded back.

In Knockbeg, Tess sat nervously on a bench in the reception area of her training centre. It was noisy with lots of people, all women, who were talking too loudly. They seemed confused, which made Tess even more anxious than she had been when Deirdre left her inside the building twenty minutes ago.

A large, red-faced woman was watching Tess and approached her.

"Hello. I noticed you look a bit nervous. I am too. Mind if I sit beside you?"

Tess looked cautiously at the woman and tried to remember what Deirdre had told her but couldn't.

"Okay," was all she could say. She knew she wasn't to say anything about not talking to strangers while inside the building.

"Thanks," the woman said and heaved her large body onto the seat, touching Tess's leg.

Tess pulled away.

"I'm sorry!" said the woman, smiling. "I'm a large girl!"

"You're very fat and you don't fit into the seat. You should ask for a larger seat."

The woman was stunned into silence. She looked closely at the young girl and couldn't see any malice in her face.

"I know, love, but they don't make seats any larger than this," she replied generously.

"Well, they should. That isn't fair," Tess said poker-faced.

The woman smiled at Tess. There was something honest about this girl that she liked, despite the insult about her weight.

"What's your name?"

"Teresa, but I'm called Tess."

"Oh, well, I'm Margaret, but they call me Peggy."

"Why? Peggy sounds nothing like Margaret. It doesn't even begin with the same letter," Tess said, slightly annoyed at this. "It doesn't make any sense." She turned slightly away from Peggy.

"Well, Tess, sometimes we just have to accept things as they are," Peggy said calmly, realising that Tess was a little "different".

Tess turned and looked at her cautiously. "My friend Dermot said that too. Do you know him?"

"No, but it sounds like good advice, doesn't it? Doesn't do you any good to always expect to understand everything. Does it?"

Tess simply nodded. She knew this. She knew she didn't have to understand everything but was always upset when she didn't. Tess wondered would she ever get to be like Dermot and Peggy.

Chapter 22

1961

By the time Maura Byrne realised she was pregnant again, she had come to accept each assault Michael Byrne inflicted upon her as a normal part of life. She did not think about the new life growing inside her and moved about her world like a ghost, a shadow of the woman she had once been. She did not even believe that she felt any real emotion any more and managed to move through each day surviving, unthinking, unfocused on anything except watching her two beloved children live as safely as they could in such an environment. She rarely went into town now but not because she was embarrassed about her bruised face as she no longer cared how she looked. She seldom attended Mass. Michael was not particularly religious and did not insist on her going, usually rising too late for Mass himself on Sunday morning due to his usual hangover. Maura's life revolved around the quiet, detached Seán and pretty Kate whose hair had since turned as black as her own and was showing signs of the fierce independent streak Maura had been known for as a girl.

Maura also lived for sleep, which had evaded her in recent years, only recently returning when her doctor had prescribed tablets so strong that some mornings she awoke with a foggy memory that Michael had returned home drunk and had inflicted his usual reign of terror on her. Her days involved dragging herself through household chores when she had a mind to do them, often relying on Kate to cook dinner for the family as she returned to bed, permanently exhausted. No one mentioned her burgeoning stomach or the fact that there would be a new baby in the house soon, least of all Michael. Maura, in her more lucid moments, thought how sad it was for this child inside her that no one, not even she, would celebrate his or her arrival. When Maura gave birth to her second daughter in the early morning some weeks later, Michael looked fleetingly at the sleeping child and went into the fields to work. The only words he uttered were that she should be called Teresa, after his mother.

Chapter 23

1971

Seán hadn't given up on finding out who the stranger at his mother's funeral was. As the woman had no family in the area, his guess was that she stayed in the small hotel in Knockbeg, probably taking a taxi to Árd Glen on the morning of the funeral. The manager of the small, somewhat rundown hotel was a man Seán had known at school even though Gerry Dunne was a few years older than him. It was a believable story that Kate had sent him asking after the woman's last name and address to send a memoriam card of their mother to. Gerry was only too happy to oblige but informed Seán that, while he remembered the woman, she had not left an address. He remarked on how quiet she was and how, on her first night at the hotel, she seemed irritated when he asked her about the purpose of her visit to Knockbeg. Dunne went on to tell Seán that he only found out that she was going to the Byrne funeral when her hackney failed to turn up and he had to drive her there himself. She had signed the guest book as Mrs Brigid Daly, Dublin, and had stayed two nights.

Seán wondered if his mother had kept in touch with this friend over the years but felt that she had probably not had any contact with her and that it was more likely that this woman found out about his mother's death in the newspaper death notices. What Gerry Dunne did remember was that, at breakfast the following morning, he heard her telling another guest from Dublin that she lived beside Croke Park but never bothered with sport and was sick of the noisy crowds of people who passed by her door whenever there was a big match on. Gerry suggested Seán try the phone book for Dalys in that area of Dublin. Instead of driving back home with this information for Kate, who seemed less than interested in his quest, Seán drove straight to Dublin, determined to find out who this woman was and how much she knew about his mother's secret life.

Before turning left towards Dublin, Seán dropped an envelope into Ciaran Brown's office, signed documents from the local doctor stating Tess was unfit to run the farm and nominating Seán as legal guardian of the sister he thought less and less about each day.

Seán sat in his truck in a side street outside of Croke Park. He had phoned directory enquiries from a telephone box who gave him addresses for two B Dalys on Cross

Street which was a small, narrow street of old redbricked houses in the shadow of Croke Park Stadium. Now that he was here, he felt a little foolish. What would he say? "Do you happen to know who my father was?" "Do you know who my mother was carrying on with?" He didn't know which of the two Daly houses this woman lived in. Were they related? How much of the story should he tell the first house before deciding if it was the wrong one? He decided to knock and ask for Brigid Daly and hope both houses didn't have a Brigid Daly inside. He could see one or two twitching net curtains of old biddies desperate to know who he was and he could feel his face redden at the thought of knocking, cold-call, at the small, rundown house directly in front of him.

Seán recognised the woman who opened the door immediately as the person who had attended his mother's funeral and was relieved that he might only have to make a fool of himself once. Brigid Daly was very short and despite being slightly overweight, she had an almost frail appearance. Seán immediately launched into an explanation for his visit, explaining that he was looking for information about his mother's life when she was younger.

Brigid Daly tried not to show how shocked she was to find Seán Byrne on her doorstep. Her heart pounded and she could feel her face flush as she listened to the tall, agitated man, her own nephew. She quickly ascertained that he did not know this as she stood nodding her head at him on her doorstep.

Before Seán finished ranting, Brigid asked him inside, out of sight of her nosy neighbours. She went into the kitchen, leaving Seán alone in the sitting room and made adequate noise to pretend she was busy making tea as the kettle hissed. She needed time to think, to work out how he had found her.

The screeching kettle broke her thoughts. After she carried the tea into the sitting room, she sat facing Seán in the somewhat old-fashioned room. An old china cabinet stood behind the door and was packed with ceramic dogs and tiny teacups full of dust. Inside the fireplace sat a small electric fire which clicked occasionally and lit up the worn red-patterned carpet. A large green-patterned sofa lined the opposite wall with a matching armchair placed directly under the window beside the PYE television. Seán could imagine her sitting there, watching passers-by, and wondered if she had seen him approaching. She could feel her heart racing and miss occasional beats. As Seán looked about the room, drinking his tea, he felt that there was something familiar about the place. He thought he had seen a photo of this room before but couldn't remember where. He was about to say this when Brigid, anxious to have this visit over, interrupted his thoughts.

"I was a friend of your mother's when we were young. But you probably know that?"

"Yes, like I said, I saw you at the funeral and the hotel in Knockbeg gave me your name. I had to do a bit of detective work to find your house though. Do you know there are two Daly houses on this street?" He smiled nervously at the stranger facing him.

Brigid's heart hurt. Seán was the image of Éamonn at that age and the resemblance was almost painful. She remained silent.

"I wanted to find out who you were," he said.

"Oh, why was that, love?"

The woman's strong Dublin accent grated on Seán but she seemed pleasant enough.

"Well, it just seemed that there was a lot that my sister and I didn't know about our mother. We – em – well – I thought you might be able to help."

Brigid coughed hard, pretending a half-eaten biscuit had caught in her throat.

"Well . . . we knew each other such a long time ago. She was a beauty, that much I remember, had all the boys after her. Myself, I was an awful tomboy."

Brigid wished she hadn't mentioned the bit about the boys but it was too late now and she could see she had got her nephew's attention. At the funeral she had wanted to hug him but instead had watched him from afar, her heart breaking with her longing to touch him, her own flesh and blood. She had been very fond of him as a baby and had not had any children of her own.

"Oh, was there any boy in particular?" Seán asked hopefully.

"Oh God no, love. Her father, your grandfather, was much too strict for that. No, just kid's stuff. You know how it is with teenagers."

Seán didn't know how it was; he was too shy to approach girls at school and any girl who spoke to him soon got fed up with his awkward, introverted ways.

"How come you used to be in Árd Glen?"

Brigid dreaded this question. She wasn't a good liar and was afraid that she would trip herself up.

"I had family there but they're all gone now."

"What was their name?" It was a small place and Seán knew that he would know them or at least know of them.

"My grandparents? Oh, love, you wouldn't have known them – before your time."

Although Seán knew he wasn't the brightest spark, he was smart enough to know when he was being fobbed off.

"Did you have any brothers or sisters?" Seán wasn't sure why he had asked this question.

"No, just me, lonely child as they say," she lied. "What about you? Did Maura have many more?"

Seán looked squarely at her, not knowing if she knew the answer but suspecting she did. He didn't answer.

"Did you keep in contact with my mother over the years?" he said instead.

"No, you know how it is, marriage, work, it all keeps you busy." Her voice was beginning to shake and she wondered if her nephew had noticed how nervous she was.

He stood up and looked about the room. He looked

at the large photo of Brigid and her husband on their wedding day that hung over the fireplace. He lifted a small black and white photo that sat on top of the television. It was an old photo of a small boy and girl sitting in a field with a collie dog.

"Is this you?"

"Yes," Brigid replied nervously.

"In Árd Glen?"

"Oh, God knows, it's such a long time ago. I look like I'm only three or so," she gulped.

"Who is the little boy" Seán asked, acutely aware that he was having to drag every ounce of information from this woman and not knowing why.

"Oh, a cousin, I think. Haven't seen him for years."

Seán replaced the photo and walked around the room, unaware of how strangely he was behaving. He was searching for something but he didn't know what.

"Have you any pictures of my mother?"

"No, love, sorry," she replied, her head slightly bowed as she sat with her hands clasped tightly together, as though she were praying.

"Have you always lived here?"

"A long time, yes, about, oh, well over twenty years now."

Seán was trying to think. He knew this visit was coming to an end and that he would have to make the most of it. He couldn't shake off the feeling that this house was somehow familiar to him.

"Did she ever visit here? With me?"

"What?" she asked, wondering if Seán knew more than he pretended.

"Was I here before? This place seems familiar to me. I think I've seen a photo of it somewhere."

"God, no, love, your mother wasn't one for Dublin. She hated it really," she replied nervously, feeling that she was digging a big hole for herself.

If it weren't for her brother and her need to protect him, Brigid would have loved nothing better than to throw her arms around her nephew and welcome him. Now this was never going to happen and they would have to remain strangers for life.

Seán sighed loudly and dug his hands into his pockets. He looked down and studied the worn, dark red carpet.

Brigid stood up.

"I'm sorry that I can't help you, love. What exactly was it you wanted to know?" She needed to know what Seán suspected.

"Oh, I don't know. I think my mother wasn't – you know – happy. I just thought you might be able to tell me a bit about her life, stuff I wouldn't know," he said, the resignation and defeat clearly audible in his voice.

Brigid felt her heart was going to break for this vulnerable, lost man. Her eyes watered slightly.

"I just remember her for her laugh, her love of life . . . she was always cheerful. That's all really, love."

Seán stood looking at the short Dublin woman. He wanted to say that she went a long way to the funeral of someone she hardly remembered but he didn't want to be rude. He knew by Brigid's expression that she knew what he was thinking. He thanked her for her time and left.

For the entire journey back, Seán mulled over how secretive Brigid Daly had been with him and he knew she wasn't telling him everything she knew. She had said that his mother hated Dublin and he knew for a fact that this was not true. He felt exhausted and wondered why he was bothering anyway. If his real father had had any interest in him he would have made contact over the years or at least after Michael Byrne had died. He knew there was no point in talking to Kate about any of this; she didn't seem to care and he couldn't understand this. One thing he was sure of was that there had to be at least one person in Árd Glen who knew who his father was.

Seán had barely driven two miles from Brigid Daly's house when she was already standing at her front door in her hallway with her coat and scarf on, her black handbag hanging loosely from her right hand. Her first reaction was to walk to her brother's office and tell him his son had been at her house, had somehow found her even though he didn't know that she was his aunt, the sister of his real father. She didn't want to tell him by phone, she needed to do it in person. She stood frozen on the red-patterned lino that covered her small square hall and ran all the way up her stairs. Suddenly, telling her brother about Seán's visit seemed like a very bad idea because Brigid had gone to Maura's funeral despite Éamonn's insistence that she stay away. She had wanted him to go with her but he refused, saying it would bring back too many memories. Brigid felt that it wasn't that, that the thought of seeing the son and daughter he abandoned was too much for him. She knew her brother had a guilty conscience for they had both known something of the life Michael Byrne had given the beautiful Maura. It could have been avoided but her brother had put his future before Maura and Seán and had never laid eyes on his daughter. Brigid had watched Kate at the funeral, her only chance perhaps to see her niece and nephew. She was the image of Maura and Brigid cried as she looked at the raven-haired girl, left now with so much responsibility – she had heard Maura's two younger children were born with some strange condition she had never heard of. Brigid couldn't bring herself to shake hands with Michael Byrne at the funeral, the cruelty he inflicted on her friend still sharp in her memory. She acknowledged that her brother had his own hand in Maura's death. If Éamonn had faced up to his responsibilities when Maura fell pregnant, she would still be alive.

Brigid thought of the man her brother had turned into and wondered if Maura, like herself, would have been disappointed. Éamonn had been so full of hope for a united Ireland. He planned on entering politics which is why he had studied law. He was a member of Sinn

Féin and hoped eventually to be part of Ireland's reunification through peaceful, political means. Brigid had even helped him in the early years, supporting marches and handing out leaflets, but had distanced herself when Éamonn started mixing with staunch Republicans who believed that Northern Ireland would never be free of British rule unless they forced it and this they believed couldn't be done through talking. Even now, Brigid couldn't understand why Éamonn gave up so easily on his ideals. A few years later when Éamonn graduated from university and began his career as a solicitor, Brigid was dismayed to hear him proudly recall how he got various "members" off on technicalities. Over the next few years she saw less and less of him although they managed never to fall out. Sometimes he would turn up on her doorstep in the darkness looking for a bed for the night. He said she was the only person he trusted in the world. She never asked why he couldn't go to his own home. She knew she wouldn't get an honest answer. When she married Joe Daly her brother visited less and less often. He insisted she never tell Joe about his political activities and she never did. Joe worked mostly in England as there was little work in Ireland at the time and it was always when he was away that her brother would call. Brigid often thought he must be watching her but again did not ask. When Joe died in a traffic accident in Lancashire, Éamonn spent more time at his sister's house. Once she had asked him if he wanted to move in – there was plenty of room and they would be company for each other. But he said it was too dangerous for her and this frightened her badly. She had promised Éamonn that she wouldn't go to Maura's funeral, which she had read about in the newspaper, but she couldn't keep her promise. She'd not had any contact with her old friend since the last time Maura had stayed in her house with Seán and so much had happened since then. Brigid's uncle was still living in Árd Glen at the time of Kate's birth and on a visit to Dublin told Brigid all the gossip, knowing she had been friendly with Maura Byrne and oblivious to the fact that his nephew was actually the new baby's father. Her uncle moved to London a few years after that and information about Maura dried up. In truth, while Brigid was heartbroken about Maura's death, she saw the sense in not attending. People had not figured out at the time that Maura had been seeing Éamonn and she didn't want to set any tongues wagging. She knew the gossip that had surrounded the family, especially since Maura's husband had died so tragically not even a year after her. It was an awful business altogether. She had followed the story closely in the newspapers and was amazed that the sweet-looking girl she had seen at Maura's funeral could have done something like that. The real reason she wanted to go was to see her niece and nephew and Maura's funeral was the perfect opportunity to mingle in a crowd without being seen. She would be able to see Seán and Kate whom she had often thought of. She had written to Maura a couple of times when the children were small but had received no reply and assumed Maura didn't want anything to do with her because of Éamonn's behaviour. She even thought she might approach Kate or Seán at the funeral. She longed to hug them but on the day of the funeral she stood in the background and went unnoticed, or so she thought. But Seán had noticed her and had gone to a lot of trouble to find her.

No, she couldn't tell Éamonn that Seán had been at her house because she never told him she had gone to the funeral.

Brigid took her coat off and sat down in her small living room that rarely saw visitors and looked at the photograph that Seán had been interested in, of Éamonn and herself in Árd Glen as children. Brigid sighed and thought what a mess it all was and how life almost never turns out as people hoped or planned. She leaned back in her chair and stared at the photo. Her house seemed deathly quiet with only the ticking of the clock and the distant hum of passing traffic to be heard, the sound of loneliness that had become her life, the sound of life passing her by.

Chapter 24

1972

Five months had passed at the institution and Tess had become as used to her new home as she could. It was play-time and she sat in the exercise yard with Leroy, the other children buzzing around them as they soaked up the rare winter sunshine.

"Leroy, what did you do?"

"What?"

"To come here. What did you do?"

Leroy reddened slightly, unsure whether to tell his friend what a nasty person he was. He thought about making something up but couldn't bring himself to lie to her. He had told so many lies already.

"Well . . . I used to be in an orphanage. Anyway, one brother . . . well, he used to . . ." Leroy looked at Tess. She was three years younger than him and he was sure that she didn't understand anything about sex. He found himself acutely embarrassed. “He used to do things to me . . . bad things. I hit him one day with his belt, over and over until I thought he was dead. I didn’t care. I just wanted to get away, to make him stop.” Leroy lowered his head. He hadn’t spoken much about this to anyone except Dr Cosgrove.

“Did you get away?” Tess asked, concerned.

Leroy laughed. This girl was so innocent. “I got away all right. I was sent here where I could be cured of Satan. Ha!”

“Was he dead?” Tess asked, her head turned to one side.

“No, pity he wasn’t. That way he couldn’t hurt any other kids.”

Tess thought for a few moments, absorbing this news. “What does orphanage mean?”

“It’s a home for orphans. You know, kids that have no family.”

“Do you not have a family?” Tess asked wide-eyed, unsure how this was possible.

“I have a mother. She’s coming back for me some day. As soon as she gets a nice flat for us both to live in.”

Tess nodded. “Is she American too?”

Leroy turned his face away from his friend and wondered when he would tell Tess that he wasn’t really American, that he made the whole thing up years ago to stop people noticing the colour of his skin. It hadn’t worked but he got used to people showing interest in his accent so he had kept it up.

"No, she's not American," he said simply, hoping to change the subject quickly. "What about you, Tess, what did you do?"

Tess looked over his right shoulder, trying to think about her answer, trying to remember exactly what the police said.

"I hit my father with a rock and he died."

Leroy's eyes opened wide, amazed that his new friend had done something like this.

"Why did you do that?" he asked, stunned, wondering if he had misjudged her.

"I don't know. I don't remember it."

"Then why did you say you did it?"

"Because they told me that I did."

Leroy stared at his friend, unsure what to say, his eyes searching her calm face. He didn't want to think she did something like that.

"Maybe you didn't do it. Maybe someone blamed you for it?"

Tess stared hard at the ground, unable to comprehend this information, memorising it so she could replay it later and try to make sense of it. The bell rang and the kids lined up in straight lines. Tess and Leroy were both deep in thought and were last to join the line as they went back inside for their lessons.

Chapter 25

1981

Sam Moran found himself at the Probate Office in the Four Courts in Dublin to view the last will and testament of Michael Byrne. Anyone had access to wills of the deceased; you just needed the person's date of death and their address to view the relevant records. He had done this sort of thing before but mostly in his junior years in a small newspaper in London where he wrote a short column on deceased estates. It was boring work but he knew that people liked reading what assets their neighbour had left behind and wrote the column for almost two years before getting a column covering current court cases which was much more to his liking.

He wasn't feeling particularly enthusiastic this morning. This story was beginning to drag out and he had more dead ends than he had ever encountered so he didn't feel confident that he would find anything unusual in Byrne's will.

When he eventually came upon the record he was looking for, Sam gasped at the information in front of him. So the gossip was true. Byrne wasn't the father of Seán Byrne. He was even more surprised to learn that he wasn't the father of the older girl either and had left the farm to Tess. He knew that Teresa Byrne wouldn't have understood this and, even if she did, he had left everything to her so why would she kill him? If she did do it, there must have been some other reason. He figured out that if Seán Byrne knew that he had been disinherited, he would have had a motive for the murder as he was mentioned as caretaker only of the farm until his sister came of age. He wondered if the police had looked into this back then. He doubted Kate Byrne had anything to do with it as the farm was never going to be hers anyway. Perhaps it wasn't about the farm? Perhaps someone had a grudge against Michael Byrne? But he didn't have anything to go on. He quickly jotted down the name of the solicitor's firm that handled the will and decided a visit to their offices on Aaran Quay might yield some more information.

Tess had sat at the same desk since starting her course in Knockbeg two weeks previously. By now, the other women in her class knew not to take this seat or the seat she preferred in the canteen. Tess's classmates, who were mostly older women, were protective of her and mothered her despite Nurse O'Connell's advice to the contrary. Overall, she had adjusted well to her new environment and was learning basic secretarial work including typing and shorthand.

Tess took her studies very seriously and soon her classmates were asking for her help and learning to ignore her comments about how they should pay more attention in class. In truth, Tess enjoyed feeling needed by her classmates. She could not remember much about her mother. She only remembered how she looked and, although she could not remember her voice, she recalled her insisting to anyone who would listen that her younger daughter was a bright girl. Tess had often heard Kate say this too but she had never believed it.

The journey by bus to Knockbeg each morning remained a tense, anxious time for her as she worried that the driver might take a different road that didn't end up in Knockbeg and she would be lost. She started memorising houses along the way or oddly shaped fields so that she would know that the driver was definitely going the right way and risked people's stares when she would hum to herself to avoid picking at her lips or hands. She made lists of the number of houses on the right of the bus between her stop and Knockbeg and often counted them aloud for the entire journey. It annoyed Tess when others told her not to worry as this did not help her; she knew things were always going to worry her. Nurse O'Connell was trying to teach her ways to solve problems when they occurred but it didn't stop her being troubled by what might happen. Dermot had told her that there are some things you cannot change and she knew this was one of them. Tess begged Kate to get Dermot to drive her instead but her sister had refused, saying she had to become more independent and that Dermot was needed on the farm. For some reason she didn't understand, the journey home didn't worry her so much as the bus made its way down the narrow country roads, dropping her off to a waiting Dermot who always pretended to have something to do near the edge of the farm at that time. He would walk her up to the house and ask her about her day. After talking to Dermot, Kate would give her tea and toast in the kitchen after which Tess helped her with housework and cooking the dinner. When Kate no longer needed her, Tess retreated to her room to work on her studies. She drew, much to Kate's annoyance, typewriter keys on the bedroom dresser to practise her speed, wiping them off only when Kate promised to price a second-hand typewriter the next time they went to Dublin. For once Tess felt like she was just like everybody else. She had a place to go to each day, a place where people asked her for help. Something she never expected in life was happening to her: she was happy.

Kate stared at the doctor as he explained Seán's test results. She had tried to waken Seán for his appointment but found him too hung-over to rouse. Despite the doctor's advice, he had continued to drink but had abandoned going to town at night. Instead he bought his drink in town and now confined his drinking to his room. Kate had tried to hide the keys so he couldn't drive but Seán always managed to threaten her enough to obtain them.

Dermot had driven her here and was waiting in the truck outside.

Liver failure, the doctor said it was and far worse than he had originally anticipated. Seán, he said, could live for years with this disease if he stopped drinking altogether. There was medication that could help with the maddening itch that he complained of but he could not be cured. Kate would have to keep a close eye on him to prevent him from drinking, which he acknowledged would not be easy.

When Kate walked back to where the truck was parked, her face pale and drawn, she didn't have to tell Dermot it was bad news. As she climbed into the truck, she felt hot stinging tears burn her eyes. She knew that although she felt sorry for her brother, she also felt sorry for herself now that she had him to care for as well. When Dermot placed his hand over hers and gently squeezed it, she did not draw it away but sat motionless staring down at her lap, the warmth and strength of Dermot's hand helping to ease her worries. She was pleased that he did not speak as she knew she would cry if he sympathised with her or tried to comfort her. When Kate squeezed Dermot's hand in return, he let her go, started the engine and headed towards home. He understood that Kate Byrne's pride could only take a little kindness and concern.

Sam Moran phoned to make an appointment at Roberts & Holford, solicitors in Aaran Quay, managing to deflect the queries of the efficient secretary as to the purpose of his meeting. He was not above pretending he wanted legal advice on a personal matter but hoped he wouldn't have to lie as this would definitely result in him being thrown out without the information he came for.

He had tried to talk to Seán Byrne one afternoon in Slattery's but found him too drunk to answer questions. A few days before he had tried to talk to Liam Kelly on the street but, as soon as he told him what he was writing about, the young Kelly went white as a sheet and ran in the opposite direction. Without thinking, Moran went after him and felt a little foolish about it later. Several people he knew saw him chase Kelly past the mart and behind Colliers Row but when he got there Kelly was nowhere to be seen. Moran wondered why Kelly would run and also wondered if the young Kelly had been questioned at the time of the murder although Moran reckoned he would have only been a teenager at the time.

When Sam arrived at the solicitor's for his appointment, he was led into the office of Éamonn McCracken, who shook his hand jovially and made small talk about the weather. Sam felt he was on to a winner and slowly introduced the reason for his visit. He watched as the ginger-headed man's face changed to an expression of shock and then anger and knew he had hit a nerve, although he had no idea why. McCracken soon composed himself and changed his previously friendly, confident manner to answering questions haltingly, stating in a dull, flat voice that while he personally didn't handle the Byrne will, his company did, and he could not divulge any personal information relating to any of their clients' affairs, living or dead. Sam tried to coax him, even tried to run his "just between us" routine but got nowhere.

"And you didn't know him personally then – never met him?" he asked.

"Like I said, Mr Moran, I didn't handle his case."

"Did you handle any legal issues for any of his family? Seems strange that he came here. It's a long way from home and –"

"What's your point, Moran? I haven't got all day."

"It doesn't make any sense, Mr McCracken – can I call you Éamonn?"

"No."

Sam, undaunted, continued. "My point is this. Like you, I'm a Dub. It doesn't really matter to me where I buy my meat, clothes, go for legal or any other type of advice. But I know the people around those parts. They don't change their habits easily. Not without a good reason anyway. Something made Michael Byrne drive over forty miles to write a will in Dublin, something made him come here specifically to you. Have you any idea why, Éamonn?" Sam was looking somewhat smug. He knew he wasn't going to get anything out of McCracken but he could at least annoy him a little before he left, or got thrown out.

McCracken leant back in his expensive leather chair and stared hard at Moran, his green eyes suddenly looking as black as coal, like small shiny black beads beneath his large red eyebrows, until the would-be journalist shifted nervously in his seat. He seemed to be thinking, his eyes darting left to right without ever fully taking them off Moran who had begun to sweat slightly.

Eventually McCracken spoke.

"I'm sorry I've wasted your time, Mr Moran. Now, if you'll excuse me, I have another appointment."

McCracken stood and moved toward the office door which was slightly ajar but stopped abruptly and turned to Sam, offering him his hand. He was a tall, strongly built man and Moran could see small white scars on his face. Then McCracken leant so close to Sam that he stiffened and pulled back, unsure of what McCracken was doing.

McCracken put his mouth close to Sam's ear. "It might be better for you, and for yours, if you don't go asking any more questions about me or my business. Do you understand me?" he whispered.

Sam took a step back and tried to prise his hand from McCracken's tight grasp. He considered making some smart comment or another but knew that if this solicitor, who knew the law, was threatening him, he had something big to hide, very big, and maybe very dangerous.

"Yes, I understand," he said in a quiet voice, his only goal being to get out in one piece and think later.

"Good," McCracken said slowly while releasing Moran's hand at the same slow speed. He opened the door and stood to one side, watching Moran walk away then turn his head nervously back before leaving the building.

There had been something in McCracken's demeanour that shook the Dubliner who was not easily frightened. Sam felt he had drifted onto something but he didn't know what. As he left the building he felt very uneasy and slightly dazed and stood for a moment looking into the polluted Liffey below him. It was almost three o'clock and he was supposed to cover an article for Talbot on illegal dumping. Despite his nervousness, he understood that McCracken had threatened him which, rather than put him off, had excited him. This story was probably bigger than he realised.

Sam decided to remain in Dublin for one drink before going home and sat in the far snug of Finnegan's pub mulling things over. McCracken had worried him and he wanted to know more about who he was dealing with. After what happened in the solicitor's office, his instincts should have told him to stop working on the story, to tell Talbot he had come up empty, but he decided to make a few enquiries about McCracken. He needed to be sure that McCracken wouldn't come after him even if he dropped the story. Perhaps he was bluffing, although he didn't think this was the case. Sam still had some contacts in Dublin, especially the not so law-abiding kind he had grown up with. He wandered down Moore Street, a street in which he had learnt all there is to know about life, a street where he had stolen his first wallet only to receive a beating he still remembered from his father who made him return it, red-faced, to its owner. He felt slightly depressed walking through these familiar surroundings, looking at the recognisable faces of people still poor despite the long days of hard work in every weather, watching constantly for the police to arrive and run you if you didn't have a trader's licence. At the end of the street, as expected, he found Rabbit Flanagan, a nickname he supposed his old friend got from his ability to run fast when the police arrived on the street. Rabbit had been adopted by a couple with eleven children of their own and, due to his strong resemblance to the family, gossip had it that he was the illegitimate child of their oldest daughter who left to work in England and never returned. Moran didn't waste any time with small talk and watched Rabbit's eyes move left to right, his wild red hair giving him an almost comical appearance. Sam told him as much as he had to. Rabbit looked around to see if anyone was listening in the busy street and Sam felt his friend was putting on the spy/informant drama a little too heavily.

"Jaysus, Moran, you don't want to be getting

involved with that lot – they'll kneecap ya if ya get in their way!" Rabbit said, his diminutive frame only barely visible above his stall.

"Wha' lot are ya talking 'bout?" Sam's Dublin accent always got stronger when he was on these streets.

"The Provos."

Sam looked at his old friend and laughed so loud he definitely drew attention to both himself and his nervous-looking informant.

"Oh come on, are ya telling me that this solicitor is involved with the IRA? That's the best yet. The cops must have hit ya on the head once too often, Rabbit."

"Ya asked me, I'm telling ya and that's the truth. He gets people off who're involved with the Ra. Few from 'round here, I know them personally. He's high up, doesn't get his hands dirty, but he's a member, mark my word."

Sam stood still and looked solemnly at Rabbit Flanagan to see if his friend was messing with him but Rabbit stared squarely back before nervously shooting glances left and right. Sam realised his friend really was frightened and changed the subject quickly, even buying some fruit to pass himself off as a regular customer before walking swiftly down Moore Street and towards the quays. He had missed his landfill story for Talbot, had discovered information he rather he hadn't but was still no closer to the truth behind the Byrne murder.

Chapter 26

1967

Maura's life had not changed much in the nineteen years that she had been married to Michael Byrne. Her parents had passed away which she took very hard despite the fact that she was not close to either parent and had resented them for making her marry Michael, a resentment she knew she would carry to her own grave. She had no relationship with her brother. Although Jimmy lived within a few miles of her, they rarely saw each other. Maura's life revolved around her three children. Seán and Kate were now almost fully grown. Her youngest, Tess, was by far the most difficult to manage and although she could be a loving child at times, she shared her father's unusual personality and watchful way.

Maura was almost eight months pregnant again and was surprised that the pregnancy had progressed this far, having endured three miscarriages since Tess was born. When Ben was born a few weeks later, Maura tried to show an interest in the child but left his care more and more in the hands of her eldest daughter. Maura found herself forgetting where she'd left things and once forgot her way home after shopping in town, walking in the opposite direction until a neighbour stopped and offered her a lift home. Her doctor said it was probably an early change of life but she didn't think he was right. She stopped taking the sleeping tablets she had been taking for years but found her memory worsening. Since Ben's birth Michael had not abused her in any way and Maura wondered if it was because he now had a son, although he showed little interest in the baby. Some days she allowed her imagination to run away with her and played her life out in a completely different way to the life she was living. Often never having met Éamonn McCracken. Sometimes she had married a man of her choice, a man she loved, and lived far away from Árd Glen, as far away as New York or Toronto, even though she had never been to either of these places. Maura found her memory of the past remained sharp even though she couldn't remember what she did yesterday. She would often forget what she was saying mid-sentence only to start the whole conversation again, much to the annoyance of her children. Once the doctor reassured her, Maura stopped worrying about her memory problems, thinking if only she had difficulty forgetting her past instead of the present, it mightn't be a bad thing at all. By the time Maura started to forget her children's names or the fact that the baby in the house was in fact hers, tests in Dublin revealed a rare progressive early dementia for which no treatment was available. Maura deteriorated rapidly and soon after Ben was one year old, she was confined to bed with Kate and a reluctant Tess caring for her around the clock.

Chapter 27

1974

After two and half years at the institution, Tess had given up hope of ever seeing her family again. The nursing staff knew not to give her the present her sister sent every year for her birthday and at Christmas as this sent her into a rage during which she inflicted deep wounds into her arms and legs and followed with a period of elective mutism during which she wouldn't even talk to Leroy or Dr Cosgrove.

Following several ignored letters to her family, inviting them in to meet with him, Cosgrove made an application to have Tess transferred to a children's home. He felt she didn't belong in a psychiatric institution but there were no places in the homes and he'd had no choice but to keep her here. He no longer tried to bring her mind back to the murder of her father. The child had no recollection of the event whatsoever and became extremely distressed whenever the murder was raised. Tess spent her time attending school at the institution and was proving herself to be a bright girl who was achieving above expectations. Cosgrove continued to keep her isolated in her own bedroom but not because he felt she was a danger to others. Rather he felt that her lack of understanding of acceptable behaviour resulted in the altercations she had with the other children. He also knew that she preferred to be alone, that she needed a quiet place where she could think. Cosgrove was worried about her as Leroy was going home at the end of the week and he knew she would be lost without him. He had told her but she did not respond and walked away from him, humming. He knew this was a bad sign. The following Friday the staff and patients gathered around a cake for Leroy as his departure coincided with his sixteenth birthday. Leroy smiled and blew his candles out. Later, when the fuss died down and the children went to their dormitories, staff allowed Tess and Leroy to sit together outside the nurses' station.

"I'll write to you, Tess," Leroy said, lowering his head to hide his tears.

"Make sure your spellings are right," Tess said matter-of-factly as she stared straight ahead, which made him smile through his watery eyes.

He could hear her humming softly and noticed she had started to rock slightly back and forth on the bench, wringing her fingers to the motion. As their conversation died, Leroy felt awkward in the silence.

"My mam got us a flat in town. It has two

bedrooms," he said nervously, even though he knew that Tess did not want to discuss his leaving.

"Leroy?"

"Yeah, Tess?"

"Are you normal now?"

"What?"

"Are you normal now? You must be because they're letting you go home."

Leroy smiled a sad slow smile at his friend. "As long as people leave me alone I am normal. So are you, Tess. Don't forget that. It's what other people do to us that makes us do bad things." He cleared his throat and shifted nervously on his seat. There was something he wanted to ask her. "Tess, can I kiss you?" he asked nervously.

"No," Tess replied, staring hard at her friend before looking away quickly.

"Please? I won't hurt you. I promise."

Tess nodded and closed her eyes as she had seen Kate do when Noel kissed her at the front door at night before he left. Her heart pounded. Leroy leant forward. He could hear the nurse coughing loudly to let him know she was watching him as he gently kissed Tess on the lips. Tess pulled back as though the kiss had hurt her and wiped her mouth with her sleeve which made Leroy laugh.

"Is that the first time you have been kissed, Tess?"

"Yes," she replied, still rubbing her mouth.

"Did you like it?"

"No, it burns," she replied, staring straight ahead and resurrecting her humming.

Leroy looked at his strange friend and laughed aloud. He wanted to hug her but knew she wouldn't let him and was thankful that she had let him kiss her.

The nurse came from behind the station, anxious that Leroy didn't try anything more than a kiss on Tess who was not yet thirteen.

"Okay, time to go to bed. Leroy, you head back to your ward."

Leroy stood and smiled at Tess, feeling his tears resurface.

"Bye, Tess. I won't forget you."

Tess stood and nodded, staring squarely at her friend, arms straight by her sides. Without a word she turned and walked away, leaving Leroy alone in the cold corridor.

Tess withdrew into herself after Leroy left and took to hiding in areas of the hospital she wasn't supposed to be in.

When Leroy was there Tess could pass the evenings in the company of the other children and staff for sing-alongs and games and managed to hide her discomfort by sitting beside her friend, who always seemed to enjoy the activities. She did not have to speak when he was there and no one expected or asked her to join in, which she preferred because she did not understand the purpose of the games, especially the ones where there was no winner.

She had long ago by chance discovered a place where she could be alone. The stairs at the bottom of her corridor led down to a hallway where the kitchen staff had their locker rooms, the door to which was always locked. Tess would hide patiently on the stairs and wait for one of the staff to emerge from the kitchens and go to the locker rooms. Once they unlocked the large spring-loaded door, she would sneak in behind them and make her way from there to the rows of disused, damp wards which were situated in the oldest part of the hospital. She would then wander through the cold dark corridors alone, glad to be far from the noise of the children on her ward. One of the wards faced out onto an unkempt garden, overgrown with bushes and tall trees and Tess liked to sit on the windowsill and paint in the silence as the daylight faded. She never ventured as far as the ward at the very end of the long corridor because she heard one of boys say that it faced out on an old graveyard for children and she was afraid that she might see ghosts there. When she tired of painting she would walk through the maze of wards alone, calling out occasionally as she enjoyed the sound of her voice echoing through the hallways before sitting on the floor of Ward B and humming to herself until the light finally faded into darkness. Then she would walk northwards towards the front of the hospital and past rooms which were now used as offices until she came to a large brown door that led directly onto the foyer. There she would wait to be "found" by the staff.

Although she liked the solitude of these wards, Tess would have preferred to be allowed to go to her own room but staff never allowed this, insisting that she mix with the other children and make friends but Tess did not know how to make friends. Other children told her off when she tried to speak to them about butterflies. Like Seán and Kate, they were not interested in these things and Tess could not understand this. When the nurses would eventually find her in the foyer, they would wonder how she had got there, knowing that no matter how much they asked her, she would never tell them.

Chapter 28

1981

Kate phoned for Dr Doyle to visit Seán at home for the second time that week. Her brother's condition was worsening and, despite Dermot's help, she found it impossible to get him to the surgery. On several occasions, she had to coax Seán from the truck as he tried to drive to town for drink. Once, despite his weakening strength, he had hit her hard in the face, Dermot moving quickly to her defence and stopping only when Kate signalled that she was fine.

Kate found it hard to look at her brother now. His skin was yellow and his teeth had begun to rot through neglect. He hardly ate and with the exception of his bulging, raised stomach, he was now skin and bone. He neither shaved nor bathed with Kate usually trying to wash him quickly before the doctor or nurse came. He had changed mentally also. When he did speak, his words were sometimes difficult to understand. Kate did not know why but sometimes she heard Seán screaming Tess's name. She would run into his room to find him pointing into thin air. The words Kate did understand she wished she hadn't as Seán used such filthy language. He was severely dehydrated and when Dr Doyle suggested he be hospitalised for a couple of weeks, Kate was relieved at the break and hoped proper nursing care would help strengthen her brother. She did not go with him in the ambulance as she would have no way of getting back to the house in time for Ben's return from school. She was glad someone else would be caring for her brother for a while and did not feel guilty as the old Kate would have done. Seán had brought these problems on himself and she was now exhausted and had long since moved beyond care or pity for her lost brother.

Sam Moran was late leaving his office in Wicklow town for the fourth time this week and was aware that Mona would think he was either carrying on behind her back or was hitting the bottle. He was doing neither – not that either activity was beyond him and he hadn't exactly been a model husband. What he was actually doing was working, finishing off mindless reports on marts, house prices, and other tedious articles that Talbot said he was falling behind on. When he was sure that the rest of the staff had left the office he would spend a couple of hours looking through archives on IRA activity in Wicklow and on the Byrne murder, hoping to find a connection.

Most Thursday evenings he would have joined the usual bar flies for a couple of pints before going home but the truth was he hadn't felt at ease since his meeting with McCracken in Dublin the previous week. On more than one occasion, he felt that he was being watched. He knew that his imagination was not running away with him. He had met plenty of rough types before and was not easily scared. What worried him more was his friend's warning that McCracken was involved with the Provos. Although logic told him that this was unlikely, it was unusual for Rabbit to be either wrong or scared and he was definitely scared. But it didn't make sense to Sam. Why would a well-educated man of McCracken's social standing be involved with the Provos?

As he left the office he pulled his collar up against the cold wind that blew around the yard noisily, scattering the fallen leaves. The sky was dark grey, threatening a heavy downpour. In a corner of the parking area, Sam thought he caught a glimpse of a figure behind a large tree and felt his heart skip a beat. If someone was trying to scare him, they were making a good job of it. He quickly got into his car, locking the door before driving swiftly away towards home.

Kate squealed nervously as she drove the battered truck through the near field, Dermot sitting beside her, white-knuckled and tense in the passenger seat. He had moved the cattle from the field earlier that morning, joking with Kate that he was afraid she would run them over. Dermot was teaching Kate to drive. He noticed over the past few days that her face looked younger, now that Seán was in hospital. She was at least getting to sleep through the night and with both Ben and Tess away all day, she had more time to herself than she had ever known.

Kate was nervous about the idea of driving at first. She wasn't sure that she would ever need to learn how to drive but Dermot had insisted, saying that if neither he nor Seán were around and Ben was ill, she would need to be able to take him to town. Kate knew that Seán might not recover and hoped that she could rely on Dermot to be around. She looked squarely at him.

"You're not thinking of abandoning me, are you?" she asked half-smiling, not wanting to make a big deal out of it but nervous just the same.

"No, Kate, I'm not, but you need to be as independent as possible, you know?"

"Yeah, you're right," Kate replied, still feeling slightly worried that Dermot had had enough of working part-time on the small farm and perhaps had notions of moving on. She had to know if this was the case and despite the jokes and laughter at her hopeless driving, the question burned in her mind for the rest of the lesson.

When they went back to the house, Kate offered him some tea and they sat in silence as they ate leftover fruitcake and put turf on the dying fire. Winter seemed to have stolen autumn's place and an icy wind had blown about the farm for days.

When he stood to go back to work, Kate followed him to the door. He turned, sensing that she had something to say.

"Dermot, I meant what I said. I like having you here. I'd hate to see you go. I . . . I need you here . . ."

Dermot smiled shyly at Kate. He wanted to hold her, to kiss her but stood awkwardly in the doorway, blushing slightly and lowering his head towards the floor to hide his discomfort.

"I'm not going anywhere, Kate, honestly. I like it here. I like being with you," he said slowly, amazed at his candidness. "You've nothing to worry about."

He looked up at Kate who seemed as nervous as he was. His heart raced as he leaned slowly forward, Kate leaning in to meet him, and they kissed clumsily and quickly in the open doorway. They separated and looked away, both of them self-conscious and embarrassed. Dermot moved forward again and wrapped his strong lean arms around her. He could feel her body tremble as he pulled her towards him and kissed her again, their shyness now dissipating. They kissed more fervently, Dermot moving her wayward curls as he kissed her neck, her face, her lips. Kate raised herself onto her toes and pushed her body into his large frame, moving her hands passionately through his thick black hair, his arms now caressing her back. They parted again and looked into each other's eyes, searching, questioning. This moment was just as she had imagined it would be on so many lonely nights in her room. It felt natural and almost familiar, as though they had always been together. Dermot smiled at her and ran his fingertips gently along her face. He kissed her once more, very gently, then he left the kitchen and went back to his work, leaving Kate smiling shyly behind the closed door.

Chapter 29

1974

Three months, two weeks and five days after Leroy left the institution, he returned abruptly and without notice. He was led by two police through the shocked crowd in the common area on the second floor where the children were having a drama lesson and were practising their new play. Tess who was sitting to one side, her fingers placed in her ears to drown out the sound of tin whistles and recorders, dropped her arms and looked at her friend. His face was cut and bruised. He smiled at her, showing two missing front teeth, and raised his arm slowly and painfully to wave at her. Tess stared after him until he disappeared from view. A strange feeling rose in her stomach that she did not recognise, something like the feeling you get on a swing but not exactly the same. She looked at the teacher whose eyes had begun to water and at the nurse who was shaking her head from side to side as she walked quickly to the teacher's side.

"Again!" the nurse whispered. "I wouldn't let her mind a dog, never mind that poor boy!"

Tess heard this but then lost track as the nurse continued to speak in a whisper and the teacher nodded, her eyes still moist.

At the nurses' station that evening Tess stayed out of view and listened carefully as the finishing shift brought the night shift up to date. Tess found it easier to hear what people said when she didn't have to look at their faces and couldn't understand why people always insisted on this. She could never find the words to tell them that if she had to look at them, she couldn't hear them and had no idea what they were asking her to do. She waited patiently until she heard her friend's name mentioned.

"Leroy Brennan returned today. The police picked him up and brought him to hospital. He's had four stitches to a cut above his right eye. His face and torso are badly bruised and he has lost two teeth. He said he has no pain but staff should check on him later," the voice said matter-of-factly.

"Do we know what happened yet?" a female voice asked.

"He said his mother's boyfriend beat him because he refused to go to the shop for cigarettes. She's saying he was fighting with kids in the flats."

Tess could hear some of the nurses make "tut-

tutting" sounds although no one spoke and they moved on to discuss the next child.

Tess did not see Leroy for the rest of the day but was pleased when he appeared in the common area that evening and quietly sat down beside her. She heard him take a deep breath.

"My mam got a new boyfriend," he said simply before raising his hands to his bruised face and falling silent beside her.

Tess knew that Leroy did not want her to ask any questions so she remained silent, glad to have her only friend back. She noticed that Leroy had reverted to his strong American accent which had mellowed in previous months.

At breakfast the following morning some of the other kids were dying to rile Leroy about yet another short stay with his mother.

"Where's your ma, Leroy?"

"Dunno," he said sharply, looking at Tess and reddening slightly beneath his light brown skin.

"Didn't take her long to dump you this time, did it?" another voice asked from the other end of the table.

"Shut up!" Leroy shouted, feeling increasingly angry and hoping to stop the conversation before it got too far. He did not want Tess to know the truth about his mother, not when he couldn't even face it himself.

"Ah, face it, Leroy. She only wants you wh–"

Leroy pushed the boy in the chest, knocking him off the bench and onto the ground before savagely beating him on the head with his closed fists. Two nurses moved quickly from the corner and separated the two, holding them back as they tried to lunge at each other again.

Leroy looked over at Tess and was upset to see that the fighting had distressed her and that she had jumped up from her seat and was now kneeling on the ground rocking back and forth. She was muttering about a lake.

The taller nurse pulled Leroy by the arm and insisted he apologise while simultaneously asking the other boy, whose face was bleeding, to apologise for upsetting Leroy. Tess quietened quickly and watched with great interest as the boys shook hands and said their sorrys before walking swiftly away. Within minutes the fracas was over and everyone returned to the table to finish their breakfast. Tess stared around at the other children and at the two nurses who had resumed their conversation in the corner as though the fight had never taken place. Something about this intrigued her. She quickly recorded each sequence of the event in her mind, anxious to remember everything and replay it later in the quiet of her usual hiding place.

Chapter 30

1981

In Wicklow town, Sam Moran peered out through the dusty office blinds before grabbing his coat to leave for the day. Over the past few weeks his days had been more or less the same. As well as his usual columns, he worked late on the Byrne case before going straight home. His new-found commitment to the newspaper didn't go unnoticed by his employer who was trying to make more of an effort to get along with him.

Sam had become more nervous of late as Mona had told him a man had knocked one morning looking for him. Naturally, she thought her errant husband had brought some trouble on himself and quizzed Sam all evening about it. Mona was partly right. Sam was sure that McCracken or one of his henchmen was watching him since their meeting but he wondered what they wanted as they knew his routine by now. Sam also knew the visit to his house was another warning, a warning which said "We know where you live, we know you have a family so keep your mouth shut" and wondered if this was the last he would hear about it.

Despite the threat, he had continued making discreet enquiries. He thought he had stumbled on something much bigger than the Byrne murder and knew that if he figured out what that was, he could find himself at the top of his game.

Sam was just about to get into his car when he heard a voice call his name. From behind the tree a man's voice told him to come over where they couldn't be seen. Sam thought about getting into his car and driving off as fast as he could as there was no one in the office to come to his aid.

As if he read his thoughts the voice said, "I wouldn't even think about driving off. I have a gun pointed at you. You won't get far."

Sam stood back from the car. He couldn't understand how he could think so clearly but he reasoned that if this bloke wanted to kill him, he would have done it by now. He figured they just wanted to intimidate him some more, make sure he would keep his nose out of the Byrne case. Sam walked slowly to the corner of the yard, towards the oak tree where the voice was coming from. He thought the accent sounded Northern but there was a howling wind so he couldn't quite make it out. He looked fleetingly to his left at the row of windows in his office building.

"I know there's no one in there, don't think we haven't been watching you, so quit the shit!" the voice said.

Definitely a Northern accent, Sam thought to himself.

"What do you want with me?" he asked, trying to sound as though he wasn't frightened.

"Come closer."

Behind the tree stood a short, stocky man, not McCracken, wearing jeans and a black jacket with expensive-looking leather shoes. He was also wearing a balaclava.

Very fucking brave, thought Sam.

"Despite our warning, you've been going around asking questions about a mutual friend of ours, haven't ye now?"

"Depends on what friend you're talking about," Sam quipped. "I have a lot of friends."

Sam felt the barrel of the gun against his cheek and fell backwards, only just managing to stop his fall. He straightened himself up and looked directly at the masked man.

"Don't get smart, mister!" said the man. "You're in no position to get mouthy. Now, we know where ye live, lovely wife by the way, nice arse. Lovely kids too, daughter looks like she'll be a looker like her oul' one. Might take a better look next time I call."

Sam swallowed hard and knew his mouth had, as usual, got the better of him. He stayed silent, waiting.

"Take this as your last warning. If we hear about

you asking questions about our friend, you won't get another chance. Do you understand what I'm telling ye?"

"Yes," Sam replied weakly.

The masked Northerner stepped out and looked around him quickly. He punched Sam twice in the face and ribs, knocking him to the ground before kicking him in the stomach.

"That's to make sure you're not a slow learner, right?"

Sam coughed hard on the cold ground and tried to catch his breath. When he sat up he felt sticky ooze coming from his face and knew he was bleeding. He let out a long groan as he stood up. He got into his car, turned on the light and looked at his face in the rear-view mirror. There was a long, narrow gash just below his eye from which blood trickled down his face, making the cut look much worse than it was. His ribs hurt. He hadn't been beaten up since he was a teenager in Dublin, preferring in his later years to talk his way out of trouble. But there would be no talking his way out of this. He knew these people meant business. Whatever it was that McCracken was hiding, it was heavy. Even though he realised the danger he was in, he already knew he would continue working on the story, the desire to know what McCracken was hiding fuelling his insatiable curiosity. He needed to know how Byrne and McCracken were connected and would have to come up with ideas to get this information without drawing attention to himself.

He drove off, looking into his rear-view mirror to check if anyone was following him but feeling slightly ridiculous as he did so. The cut below his eye had started to bleed more profusely. He knew he was facing a long night of interrogation from Mona and spent the journey concocting a story even she would believe.

Kate was worried. The letter for Tess from her training course stated that they had found her work experience in Marshall's Art and Craft Centre in Glenmire, a larger town about twenty miles from Árd Glen. Kate did not like the thought of Tess in a town where no one knew about her difficulties. At least in Knockbeg, some of the women doing the course with Tess had been from around the area and knew the family. Nurse O'Connell tried to reassure her, reminding her how worried she had been when Tess started the course. Kate was pleased to see the changes in her younger sister who, although anxious about the two-week work experience, was also excited about her "first job". Kate finally relented and was pleased that, as there was no daily bus to Glenmire, Dermot would have to drive Tess there and collect her each day. The work experience wasn't due to start for another four weeks and perhaps by then she would be confident enough to drive Tess there herself.

Delighted that her sister had agreed to let her go, Tess jumped around the room excitedly. She couldn't wait to show her new boss how well she could type and answer the phone. Later, when the reality of the upcoming change set in, she withdrew to her room, making lists of all the things that could go wrong.

Later that day, when Kate visited her brother in hospital, she found him propped up in bed. A drip slowly fed fluid into a vein in his left arm and his skin was covered in a light pink lotion. He was shaved and bathed and looked like he had already put on weight. Kate hadn't visited the first week, pretending to her older brother that Ben had been sick and that she hadn't wanted to bring any infection into the hospital. The truth was she hated seeing Seán so ill and, besides, there was a small part of her that was still smarting about him hitting her only a couple of weeks before. She wasn't sure if her brother was annoyed that she hadn't visited sooner as he looked sleepily in her direction with no particular expression on his face. She looked around the ward, which had a long row of beds on either side, each placed directly under a long narrow window. The room was sparse and clean with each bed covered by crisp white sheets and pillows with a small wooden locker by its side. There were no flowers, no colour, and the ward was silent as seven or eight men lay on their beds sleeping. Kate wondered if Seán was sedated as his eyelids were half closed.

She told him that she was learning to drive and he showed some interest. She told him about Tess's work experience but could tell that he didn't want to hear anything about his youngest sister. He asked her about the farm. Kate hadn't heard Seán express an interest in the farm in years and wondered if he was going to recover and return to the man he had been.

After sitting by his bedside for some time she could see that he was tired. As she rose to leave, he gently caught her hand and shook it. He had tears in his eyes. When Kate asked him what was wrong, he simply shook his head. She kissed her brother on the forehead, something she had not done in a very long time and promised to return in a couple of days. When she reached the top of the large, old-fashioned ward, she looked back. Seán was waving weakly at her. She could see that he was smiling. She waved back and slowly walked out of the ward down several long corridors towards the exit and cried all the way home.

Tess screamed with excitement. She had passed all of her exams and her group were going out to a hotel in Knockbeg for dinner. Kate knew better than to express any concern and made sure someone in the group was responsible for Tess during the evening, her friend Peggy agreeing to collect her and drop her home at the end of the night.

When Peggy arrived she assured Kate that she had gone through all of this worry with her own daughters who were now married with daughters of their own. Kate wondered if Peggy thought she was Tess's mother and felt slightly irritated by the large jolly woman. Kate knew that people thought she was overreacting in her concern for Tess. She knew that no one understood her worries, no one except Dermot who seemed to understand her younger sister well.

Rather than eat alone, she had invited Dermot for dinner after she put Ben to bed. When the meal was underway, Kate ran herself a bath. She stood naked, looking at herself in the mirror that had been broken as long as she could remember. She didn't have a bad figure. She admired herself briefly before lowering herself into the warm water. It was hard to know where the years had gone since her mother died. Somehow her life seemed to end then and was replaced with an existence which involved caring for almost every member of her family except herself. Kate made an effort to soften her mood; she didn't want to be in bad form when Dermot arrived. Things weren't so bad. Ben was improving and the health service had even offered her weekend respite where they would take Ben into one of their houses to give her a break, but so far she hadn't availed of it. She didn't feel ready for anyone else to care for Ben. Tess, too, was making progress. Kate was amazed that she wanted to go on the night out without knowing what was on the menu and half expected a phone call asking her to come and collect her distraught sister. She worried about this as she knew it would set Tess back months.

She had ironed a dress she hoped Dermot had not seen her wear before and placed her good underwear out on the bed, blushing slightly as she had no intention of Dermot seeing her underwear, good or bad. When she was ready she looked approvingly at herself. Her dress was a deep red that complemented her dark hair. She put on some lipstick and stood staring at the woman in the mirror.

When Dermot arrived he took Kate by surprise by kissing her at the door. She blushed slightly which made her feel like a silly teenager and not the elegant woman she had seen in the mirror only minutes before. She found herself looking behind Dermot and into the yard, as though Seán would appear and ruin her night. They ate slowly, Dermot complimenting her cooking and Kate laughing at how silly this "date" was as she had cooked his meals for months now, albeit less fancy ones. Dermot had brought a bottle of sherry, unsure if Kate drank. She didn't and neither did he but neither wanted to offend and each had a large glass of the sickly sweet brown liquid that made them both a little tipsy. After dinner Kate cut slices of cake for them both and they sat on the floor beside the fire in the seldom-used sitting room and talked about their lives, Kate leaving out many events that were still too painful to discuss. They talked about their individual dreams, or at least Dermot did, for Kate had long since abandoned hers. Dermot told her about his plan to buy his own farm, about the falling out with his father. She was the first person in Árd Glen he had told this to and the significance of this was not lost on him. They talked about their families and Kate's hope that Seán would recover and run the farm as he had done as a younger man. There weren't any of the long, awkward silences that Kate had been dreading and they sat talking until both of them fell into a comfortable silence and looked peacefully into the flickering fire. After some time, Dermot reached over and kissed her on the forehead, then the neck, his hands caressing her shoulders. She shuddered at his touch and when he whispered, "Is this okay?" she nodded, too scared to speak. After they kissed passionately for what seemed like an eternity, Dermot stopped and looked lovingly at her. He moved her around to face away from him and pulled her body against his, covering her bare arms with his as they rested there, taking long, even breaths in harmony with each other.

At last Kate turned to look at him, a look that said: "It's okay, I'm ready." His eyes searched hers. He stood and helped her to her feet. They kissed again and walked arm in arm down the hallway to her room, closing the door behind them.

After three unmerciful days of the silent treatment, Mona Moran was finally talking to her husband. She had tried to find out what he had done to receive such a beating and felt that his refusal to go to the police meant it must have been something illegal or at least underhand. She worried that it might be an aggrieved husband as she suspected her husband had been unfaithful to her over the years – though she had no evidence of this and preferred not to think about it. She worried that Sam had got himself caught up in something and wondered if she should speak to her father about it. He knew people in lots of high places. She only agreed not to when Sam pleaded with her to drop it for all their sakes. This really worried her, as she had never seen her tough Dublin husband frightened before, and she finally agreed to let the subject drop providing that he never came home looking like that again.

The following Saturday, Sam knew it would be a good day to observe Rabbit Flanagan from a distance in the busy market street. He made an excuse that the whole family needed a day out in Dublin and that it would be nice to call into his younger sister Abby while they were in the area. Sam knew that Mona hated Abby and that the feeling was mutual, his upper-crust wife never having taken to his "salt of the earth" sister. The day was cold but the sun shone in a clear blue sky. A brass band was playing as they made their way down Henry Street. Sam hoped the band would be turning right down Moore Street where he could hide behind them and get a good clandestine look at his friend Rabbit. He felt bad that he had dragged him into this mess and was worried that they might have roughed him up or worse. He wanted to make sure his old friend was okay.

Sam was disappointed when the band kept going straight towards Mary Street and he had to make his way down Moore Street without their cover.

He left Mona and his two daughters looking in

clothes shops and walked on with his young son by the hand. At the end of the street he could see the back of Rabbit's unmistakable wild red hair. Sam walked on, careful to stay well out of sight behind the throngs of Saturday shoppers. When his spoiled youngest child kept whimpering for an ice cream, he squeezed the boy's hand tightly to quieten him, promising him one when they got back to O'Connell Street and pressing some coins into his other hand. They were now quite close to Rabbit's "stall" which was made from the base of a pram and stacked high with packets of toilet rolls and washing powder. Sam could see that Rabbit was trying to sell illegal bangers for Halloween to some teenage boys who were brave enough to haggle with him, the bangers hidden in the pram out of sight of the police. Sam didn't know how his friend made a living this way. Street trading was in both their blood but Sam hated it. He was the type of man who needed a regular pay packet.

Sam could still hear the band play in the distance and the occasional call of the traders "Get yer oringis 'n' apples!" as he moved closer, carefully searching the crowd even though he felt a little silly. What would the Provos be doing here on Saturday – stocking up on bananas? Still, someone had seen him talking to Rabbit that day and he knew McCracken could have got someone to follow him from his office.

Then Sam cringed as he got a side view of his friend's bruised face and cut lip. He moved closer to his friend's stall as his son squirmed and moaned, trying desperately to loosen Sam's grip on his small hand. Sam held tighter as the boy pulled away, yelling that he would tell his mammy. When Sam loosened his grip his son fell sideways onto the ground, his ice cream money falling everywhere on the busy path. He started to shout and scream at Sam who put his hand over the boy's mouth to quieten him while simultaneously looking over his shoulder toward where Rabbit stood less than ten yards away. He saw that his friend was looking through the crowd and directly at him. Sam gasped at Rabbit's half-missing right ear. There was a long jagged gash from his jaw line ending millimetres from his throat. It was only a flesh wound but someone had wanted to frighten his friend badly. Rabbit stood and looked for a brief moment at his friend, his eyes giving nothing away, no expression, no emotion. He blinked briefly and lowered his head before turning back to his stall.

Sam turned and pretended to look into a shop window while he gathered his thoughts. His stomach churned and he could feel tears springing to his eyes. He wanted to tell Rabbit that he was sorry but knew that his friend was signalling to him to go away. After a minute he began to walk back in the direction of Henry Street, hauling his protesting son after him by the hand, hoping that some day, when it was safer, he could make it up to his friend. But today was definitely not that day.

Chapter 31

1974

Two months after Leroy returned to the institution, Tess sat silently in Dr Cosgrove's office for her weekly session, her mouth moving slowly as though she was about to speak. Tess spoke less and less these days and Cosgrove watched her closely, knowing she was about to launch into one of her rare questions and relieved for the distraction because he did not want to tell her that, despite four letters to her siblings, he'd had no contact from them. He didn't want to upset her and knew that she was trying hard to follow the hospital rules.

Tess had spent a lot of time thinking about the lake since Leroy's fight and had tried hard to remember herself hitting her father on the head the way Leroy had hit that boy but no matter how hard she tried, the only thing she could remember was seeing him at the water's edge. She didn't remember how the blood got on her dress. She knew it was a secret but could not remember why and it frightened her to think about it. For some reason she could not understand, she always put her hand into her mouth to feel her front teeth when she thought about the blood on her dress. It made no sense to her. She didn't want her daddy to die even though he drank the farm money and was not kind to Seán. She wished she could remember hitting him so that she could apologise and go home. So much time had passed since she came to the hospital that she wondered if she should apologise anyway and get back to her normal life. She decided she would ask Dr Cosgrove today.

"Can I ask a question?"

"Yes, Tess."

"If I say I'm sorry for hitting Daddy, can I go home?"

Cosgrove, who had been sitting lazily in his large leather chair suddenly sat bolt upright, hardly able to believe what he had just heard.

"Did – did you hit your dad, Tess? Is that what you're saying to me?"

"No. I don't think so."

"Then what do you mean, Tess?"

"You have to apologise for bad things so people won't be angry with you any more. Mark had to apologise for annoying Leroy and Leroy had to apologise for hitting Mark and now they are not angry with each other. I don't want Kate to be angry with me any more so I am going to say I am sorry."

Cosgrove studied Tess carefully. He was unsure of

the correct approach to take and thought carefully about his response.

"Tess, you don't like when people lie, do you?"

"No."

"If you apologised for hitting your dad, would you be lying?"

"Yes, but I want to go home. I can be sorry for lying as well."

Cosgrove cleared his throat. He knew that Tess was ready to go home. He needed to speak with her siblings directly to find out why they didn't respond to his letters. He felt that it was wrong to keep her here but without alternative accommodation he had no choice but to leave her where she was.

"Tess, I think you should stay here for another while, just until your family are ready for you to return. You have exams, don't you? You don't want to leave without getting your certificate, do you?"

Tess thought about this, her head moving slowly from side to side. "No."

"Then will you stay here a while longer and let me see what I can arrange?"

"How much time longer?" she asked innocently.

Cosgrove swallowed hard. He had built up a trusting relationship with Tess and did not want to lie to her.

"I'm not sure, Tess. That's the honest answer. But I will talk to you about it after your exams. Is that okay?"

Tess stared hard over Cosgrove's shoulder and focused on the light green paint on either side of his window.

"That's okay," she said flatly, unsure what exactly she had agreed to.

Chapter 32

1981

Sam Moran made himself his fourth coffee of the morning and stood at his untidy desk looking out onto the yard where he had been attacked only two weeks previously. His ribs still hurt when he coughed which was bad luck as he also had a chest infection and this meant he was coughing nearly all the time and sat slightly hunched over his desk. The bruise under his eye was almost gone which is more than he could say for poor Rabbit who had obviously got a much worse going-over than he had. He didn't think Rabbit had told them where he lived – McCracken could've got that information himself as Sam had told him the name of the newspaper he worked for and he knew that someone had been following him for a few days before he was beaten up outside the office.

Sam considered forgetting about the story but

couldn't understand how McCracken fit into the picture and found himself intrigued. He did not want to let bullying tactics get the better of him. If he was to really get into proper reporting, he couldn't let a couple of threats get in his way. Moran wondered how a small farmer in Wicklow with no known police record could have any connection with the IRA and also wondered what connection McCracken had with Árd Glen. Someone out there had the answers and if Sam didn't ask the questions, another reporter might do it for him and snatch what could be his big break from under him. He was worried though, not about himself but about the subtle threat to his family. He returned to his desk and flinched with pain as he sat down, and wondered if this was a reminder to keep his thoughts to himself.

By the time Tess returned from her night out, Kate had already risen from the bed she had shared with Dermot and was sitting in the kitchen beside the range as though nothing was different, as though she wasn't any different. She had said goodnight to him at the back door and they had stood drinking each other in, trying to memorise the night as though it might be their last. She wished she could tell Tess about the night like sisters often do but she needed, at least for now, to keep this to herself. Also she didn't feel it was appropriate to tell Tess who, despite being twenty-one, probably knew very little about men.

Kate didn't feel ashamed. She didn't regret it. She

doubted she ever would, regardless of what came of their relationship. At eleven thirty Peggy woke Kate from her dreamlike state when she burst in the back door, talking excitedly about how Tess had not eaten a thing. Tess stood silently beside her noisy friend but appeared to be smiling, albeit nervously. Kate watched her carefully, looking for signs of distress, but there were none.

Instead, when Peggy left, Tess went to the fridge and greedily ate Kate and Dermot's leftover cake. When she finished eating, Tess looked at her sister and cocked her head to one side as she always did before asking a question.

"Kate, are you sick?"

"No," Kate replied, frowning slightly, unsure what her sister meant. "Why do you ask?"

"Your face is different, Kate. It looks hot," Tess looked closely at her sister before returning to the fridge for more food.

Kate smiled to herself. She felt different. She felt happy. She felt enthusiastic for the future and, what was even better, her sister seemed, for once, to notice.

Chapter 33

1974

Kate sat quietly in the kitchen, her hands clasped tightly on her lap, as Seán read the letter that had arrived in the post that morning.

"Well?" she asked as her brother put the letter back into its envelope and threw it onto the kitchen table

"Well, what?" Seán asked sharply.

"Well, what should we say? Do you think it'd be all right for her to come home now? They say she's much better now." She noticed the slight nervousness in her own voice and wondered how her brother had come to have this effect on her.

Seán glared at his sister. He knew she wanted to bring the girl home, he knew she missed her and was so upset that she could not even bear to see her in the institution. The poor fool had travelled to Dublin twice and had only got as far as the front door of the hospital on both occasions. In the beginning Seán, like Kate, had been upset to think of Tess there, away from them and frightened, but that was before he knew that Tess owned the farm he thought was his, the house he lived in and even the chair he sat in. Seán's feelings for his younger sister were gradually replaced by resentment and he didn't want her in the house even one day before he had to.

He rubbed his hands together and looked out towards the back yard, waiting for his hangover to ease before he tended the stock. He ran his hands over his unshaven face. His knew his hair was dishevelled and his eyes bloodshot from his nightly visits to the pub. He was in no mood for Kate's nagging.

"I'm saying no, Kate, not yet," he said loudly, hoping to make his sister nervous as he knew she hated to fight with him.

"But, Seán – it's –"

"No, Kate, and that's final."

"Why Seán? What have you got against her? She's just a child." Tears welled in her eyes and she lowered her voice slightly in case she started Ben off.

"She's grand where she is, Kate. They're taking care of her. Needs help after what she did."

"But they said she's –"

"Enough, Kate!" Seán roared before opening the back door and banging it behind him, causing Ben to stiffen in his chair and start to cry.

Kate looked at the letter from Dr Cosgrove and

wondered what he thought of them, what he thought of her. Maybe she would write to him and explain things, explain the situation with Seán.

She sat back down in her chair beside the fire, having successfully calmed Ben, and cried silently over the dying flames.

Chapter 34

1976

Two more years passed and Tess adapted to and accepted life at the institution. She no longer expected her family to return for her but had calculated that if they did, her good behaviour of not biting had brought her three thousand, one hundred and sixty-eight steps closer to home. Tess wasn't sure how close to home this would have brought her as no one could tell her how many steps it was to Árd Glen from here, not even Leroy whose mother had not come back for him and who had become her very best friend.

Dr Cosgrove had asked her how she would feel going into what he called a foster home but she had screamed and he never talked about it again. He had told her that her sister and brother had a lot of work to do with her younger brother and the farm but that they hadn't forgotten her and were looking forward to seeing her when they had more time. Tess knew this was a lie and made Dr Cosgrove apologise for it. She had learnt to apologise herself now but sometimes got confused and found herself saying she was sorry to children who called her names. She was trying to be as normal as she could and now spoke occasionally and answered questions when she understood them.

She spent her days at her lessons and had passed her Intermediate Certificate exam, the teacher informing her that in two more years she could sit her Leaving Certificate exam. In the evening she continued to draw, the nurses and orderlies often buying her paper and paint from their own money.

Leroy told her that they would have to move to another place when they were eighteen as the hospital was only for children. This terrified Tess and she worked even harder at being good, just in case Kate was no longer angry with her and would let her come home. Even though she could remember the fields and the house very well, her memory of Kate's face was beginning to fade and Seán's too. When she thought of Ben he was always screaming so she tried to get him out of her mind quickly.

As well as her paintings of the lake, Tess started to draw the house as often as she could from memory. She began to have nightmares that she was alone on a country road, counting steps as she walked but getting no nearer to her house. She didn't recognise any of the landmarks and the mountains were not the same as the ones near her home. There was no lake to be seen and she couldn't remember what her house looked like. She would start calling out Kate's name which always woke her up, leaving her afraid to return to sleep. On these nights she would get up and draw the house over and over again in the dark room, humming and rocking and looking forward to the morning.

Chapter 35

1981

When Kate returned to the hospital to visit her brother, she found Seán sitting in a small lounge room with a group of men from his ward which pleased her as Seán had always been shy and had never been good at socialising. Even when her brother went to the pub, he usually drank alone, only talking to others who spoke to him first. Still, she knew that this was probably because he had more in common with these men who, he informed her, all had drink problems. Most of the men's marriages had broken down, with some families refusing to visit.

Seán hugged his sister awkwardly and avoided making eye contact with her. He asked how things were going for her and seemed to be showing more interest in her life than he ever did which unnerved her a little as there was no way that he could know about what had developed between Dermot and herself. Kate filled him in on developments at the farm, how Dermot was doing more hours than they paid him for. She told him about Ben and his new-found independence. He was now able to give Kate a sign when he wanted a drink or something to eat which Nurse O'Connell had taught Kate to understand. He even signed when he was tired and wanted to go to bed which had put an end to his usual half hour of screaming each evening. Kate didn't mention Tess or her work experience, knowing Seán had no interest in poor Tess's progress. This saddened Kate as nothing that had happened to Seán was Tess's fault. Tess was, after all, their mother's child, the same as Ben was, but Kate knew Seán's ill feeling towards Tess was more about the farm than anything else.

After a few minutes Kate ran out of news, and began to tell him even about elderly neighbours who had died, the kind of thing he normally showed no interest in.

He looked away from her and gazed out of the tall window on the opposite side of the ward. As he sat in his chair he tapped his foot nervously on the grey linoleum and then she realised he had something to say, something he found hard, and she decided to break the silence.

"What's wrong, Seán?"

Seán thought for a moment and took a long deep breath before looking down at his slippered feet.

"I might be going home soon, in a couple of weeks, I think."

Kate smiled. Her brother's speech didn't seem so slurred since he had come into hospital. "Well, that's great, Seán. You must be delighted."

"Yeah, I am," he replied, beginning to tap his foot on the floor again. "I – em – I know I caused you a lot of worry, Kate. They have meetings here, we sit around and talk about – the drinking." He reached out and held her arm gently. "Anyway, I know now how hard it was for you. I hurt you and the family. I ruined your life."

"What do you mean?" Kate asked, pulling her arm away from him.

"The drinking, Kate, spending money we didn't have. Even though Michael Byrne wasn't our father, I turned out exactly like him. I even . . ." He started to cry and closed his eyes, trying to stop his tears.

Kate had not seen her brother cry since he was a little boy. "What, Seán?"

"I even – hit you. I'm sorry, Kate, I'm so sorry. I can't believe I hit you – not after – not after how he hurt Mammy. What happened to me?"

Kate dug her nails into her thigh. She didn't want to cry. She knew that if she did he would clam up and change the subject. She needed to hear what he had to say. It was important for both of them. Important because only when the air had been cleared between them could they begin to move on and try to rebuild the life they'd had before. She took a breath and waited. He was crying loudly now. Two men who had been lying on their beds reading stood up and left the ward. Others, too sick to move or care, stayed put and Seán seemed oblivious to their presence. Kate stood and wrapped her arms around her brother, hugging him close and shushing him as though he were a small boy.

"It's okay, Seán, you were sick and now you're better. You're going to get completely better now." Kate didn't know what else to say. She knew his liver damage was permanent and that he needed to stop drinking completely to see any sort of a normal life span.

Seán cleared his throat. He had more to say. "Kate, what I'm asking is – is it okay for me to come home?" He started to cry again, tears and snot running down his blue striped pyjamas, a wreck of a man.

Kate began to cry, unable to hold back the tears. "Of course, Seán! Of course you can come home. Why did you think anything else?"

She knelt on the floor beside her brother and he flung his arms around her. They stayed there, brother and sister, wrapped around each other, crying and laughing, drying tears, erasing memories, Kate forgiving and looking forward to a fresh start. Seán looked down the long ward which had eleven beds on each side, all occupied by drunks like himself, most with nowhere to go. Some of the men were well enough to leave but were waiting on the hospital to find them a hostel or homeless shelter to live in. It had scared him. If he had owned the farm, he would have come home anyway and thrown Kate out if she didn't like it. But the truth was he was a drunk with nothing to his name. He needed Kate on his side. He really did plan to stop drinking. The older men here, some too far gone for help, had worried him. He didn't want to live like them, to die like them and vowed never to take a drink again.

As she paced the hall, anxiously talking to herself in hushed, secretive tones, Tess referred to her list of "What could go wrong and what to do next".

It was her first day of work experience. Even though Dermot would go with them, Kate was driving as he insisted she needed all the practice she could get. Kate didn't think it was the best morning to start as they were already running late. She was under pressure to get Tess there on time and felt that one anxious woman was enough on the journey. She could never understand how these lists of Tess's made her feel calmer.

By the time they pulled up outside Marshall's Art and Craft Centre, Dermot almost had to restrain Kate from going into the neat, posh-looking gallery to meet the manager. Tess had already met Marcus Gill and hadn't liked him and Kate worried that her vulnerable sister might not be treated well. Dermot stood outside the truck and spoke quietly to Tess, calming her. The scene made Kate slightly emotional. She saw how gently Dermot treated Tess and how he cared for her. It made Kate happy as, if things did work out between herself and Dermot, Tess would always be with them and she hoped that Dermot would accept this. Kate watched from the truck as Dermot hugged Tess loosely, knowing she would raise up her shoulders and squirm when touched. Tess smiled at him and waved to Kate before walking confidently into the shop. Kate had no idea what Dermot had said to her and didn't ask but it had worked.

Kate was beginning to relax about Tess when the phone rang. A woman introduced herself quickly as the receptionist at Marshall's Art Centre. Kate's heart skipped a beat as the panicked woman asked her to come immediately and collect Teresa. There was an incident and the manager urgently wanted her calmed down. Kate could hear Tess screaming and was torn between driving there as fast as she could and trying to speak to her on the phone. Then she judged by the pitch of Tess's screaming that she had better go to her. She had expected incidents like this to occur in the training centre and, when they hadn't, she'd wondered if Tess had grown out of her outbursts.

Dermot was not around and Kate trembled as she put the keys in the ignition, glad she had driven to the gallery that morning as it gave her some courage. Glenmire was a large, busy town full of fashionable boutiques and restaurants. Kate rarely had any reason to go there. Everything she needed, which wasn't much, could be bought locally.

The drive seemed to take an eternity, during which Kate's mind raced with thoughts of what might have happened. She hoped it was something simple like someone touched Tess's lunch or used the cup she had brought specially with her. By the time she arrived, Tess was standing in the middle of the gallery, shaking and sobbing. The few customers who had stayed stood staring at Tess. The manager stood against a wall, both hands to his face. Kate looked at him and worried that he was injured, that Tess had attacked him but, when he lowered his hands, she realised he was simply at his wits' end. When Kate approached Tess, she flung herself at her, screaming to go home. Kate smoothed Tess's hair which their mother used to do to calm her. The receptionist helped Kate get Tess into the truck with Kate promising to phone later to find out what had happened.

The two drove home in silence with Tess sitting for the entire journey with her hands covering her face, her fingers split open enough to look through them. When they arrived back at the farm Kate helped Tess into bed. She thought she would have to give her one of the tablets the hospital had given her when she was discharged but she fell asleep immediately and slept soundly for four hours while Kate sat rigid in the kitchen. From the look of the staff at the gallery, Kate doubted anyone did anything to her sister. No doubt Tess had simply had difficulty with the change of environment. She should have stuck to her instincts not to let Tess go there.

Kate felt exhausted. It was always going to be like this with her sister. How could she expect to live a normal life when everyday changes caused such a violent reaction? She would call Nurse O'Connell and tell her what had happened. Maybe Tess could finish her work experience in a local shop or something, somewhere people knew her and she knew exactly what to expect.

When Tess finally rose, the bus had just pulled up with Ben and Kate knew she would not have a chance to ask her sister what had gone wrong until she put him to bed later that evening.

Tess looked ashamed and stood briefly in the kitchen, returning quickly to her room before her brother, who she could hear screaming from the bus, came in.

Tess walked gingerly into the kitchen when she heard Kate putting Ben to bed for the night. She had stayed in her room all evening, knowing Kate was upset with her. She was starving and quickly ate her dinner which had been kept warm in the range. She did not want to fight with Kate and wished she hadn't behaved as she did in the work experience. They would never have her back now and she felt as though she had failed. She had managed to get through her training programme and, even though she knew she had upset a few of her classmates, they had forgiven her and she had made a list of the things that upset them so she wouldn't say them to anyone else ever again. Tess knew that Nurse O'Connell had smoothed things over on more than one occasion at the training centre but it had never been as bad as today and she believed that even Deirdre couldn't fix this.

When she had arrived at her work experience, people were friendly. Ann, the receptionist, offered to hang up her coat and had frowned at Tess when she refused. Tess had lost a good coat as a child and she didn't want it to happen again. Tess did not like the manager who she felt spoke like a girl but she did not see much of him that day and he did not speak directly to her even once. A girl named Siobhán was supposed to be showing her around but spent the morning talking to someone named Mike on the phone and Tess did not know what she should be doing. She was worried that customers might be trying to get through and the shop would lose business unless Siobhán got off the phone. Besides, Tess had practised saying "Good morning, Marshall's Art and Craft Centre, how may I help you?" with Deirdre and Peggy for hours. The small switchboard was exactly the same as the one she had trained on and now she wasn't going to get a chance to do it. No one told her where the toilets were and she didn't want to ask. She needed to go badly but still behaved herself and did what Dermot had told her to do. By the time she had drunk tea from her own cup, she was beginning to wet her underwear and began to cry. Ann helped her and showed her where the bathroom was and Tess felt all right then. When Ann brought Tess back to her work station, Siobhán told her off for going missing and said she should have gone to the toilet on her break. Siobhán picked Tess's cup up and asked what was wrong with the cups there – did she think they had a disease or something? When Tess began to sob Siobhán went for Ann, saying loudly, "How am I going to put up with *her* until six o clock?" and this was why she became upset. Deirdre had told her she would finish at five o'clock and Kate would be returning for her then. Kate wouldn't know that she had to stay in the gallery until six and might drive off thinking she was lost and she might never find her way home. Tess felt that she couldn't breathe and began to scream. No one could calm her down even though people tried. Ann tried to hug her which made her scream louder as Ann was a stranger and you shouldn't let strangers touch you. She heard the manager with the girl's voice tell someone to ring the police and she screamed harder because the last time someone phoned the police they had sent her away and she didn't see Kate for years. She started to scream for Kate and she heard Ann insisting they ring Kate and not the police.

Tess recounted all of this to Kate beside the fire. Kate's heart broke but she put on a brave face for her sister. She felt that it wasn't worth putting Tess through all of this for her to have a "normal" life because what was "normal" anyway? Kate's life? Seán's? There was no such thing as a normal life. Tess would be fine here with her. She could help around the place but there would be no more training or work outside for Tess. It was too hard on her and Kate was going to make sure she protected her vulnerable sister from now on.

The two sisters settled into their usual evening routine. Tess was quieter than usual as they sat beside the fire watching television.

Later, she seemed to have recovered from her ordeal and Kate smiled as she gave her usual "I have a question" expression.

"Kate, do you like Dermot?"

Kate threw her head back and laughed quietly. "Yes, Tess, I do like him. Are ye satisfied, little Miss Matchmaker?"

"I mean, Kate, like you liked – em –" Tess knew mentioning Noel Moore upset her sister.

"Like what, Tess?" Kate asked smiling. She was enjoying this conversation as she had no one to tell about her relationship with Dermot. If you could call it a relationship since they didn't spend much time together.

"Like . . . like Noel?"

Kate gazed at her sister who looked nervous. "Tess, I like him even better than Noel, how's that?"

Tess simply nodded and smiled, feeling she understood.

The two fell silent beside the fire, Kate thinking of a life with Dermot, away from this farm and the hardship it had brought her while her sister dreamt of Dermot marrying Kate and running the farm and then there would be no need for Seán to stay here fighting and shouting. Finally, her list was beginning to work.

Sam Moran had reached a dead end. Despite spending

hours looking through old microfilms at the larger newspapers, none of the articles on Byrne's death made any reference to Republican ties. He even searched through photographs taken at the time of the death, not sure what he was looking for, but had come up with nothing. He found a photograph of McCracken in a Dublin newspaper, standing on the steps of the courthouse having successfully defended a murder case. He cut it out and brought it to Mattie Slattery, hoping the publican might recognise him.

Sam looked around him to ensure no one was listening, placed the photo on the bar and ordered a pint from the publican.

"Mattie, you don't happen to recognise the man in this photo, do ya?" he asked half-heartedly.

Mattie picked the up the black and white photo and peered closely at the grainy image in front of him, shaking his head. "Nah, Sam, who is he?"

Sam wasn't sure if he should say McCracken's name out loud and checked to ensure there were no eavesdroppers.

"His name's McCracken. I think he had some links to Árd Glen. He has red hair, big fellow."

"There are no McCrackens around here, Sam. It's not a Wicklow name."

"Could he have been passing through, working maybe?" Sam asked hopefully.

"I'd know if I'd seen him around. How long ago do you think he was here?"

"Not sure. It was ten, eleven years ago, maybe even further back."

"Is this something to do with the Byrne thing, Sam?"

Sam looked around the quiet bar again. He could hear two or three voices behind the snug. He couldn't help but feel a little nervous, especially as he still had no idea exactly who he was dealing with and what they were capable of.

"I think so, I – I'm not sure. You definitely don't remember seeing him?"

"No, Sam, and if he's a drinking man, I'd remember him. Mind you, the missus and I were in England for years – didn't come back until '56 to take over the pub when my father died. Maybe it was further back than you think."

Sam thought about this but it didn't make sense. McCracken had to have ties to Árd Glen, at least up until Byrne was murdered. He wondered if he had it the wrong way around, if Byrne had ties to Dublin rather than McCracken to Árd Glen.

"Did Byrne go to Dublin much, Mattie? Maybe he knew McCracken there?"

"Ha. You didn't know Byrne. He was an odd sort. Roamed the farm by day, sat here at night. Doubt he had much truck with Dublin. But how do you think this man is involved?" Mattie was hopeful for a bit of gossip.

"Oh, just someone I know mentioned him, that's all – it's probably nothing," said Sam, knowing he wasn't fooling Slattery one bit.

Moran finished his drink slowly and sat at the bar mulling things over. He had to try to talk to Tess Byrne. He had to get to her without the sister around. He was going about this the wrong way around. If he got to Tess Byrne, he'd get the story straight from the horse's mouth.

Chapter 36

1977

Tess blew out the candles on her 16th birthday cake, surrounded by nurses and children, her friend Leroy beaming as he presented her with a present of a wooden box of coloured pencils – her paint always running out far too soon and frustrating her. Leroy was now nineteen years old and had left the institution six months before. Leroy's mother had never returned for him and Cosgrove had helped him find accommodation locally and had organised a job for him in the adult wing of the hospital so that he could keep an eye on the vulnerable young man. Cosgrove wondered if Tess would have to be accommodated in the adult wing in two years as, unlike Leroy, he did not believe that she could live independently. He did not want this for Tess who had become a favourite with many of the staff over the years – by now they had learned how to interact with her and even asked her to help with the younger children.

Tess held thc pencils in her hand and said "Thank you" in a low hushed voice which brought tears to some of the staff's eyes as even now Tess rarely spoke. As she blew out the candles on her birthday cake, Tess made her wish. The same wish she made every year: to go home.

Chapter 37

1981

Seán stood at the front door of the hospital, waiting for his sister to collect him. He was glad she was now driving as he didn't want Dermot to see him here. Seán always felt that Dermot saw right through him and he didn't like spending any more time in his company than he had to. He planned on working on the farm immediately and planned to get rid of Dermot as soon as he was strong enough to run it on his own.

On Kate's last visit a doctor had arranged to meet with her and explained that while Seán needed an intense addiction programme in a specialist hospital, there were no beds there at present and now that he was medically fit enough to go home, there was no reason to keep him in hospital. They would write to him directly but in the meantime Kate had to ensure he didn't have any access to alcohol and that he didn't go out alone.

The doctor assured Kate that, as well as Seán looked, alcoholism was a disease and it would take only one drink to set him back. Before Seán was admitted Kate would have thought her task impossible but now she felt the worst was behind them and that she might at last have her brother back.

Seán smiled warmly at his sister when she arrived but as they drove towards home, fell silent and looked once more the sullen man he had become. Kate wanted to ask him what he was thinking but was somehow afraid to ask, afraid of what his answer might be. She wanted to hold onto the feeling that today was a new beginning for them both and stayed silent for the whole journey home, turning up the volume of the radio to drown out the unbearable sound of silence.

Seán woke to his first morning at home. He was glad to be back even though he had received a lukewarm welcome from Tess. Bitch, he thought – if she knew she owned the farm, she'd probably run me off. Even Ben who he had actually missed seemed to ignore him, pushing him away when he tried to play with him. Only Kate seemed genuinely pleased to see him. He had not yet seen Dermot who he understood would be working later that morning. He was dreading that and had started to dislike the clean-living man who never took a drink despite his aunt and uncle owning their own pub. Idiot, he thought, as he made his way to the kitchen.

After breakfast, he went out to the barn to help

Dermot who was trying to start the old tractor yet again. Kate knew they needed a new one but there was no way the bank would loan them the money, the farm only making a meagre income for the past few years. Kate could hear both men talking and watched Dermot walk away, leaving Seán to complete the makeshift repairs. She wondered when to tell Seán about her relationship with Dermot but no matter how she worded the conversation in her head, it seemed childish and she thought it best to wait until Seán had settled in again.

Tess, who had been moping around the house for three days, followed Dermot out to the field where he was working.

"Dermot, I'd like to give my work experience another try but Kate said it's too hard on me and I'm better off here with her."

Dermot thought before responding, eyeing a sad-looking Tess who was like a fish out of water hanging around the farm all day. He had also noticed that Tess didn't like being around Seán. Dermot thought it was because of the business with their father all those years ago but never asked Kate, preferring to mind his own business.

"You got very upset, Tess. Kate is just worried about you, that's all."

"I know but I didn't stop and think like Deirdre said when someone said something I didn't understand. I didn't keep my dignified like you said."

Dermot laughed. "Dignity, Tess!"

"Yes, dignity, Dermot."

"And you want to go back to the same place, Tess. Is that a good idea?"

"I have to learn, Dermot. I liked the paintings on the wall and the building. I just have to learn to keep people simple."

Dermot laughed loudly. "If only it were that easy, Tess. People aren't simple, they aren't easy to understand. What you need to do is not lose your temper and learn to ask questions. Proper ones, I mean, not personal questions, remember?"

Tess nodded.

"I don't know, Tess. If the same thing happened again, Kate'd kill me."

"No, she wouldn't, Dermot. She said she likes you – better than Noel Moore!"

Dermot stood and looked at the odd girl before him. Sometimes he felt she was smarter than she pretended to be and was manipulating him as he couldn't imagine Kate making that statement even though he knew they were becoming close.

"Oh, she did? Is that the truth, Tess?"

"Yes, Dermot, I don't tell lies."

Dermot shook his head and got back to his work, laughing.

"Okay, Tess, I'll talk to Kate but you better protect me when she comes after me with a sweeping brush!"

Tess laughed and ran back to the house. She knew Dermot was making a joke.

Dermot didn't know how he was going to get Kate alone without Seán being around. He had got used to being the man of the house while Seán was in hospital and wasn't too happy that he was back. He didn't mean the man any harm and felt sorry that he was so ill but he could sense that Seán Byrne didn't like him and probably wouldn't take it too well when he heard that Dermot was seeing his sister. A fool could see that Seán relied on Kate and he wouldn't be too happy with anyone who planned on taking her away. Dermot wondered where exactly he would take Kate to. His father had not contacted him in months, the only contact from home being an invitation to his sister's wedding in January. He hadn't made up his mind whether or not to go as he still felt embarrassed at how he had left things back home and didn't want another row with his father. He also knew that if things worked out between him and Kate, he would be taking Ben and Tess on too. He admitted to himself that this was not exactly the married life he had planned but if he wanted Kate, and he did, her two younger siblings would come with her and he accepted this.

When Dermot entered the kitchen, Kate was washing up, humming to herself. She had not seen him come in and jumped when she heard the back door close loudly.

"Oh! Dermot, you gave me a fright!"

"Sorry, don't know my own strength!"

He bent over to kiss her and Kate moved away, glancing out the window towards her brother who was trying to fix the tractor and getting nowhere.

Dermot tried not to show his annoyance. "We'll have to tell him sometime, you know!"

"I know, just not yet – let him settle in, okay?"

Dermot glanced out the window at Seán who was removing parts of the engine he didn't need to. He didn't seem to know what he was doing.

"He won't let me fix it. I'd have had it done by now. Don't know what's the matter with him." He felt slightly annoyed at the way Seán Byrne had treated him earlier, directing him off to do other work without so much as a please.

"Ah, just let him at it. It's a while since he did anything around here. You don't need the tractor today, do you?"

"No."

"Well, if he hasn't fixed it by tomorrow, I'll talk to him. That's fair, yeah?" Kate asked hopefully, anxious to keep everyone happy.

Dermot shrugged. He hoped Kate wouldn't always be defending her sour brother.

"Kate, it's about Tess . . ."

Kate swung around from her dishes, frowning. Tess had tried to talk her around about going back to her work experience this morning. She should have known that she would try dragging Dermot into it. She narrowed her eyes at Dermot and listened.

"Kate, she's lost here. She has nothing to do all day."

"No, Dermot, you weren't there. She was so upset. I can't put her through it, I can't."

Silence permeated the room. Was this their first fight, their first disagreement?

"I don't know why she wants to go back anyway. She misunderstood almost everything that happened that day and –"

"She wants to learn from her mistakes, Kate. Don't we all?" He touched her face gently, having made sure that Seán wasn't looking their way. "And . . ." Dermot knew he was treading on dangerous ground, "and she doesn't seem to like being around Seán. I'm not getting involved in your family business, Kate, but she seems – well – scared of him for some reason."

Kate nodded. She was aware of the tension between the two ever since Tess came home. She didn't understand why Seán had to be so rude to Tess, shouting at her if she didn't move quickly enough. He had been much better with her before Michael Byrne died.

"I know, Dermot. I know how he treats her. I've tried talking to him but it's no use. He won't listen to me."

"Then give her this chance to get out of here, if only for a few hours each day. Give her a chance to learn where she's going wrong."

Kate looked at Dermot, feeling guilty. She was only trying to protect Tess but maybe the treatment Tess got in her work experience was better than the treatment she got here at home? Maybe she would learn how to behave but Kate doubted it. She shook her head and looked up at the waiting Dermot.

"She really has you wrapped around her finger, hasn't she?"

"She can go back then?"

"If she wants to."

Dermot laughed and was about to find Tess to tell her when they heard a "*Yippee!*" coming from outside the kitchen door which was slightly ajar. They laughed together as Tess had been eavesdropping all along.

"Okay, Tess," Kate shouted, "don't get too excited. It's not definite. Deirdre will have to ask or maybe beg them to take you back, okay?"

But Tess was still laughing in the hallway.

Chapter 38

1978

Leroy Brennan sat on Tess's windowsill and looked out over the hospital grounds, his right leg moving back and forth as his friend sat on her bed drawing him.

"My mam's back," he said casually.

Tess looked up in surprise but said nothing.

Leroy moved his glance back towards the window and looked out at the city skyline. He liked his new flat and had even bought some cheap furniture for it. He liked the job Dr Cosgrove had got for him in the adult hospital and the staff were nice to him. But he wasn't happy. He had been in this hospital most of his life, only leaving to try out a new foster home or whenever his mother came back for him. He had hated it here most of the time and yet he came back twice a week to see his only friend. He felt lonely and knew that there was something missing from his life. He sighed and decided to change the subject.

"Has Dr Cosgrove heard from your sister, Tess?" he asked gingerly, knowing that Tess was now almost an adult and that somehow Cosgrove had managed to keep her here.

"My brother's sick," she said simply before picking up another pencil to finish her drawing. "There, finished. Do you like it, Leroy?"

Leroy studied the drawing and was amazed that it looked just like him.

"It's great, Tess. You should become an artist and get paid mad money for your paintings."

"Mad money?" she asked, tilting her head to one side.

"I mean lots of money, Tess," he said smiling.

He felt sad for this girl who was still here after all these years and wondered what would happen to her if her family did not take her home. He hoped she wasn't going to spend the rest of her life here. There was a time that he hoped she would be interested in him as a boyfriend. She was beautiful although he knew she did not know this. He loved her long black hair and her pale face. He even loved her sad distant eyes that never seemed to look directly at him. But he knew that she had no interest in that kind of love and looked on him as a friend. He stood and walked towards the door.

"Leroy?"

"Yes, Tess?"

"Your teeth never grew back, Leroy," she said simply, looking at her sketchpad.

"What?"

"When your mam took you and your teeth were gone, they never grew back," she said, staring into space.

Leroy looked at his friend, unsure if she meant something deeper or was simply recalling what had happened the last time he was with his mother.

"No one will hurt me, Tess, I promise," he said as he left the room, closing the door quietly behind him.

Chapter 39

1981

Kate heard Seán shout out in pain and rushed out to the yard where her brother had been tirelessly trying to repair the tractor for three days. She had insisted he come in for some lunch and noticed Dermot had not come in to eat all day and hoped there hadn't been more words between them. Seán's right hand was bleeding heavily where he had caught it in the engine. Kate wrapped a towel around it and hurried him in to run the cut under the tap. The cut started three inches past his wrist and traced its way across the palm of his hand towards his thumb, narrowly missing the artery in his wrist. Kate felt it needed stitches and offered to bring him to town to see the doctor. At first Seán wouldn't hear of it but surprised Kate by relenting later when the pain got the better of him. Ben would be home in less than an hour and Kate had to leave Tess with written instructions on what to do as Dermot had already left to work in his aunt's pub and wouldn't be back until the next day.

In the doctor's waiting area Seán seemed on edge. Kate tried to keep him talking, thinking it strange that the pain was getting the better of him when he would have had many cuts like this on the farm over the years and would have hardly noticed them. The doctor's waiting area was crowded with elderly people and a crowd of coughing children. Kate became increasingly worried that Tess wouldn't cope with Ben on her own. She could feel the palms of her hands start to sweat and began to think she should take Nurse O'Connell up on her offer of respite for Ben. She was tempted to ask the secretary if she could use the phone to check on Tess but there always seemed to be someone standing at the reception desk and she didn't want people to hear her conversation.

Kate tried to read a magazine but kept looking at her watch. Eventually, the worry got the better of her and she decided to phone Tess from the phone box outside the post office, less than a minute's walk from the surgery.

Kate hurried down the path while searching in her purse for the coins needed and dialled the number quickly. When it had rung seven times Kate could feel an overwhelming panic rise up in her. She worried that Tess might hurt Ben if he kept screaming, and then she felt ashamed of the thought.

When Tess finally answered on the tenth ring, Kate could not hear Ben in the background.

"Tess! Is everything okay? Where's Ben?"

"He's in the kitchen, Kate," Tess answered calmly. "He wouldn't stop screaming when he didn't see you so I gave him my painting book and crayons. He loves them and I usually won't give them to him because he bites them and puts spit on them and . . ."

Tess rattled on and on and Kate sighed with relief. She told her she would be home as soon as possible and to give Ben some mashed potato, not too hot, if she wasn't home by six.

She smiled as she heard Tess say, "I know, Kate, I'm not a baby, you know!" and rushed back to the crowded doctor's office.

When she returned, she moved quickly through the crowded room with her head down, stopping at the back row where she had sat with Seán. She raised her head to sit down and found that her brother was gone.

Sam Moran couldn't believe his luck when he saw Kate Byrne helping her brother from the truck and into the doctor's surgery. He had been in Slattery's and knew Dermot Lynch was working so assumed that the younger sister was alone in the house. He returned to his car, forgetting the story he was supposed to be working on and drove towards the Byrne farm outside town. He parked behind thick scrub, thinking he could walk up the path unnoticed.

But Tess had already heard him and knew that a strange car had driven onto the property. She looked out and couldn't see anything but waited, hoping it was Dermot in a different car coming to sit with her. She did not like being alone but wanted Kate to know that she was grown up. Neither did she like looking after Ben who she had just managed to quieten but she knew it wouldn't be long before he started screaming again. She had planned on working on her list by teaching him to speak.

She gasped as she saw a stranger walk slowly and quietly up the front path. She could feel her heart thump and tried to remember her emergency list of what to do with strangers. She watched the stranger look through the glass in the front door and stood transfixed, her heart pounding so loud she was afraid he could hear it. Her eyes followed him as he walked around the side of the house towards the kitchen. Her heart leapt as she thought of Ben who she had left on the kitchen floor rocking and humming with her good crayons in his mouth, full of spit. She ran down the hallway and glanced into the kitchen, anxious to remain out of view. She saw the man place his two hands around his eyes and peer through the bright kitchen window. He knocked loudly when he saw Ben and knocked harder when the boy did not answer first time, the noise startling her brother, making him scream again. Moran started to call out loudly and Ben rocked back and forth so severely he hit his forehead off the table leg and started to cry. Tess, who had hoped to hide until the stranger went, ran into the room and tried to soothe her brother like Kate always did but it did not work and Ben became more and more agitated, knocking his head twice more off the table. Tess ran to the phone and lifted the receiver but she did not know who to call. She heard the man say "Miss, I just want to hear your side of the story" but she did not know what story he was talking about and felt tears well up in her eyes as she did not know any stories.

"Miss, could you let me in, please! I'll only take a minute of your time," Sam shouted shamelessly, knowing he was causing severe distress to both the boy and his sister.

Tess felt her hand rise to her mouth to bite herself but resisted the urge and lowered it. The man continued to bang on the window, shouting, and she could think of nothing else to do except shout "Help!" down the phone, pressing all the buttons until the man ran out of the yard and around to the front of the house.

Tess ran down the hall and listened as he got into his car and turned the engine on. She drew a sharp breath as she saw him reverse into the driveway, thinking he was returning, but was relieved when he drove off in the direction of the town.

Tess stood in the hall frozen for several minutes, trying to absorb what had happened and what the man wanted from her. She walked back to the kitchen where Ben was whimpering quietly from his sore head which was not bleeding and gave him more of her crayons. She then returned to stand at the bottom of the hallway which had no windows for strangers to look into and waited for Kate to return.

Kate had already looked for Seán in one of the town's three pubs and had not found him. She felt guilty that her first thoughts were of him heading to the pub but there was nowhere else in this town to go. She walked hurriedly to the other end of town, to Slattery's where Dermot worked. She was aware of her breathing and could feel her chest rising and falling quickly with each gasping breath as she quickened her pace. She could feel the panic rising in her with each step she took and with each passing moment. Her heart pounded and sweat began to roll down her back. She knew that if Seán had even one drink he would go back to his old ways. She didn't want to trouble Dermot but Seán used to drink there and she thought he might have sneaked into the bar unnoticed for a quick drink, hoping to get back to the surgery before Kate finished phoning Tess.

Dermot looked up when he saw Kate enter the lounge and instinctively knew that something was wrong. She beckoned him to the door as she didn't want to talk in front of the customers. Her Uncle Jimmy, just off the Dublin bus and having his usual on the way home, nodded to her.

"Kate," he said as he tipped his cap.

Kate ignored him. She had not spoken to her uncle

for years – the memory of him trying to point the finger at Seán for their father's death still made her angry. Dermot followed her outside and she explained how Seán had disappeared from the surgery. He could see she was worried sick, her voice falling and rising as she recounted how she had left him for just a few minutes. He went back inside to ask his aunt to watch the bar while he helped her look for Seán.

As he walked through the bar Jimmy Kelly caught him by the arm and leaned towards him, the smell of drink and cigarettes almost choking him.

"Anything wrong, son? My niece looked like she's seen a ghost."

Dermot wanted to give Kate's uncle a smart answer or better still tell him to mind his own business but thought the better of it.

"No, Jimmy. She has a flat tyre, that's all. Back in a few minutes."

Dermot found Seán in Massey's, a quiet pub frequented by older men who didn't care about the pub's rundown appearance and dirty glasses, the owner himself being a little too short-sighted to ensure the place was kept clean. Luckily it was quiet with only two men sitting at the bar together, Seán sitting at the other end alone. He had a large whiskey in front of him and an empty glass, obviously about to start his second. Dermot walked casually up to him and sat down, refusing the offer of a drink from the octogenarian bartender.

"What do you want?" Seán snarled loudly.

He seemed to be already drunk which Dermot couldn't understand.

"Keep your voice down, Seán. Kate's outside. She's worried sick. She left Tess looking after Ben and has to get home. Now, will ye come with me, Seán? Let's get that hand seen to."

Seán's hand had stopped bleeding, the towel tied around it stuck to the hard blood around his wound. He tried to stand up but fell backwards, saving his fall with his one good hand. Dermot had just reached out to help, thinking Seán was rising to leave with him, when Seán recovered his balance and swung a left fist into Dermot's jaw. Dermot, taken off guard, fell sideways and crashed into the bar. The two elderly men looked on amused at the free entertainment but did not move. Dermot tried to restrain Seán and was amazed at the thin man's strength. Seán flailed and with his injured hand tried again to punch Dermot who by now had twisted Seán's good arm behind his back. Seán grimaced with pain and Dermot loosened his grip whereupon Seán pulled his hand free and hit Dermot again, knocking him onto the filthy bar floor that probably hadn't been swept or mopped in weeks. Dermot stood up, looked at Seán and weighed up the situation. He didn't think it was possible to reason with him and knew he would have to overpower him. He didn't like the idea of hurting a sick man but knew he had no choice. He lunged at Seán, punching him hard in the jaw and knocking him out.

As Dermot stood the dazed Seán onto his feet, one of the old men said, "Yes, that's how it was done in my day, lad. He'll have a sore jaw tomorrow, by God!" before lifting his pint and looking towards the black and white television perched high in the corner. The Angelus had begun and the six o'clock news would be on soon.

Outside, Kate watched ashen-faced as Dermot helped a bloodied Seán into the truck. Dermot accompanied her on the journey home – he would have to borrow the truck to get back to town and would deliver it to her early the following morning. It was lucky that he went with her as halfway home Seán started to come to and began waving his hands about, trying to grab the wheel. Dermot had to pull over and let Kate drive so he could sit between Seán and her, hoping his bulk would prevent Seán from trying anything stupid. After a few slurred protests, Seán fell into a drunken sleep and Kate and Dermot drove in silence, the reality of the situation seeping deeply into their minds. Seán would never recover and they both wondered how they would cope with him in the future.

Back at the farm, Dermot helped Seán from the truck as Kate ran ahead into the house to warn Tess, knowing her sister hated the sight of blood.

Tess was in the hallway where she had stood for almost an hour but for a few attempts to quieten Ben who had now at last fallen asleep on the kitchen floor. It occurred to her several times to pinch him to make him stop screaming but she didn't want to hurt him. So she stood in the hallway away from him and out of sight of the man who had wanted her to tell a story, should he come back, and waited for Kate to return.

Kate told her that Seán had been drinking and had fallen and got hurt and Tess didn't have time to tell her about the man who had come and shouted. As the others passed her in the hall, she could smell drink from Seán and wondered why he would drink again when he could die. She covered her eyes as she thought about him becoming a skeleton. She worried about being dead and didn't like to think about the skeleton she knew was inside her. When Seán was safely out of view she went to her bedroom and sat on her bed. Then she remembered she should rescue what was left of her crayons from the sleeping Ben and, besides, she should tell Kate about the man who shouted in case he might come back.

Dermot and Kate were in the kitchen, talking quietly, so Tess stood outside the door, listening to see if it was about her work experience. Peeping in, she gasped when she saw Dermot kiss Kate on the lips like Noel Moore used to do when Tess was a little girl. Then Kate turned around and saw her and smiled, telling her to come in. Tess wondered whether she should apologise for seeing them kiss because it was personal or whether they should apologise to her. She didn't know so she said nothing.

"Well, goodnight, so," said Dermot awkwardly. "I

have to get back to work. Now be sure to phone me if Seán wakes up and gets aggressive." He didn't want to leave them but he had to get back to his aunt who was working the bar alone in his absence.

After he had left, Tess gathered up her sketchbook and crayons, the ones that didn't have spit on them, and Kate asked her what happened to Ben's head and did not believe her when she said a man made noise which frightened him. Kate looked angry. Shaking her head and tutting, she made Ben get up from the floor and led him away to his bedroom.

Following her, Tess was glad to see that Kate locked Seán's bedroom door to be sure he didn't get back out that night.

Chapter 40

1981

Sam Moran sat at the newspaper's weekly staff meeting and cringed as Talbot asked for an update on the Byrne article. Talbot listened as he went through the ups and downs of his investigations which to date hadn't resulted in anything except his being threatened which he kept to himself, fearful that Talbot would call him off. When Sam finished he watched Talbot nodding and waited.

"Right. Well, it seems that's going nowhere really so let it go," Talbot said matter of factly. "It was worth a try of course but it's been a costly exercise, so forget it, Moran. I want you to work with Kenny, show him the ropes."

Sam looked at the new freckled-faced apprentice and winced – he didn't even look old enough to drink.

"Could I have two more weeks, just two? I know I'm

onto something," he asked, the sound of desperation audible in his voice.

"Sorry, but you've been chasing this story since February. I know you're keeping up with your regular work but it's costing money. Let it go, Moran."

Sam sighed and slumped into his chair. He paid no attention to the rest of the meeting and watched his new shadow Kenny take notes and show enthusiasm, something he felt he seriously lacked at the moment.

Kate slammed a plate of toast on the kitchen table in front of her brother who sat, head in hands, looking down at his breakfast like a scolded child. Seán looked up at his sister who stood red-faced at the kitchen sink. He could see the veins bulging on her neck and was weighing up whether or not this was a good time to apologise and try to smooth things over with her. He could see that worming his way in was going to be harder than usual.

"Kate, I'm sorry – I –"

"Don't Seán, don't! Your apologies mean nothing to me any more. Your promises mean even less. You're a drunk, Seán, and neither I nor Tess nor Ben can depend on you for anything."

"Kate, no, please – I'll –"

"You'll what? You'll change? Turn over a new leaf. Is that it, Seán? Well, I've heard it many, many times before and you know what, Seán, even you don't believe it. If it wasn't for the kids I'd leave here, wash floors in

Dublin if I had to. At least I could go to bed at night knowing peace. No, Seán, you save your sorrys for they mean nothing in this house any more. From now on you'll do as I say. No keys to the truck because you won't be going anywhere without me any more. You can work on the farm if you're able but your days of telling me what to do, of roaring abuse at either me or Tess, are over!"

Seán sat open-mouthed at the table. He had seen his sister cross before but there was something different about her this time. She seemed, well, unafraid of him. He sat for a while looking at her until she began to bang dishes around in the sink which made his head hurt. He rose slowly from the table, considering trying another tactic but thought better of it. He could see Dermot pulling up outside in the truck and rubbed his sore jaw, remembering the farmhand's punch that sent him flat out on Massey's floor.

Seán returned to bed, unsure what else to do with himself. He wanted to explain to Kate that the pain from the cut in his hand was unbearable, that he couldn't wait another minute for the doctor to see him.

He honestly hadn't thought about having a drink and still didn't know when the idea first came to him. He had found himself standing in the surgery and moving one foot in front of the other towards a pub he rarely frequented. He ordered a large whiskey, his first since he entered hospital which was now over five weeks ago. Within a few minutes, the pain in his hand seemed to ease but had not gone altogether. He ordered a second double and drank it as quickly as the first. He felt slightly dizzy and was amazed that the drink affected him so quickly. He used to be able to knock back five or six large ones before feeling even slightly merry. He had just ordered his third drink which sat on the bar, one for the road, when Dermot walked in, looking for trouble. It was none of his business what Seán did and he wondered why Kate had gone to him for help.

The thought had crossed his mind before that Dermot might have an eye for Kate and this worried him greatly. He was trapped here in this house with Kate. He needed her to look after him. If the doctors were right, he would never be a strong man again, would be dependent on help. If he started drinking again, like he had been, he would be dead within a few months. Some choice, Seán thought. He could hear the voices of Kate and Dermot in the kitchen. He strained to listen but could not make their words out. He wanted to get out of bed and put his ear to the door but found he was snug and warm and didn't want to rise. Within minutes he had drifted off to sleep, smiling at dreams that would never come true.

Tess stood nervously in the front hall where she had positioned herself more than twenty minutes ago and stood, statue-like, looking at the front door as though she had never seen it before. Kate knew not to interact with Tess when she was like this and busied herself with Ben before the school bus came to collect him. It was Tess's first day back at the arts and craft centre, Deirdre O'Connell having met with the manager twice to smooth things over and give some advice to the staff on how to interact with Tess. Deirdre explained that sudden changes to Tess's routine caused severe anxiety so her day needed to be kept as routine as possible. She explained how Tess would need prior notice of any changes to give her enough time to adapt and how Tess's receptive language was extremely literal so staff should not use colloquial expressions or idioms. Gill still seemed reluctant to take the strange girl back, only relenting when the community nurse reminded him that if people who were different weren't given a chance, it would be a boring world. Deirdre O'Connell was no fool and knew this would trigger a positive response from the mild-mannered manager.

Before driving Tess to Glenmire, Kate looked briefly in on Seán who was still sleeping, leaving his bedroom door unlocked in case he needed to use the bathroom. Without the truck, he could not get up to much trouble in her absence. When they arrived at Tess's work experience, Kate could see Deirdre waiting for Tess in the foyer. Kate waved to her and signalled that she would phone her later. She wanted to talk to her about Seán. Perhaps they could take him back into hospital or see if he could get on that addiction programme earlier. Kate knew her brother was slipping and while she felt a kind of numbness towards him, she knew that if she didn't do something, Seán would be dead by Christmas.

By the time Kate returned home from dropping Tess to Glenmire, Seán was missing from his bedroom. Kate searched for him in each room but he was nowhere to be seen. When she entered the kitchen, she stood open-mouthed. The bottle of sherry that Dermot had brought for their date lay empty on the kitchen floor. She had completely forgotten about it and had placed it in the cupboard, saving it, hopeful for another similar evening with Dermot to occur. Every cupboard door stood open, drawers lay upturned on the ground, forks and knives strewn everywhere. Kate slumped down on a kitchen chair, unable to believe that this is what her brother had come to and knowing that she could no longer manage Seán on her own. The old metal tea canister that Kate kept money in was upturned, its contents of fifteen pounds emptied and gone. Seán had even put his hand into the flour jar – searching for what, Kate didn't know – and had spilled flour everywhere. Kate sat and looked at the mess for a few minutes, her eyes absorbing the scene. She had come to the end of the road, she could no longer help Seán, and she no longer wanted to. She thought of phoning Dermot who would be setting up the pub for the day but she was aware that their last few conversations were all about problems, her problems. She longed for a normal conversation with this man that she had begun to love.

Kate walked down the hallway and phoned Deirdre O'Connell who would hopefully be back in the dispensary by now and arranged for her to call that afternoon. Kate hoped Deirdre would organise an ambulance to take Seán back to hospital as soon as possible as she felt she couldn't sleep under the same roof for another night with her unpredictable brother. When she put the phone down, she did as Deirdre said and looked for Seán in the nearby fields, knowing he could not have got far without a car. She searched the fields nearer to the house first, calling his name, feeling the panic rising inside her. She walked to the outer fields where she found him, lying in the field that led down to the lake, the field where they used to play as children. At first she stood some twenty feet from him and looked at the scene as though she were watching a movie, eventually moving toward him and kneeling beside him.

Seán lay on his side in the long grass sobbing, spit and tears running down his neck and soaking the crumpled grey shirt that he had slept in the night before. She placed her hand on his arm as he lay there. Beside his head lay a pool of blood-streaked vomit which alarmed Kate though she tried not to show it. She tried to lift him but found that even though he had lost a lot of weight, she could not move him. She sat there for some time, silent, as Seán's sobs gradually died down to a whimper.

Finally she spoke, her voice gentle, sad, resigned.

"How did it come to this, Seán? What happened to

you along the way? Look what you've become, lying in this field – hopeless – and all because of some land!"

Kate realised that her words were directed more to herself than to her brother who was distraught, unable to listen to or answer her. The sky above them was dark grey and a heavy rain began to fall, soaking the pair. She could hear the gentle lap of the lake in the distance. She rarely came down here – it was too near where her father had died and she found it eerie. They kept stock here at different times of the year but she knew even Seán didn't like coming down here and she wondered why he had chosen to lie drunk in this field above any. Maybe he thought she wouldn't find him here – he knew she hated this field.

After some time she managed to get him to his feet, following which he vomited again. He bent over and grasped his stomach, a fierce pain gripping him as he moved. They walked slowly back to the house, Kate supporting her brother. The walk was mostly uphill and she sweated under his weight as he limped beside her, exhausted and feeble. She could feel his ribs beneath his shirt and it brought tears to her eyes. She wondered when this pain would be over for him as she no longer believed that he was going to recover.

As Glenmire was on her rounds, Deirdre O'Connell had offered to collect Tess on her way and bring her home. She knew that Kate could not leave her brother unattended. When they arrived Kate had already helped Seán into bed where he lay asleep and at peace.

Deirdre listened carefully as Kate told her about Seán's drinking since he was discharged from hospital.

"I can't cope with him any more, Deirdre. I'm at my wits' end. I have enough to cope with. If he does this again – if he drinks any more – he'll – he'll have to leave here."

Deirdre agreed that Kate could not manage Seán alone and that he needed to be in hospital. She phoned Dr Doyle from the house, informing him of the situation and requesting he organise for Seán to be admitted as soon as possible.

By the time Deirdre left, Kate felt reassured and set about making dinner for Tess and Ben. Later, Dermot called in to check on things and stood protectively outside Seán's bedroom while Kate brought food in to him, worried that he might become aggressive as he hadn't had a drink since early that morning. Dermot had collected medication that afternoon from Dr Doyle to help Seán sleep and as Seán finished the last of his tea, Kate gave him the tablet, hopeful for a peaceful night's sleep. When they returned to the kitchen, Tess had retreated to her room. Her first day back at work experience had gone well and she was copying paintings from the craft centre from memory onto her sketchpad. She was thinking about taking them in to Mr Pascoe, who liked paintings and had seemed much nicer to her today.

When Kate had checked on Ben and found him sleeping soundly, she sat with Dermot in the sitting room. They had not made love since that first night and she longed for that closeness again. When she was sure

Tess had finally drifted off to sleep, they made love, more urgently and fervently than the first time, in the sitting room that had once been her mother's bedroom. Afterwards, as they lay in each other's arms, Kate did not feel guilty about the brother who lay ill in the room not twenty feet from her. She deserved this happiness, she needed it.

When Dermot left, Kate checked once more on Seán who seemed to be smiling in his sleep. He stank of vomit and sweat and she would have to wash him tomorrow before the nurse came.

She realised that Tess was awake and was watching her as she undressed and slid into bed, exhausted.

"Kate?"

"Yes, Tess?"

"Do you love Dermot?"

Kate felt her heart skip a beat, fearful that Tess had seen them.

"Tess, did you come out of your room?"

Tess remained quiet before answering. She could detect the sharp tone in Kate's voice.

"No, Kate, it's just my questions. Sorry. It's personal. I apologise."

Kate smiled to herself in the darkness. "It's okay, Tess, and yes, I love him, God help me."

Kate rolled over and though she expected a peaceful night dreaming of Dermot and their future, she dreamt of her mother walking through the same field she found Seán in earlier that day. She was walking arm in arm with Kate's grandparents. They all looked happy, as if her mother had forgiven them for making her marry Michael Byrne.

When she awoke at four in the morning, unable to sleep, she went to the kitchen and made tea. The room was cold and the air felt damp. There was something about the dream she'd had that made her feel uneasy. She opened Seán's bedroom door to check on him and found him sound asleep. Her mother used to say you dream of the dead when they are trying to send you a message but what was the message? Forgive Seán? Make amends to him? She didn't know.

When Kate returned to bed, she lay awake and watched the sun rise and attempt to shine through a wintry grey sky.

Chapter 41

1981

Kate woke with a start at eight thirty and realised she had not heard the alarm go off, having returned to a deep satisfying sleep after her broken night. She jumped out of bed and shouted to her sister to get up. Tess would normally have been awake and impatiently waiting on Kate to drive her to Glenmire. Kate felt the strain of Seán's behaviour was affecting the whole family. She dressed quickly and shook Tess, then ran into Ben and Seán's room on the opposite side of the hallway. Both were sleeping soundly. She had a foggy memory of Ben's school bus beeping its horn outside and realised they must have driven off when they saw no sign of life. She would either have to keep Ben home or drop him to school after she dropped Tess off. Kate quickly dressed Ben and fed him toast in the kitchen. It was the quickest breakfast she could muster up and Ben screamed throughout the meal, anxious about the change in routine, and rocked violently back and forth on his chair, giving Kate a headache. She tried not to shout at Tess who was talking loudly to herself about her hair and for some reason was still in her nightdress. Leaving Ben alone, Kate walked down to Tess's room and held her anxious sister gently by the shoulders, calmly telling her that she had five minutes to dress, that she would do her hair when she was dressed and she would have to eat toast in the car on the way to Glenmire. Tess walked quickly away and started rooting through her drawings in her room. Kate, sensing a row brewing, walked away deciding that if they all stayed home today it wasn't the end of the world.

She could hear Tess say "It's all your fault!" over and over and could feel herself becoming irritated at her sister's rantings.

"Whose fault, Tess?"

No answer.

"What are you saying, Tess?"

"It's all his fault!" Tess screamed, biting her closed fist hard.

Kate could hear Ben joining in the screaming from the kitchen. It was almost more than she could bear.

"Who is *he*, Tess? Who are you talking about?"

"Him, him!" she screamed, pointing at her own face and running back to her drawing.

Kate sighed heavily and wearily walked back into the kitchen. She stopped at Seán's bedroom door, looking at him as he lay face down motionless in his bed, and wished her brother was able to help her. There was a time that he would dress and feed Ben when Tess was a younger, more difficult version of herself. The sleeping tablets are obviously doing their job, she thought to herself.

As Kate washed Ben's face and hands roughly by the kitchen sink, Tess appeared in the doorway, ready and waiting, having brushed her own hair and tied it back with a white hair-band. She appeared calm and Kate decided not to rock the boat by asking her sister to explain her outburst a few minutes earlier. She smiled at Tess and walked Ben, who was still screaming, to the door. She sat Ben in the truck and waited for Tess before running back into the house when she did not appear, the stress finally getting to her. Tess was not in the kitchen or the bathroom or her room. Kate looked in the tall wardrobe in their bedroom and in the cupboard in the hall where Tess sometimes hid but could not find her. She returned to the bedroom to look under Tess's bed and then ran back to the kitchen where through the window saw her sister tying a note to the tractor in the yard.

Kate opened the window quickly. "What's that, Tess?"

"It's from me, Kate, for Dermot," Tess replied flatly.

Kate looked at her sister, thinking carefully before speaking, hoping Tess had not written anything about their relationship in the note.

"What does it say, Tess?"

"It's personal."

Kate had to be wary as she could see Tess was in a bad mood about being late and she couldn't afford to set her off.

"Does it say anything about me, Tess?"

Tess gulped. "Yes."

"Do you want to tell me what is says about me at least?" Kate was trying hard to conceal how irritated she was.

Before Tess had a chance to answer, Kate heard the truck engine roar and turned horrified towards the front of the house where the truck was parked.

"Oh God no!" Kate screamed, the reality of what was happening dawning on her as she ran as fast as her trembling legs could carry her. She heard the engine rev again as though someone was accelerating out of the driveway and reached the front door of the house in time to see Seán drive off with Ben screaming in the back. Kate screamed as loud as she could and saw Seán turn back and wave at her, laughing as he drove the truck towards the main road.

Tess stood rigid at the back of the house, her sister's screams pinning her feet to the ground. She stood wide-eyed, unable to move, even as she heard Kate scream louder after the disappearing view of the truck in the driveway.

Tess eventually followed Kate into the house and went directly into the sitting room to hide behind the sofa. She could hear Kate call someone on the telephone as she rocked back and forth and hummed gently to herself in a low scared voice. Kate had phoned the police, trying to calm herself down enough to give them the number plate and description of the truck. She phoned Dermot who insisted on driving the roads looking for Seán, hoping to stop him on the main road towards town. Kate rang Deirdre O'Connell who was not in her office, leaving a frantic message for her to call as soon as possible. When she could do no more she fell into a crumpled heap on the kitchen floor and wept uncontrollably.

"Please, God, don't let him hurt Ben, please! Please God in heaven, bring Ben safely home! Please, Mammy, if you're listening, help Ben! God, what will I do? What will I do?"

Tess came from behind her safe place and, going to the kitchen, put her arms around her howling sister and they sat there on the floor, neither of them speaking. After a few minutes, Tess began to feel uncomfortable under Kate's tight hold even though she knew that Kate needed this hugging. She squirmed and freed herself from her sister, returning to her space behind the sofa in the sitting-room where she stayed until the loud siren of the police car pulled up noisily on their gravel driveway, nearly deafening her.

When he reached the main road Seán swung the battered truck left towards Knockbeg, knowing Kate would expect him to take a right towards their village. Seán headed for the bigger town knowing no one would think of looking for him there, thinking instead that the idiot brother of Kate, child of a whore and God knows which father, would drive directly to his own town to drink. What he hadn't planned on was taking his brother with him and he wondered what he would do with Ben when he arrived at the pub. He couldn't take him in with him and might have to lock him in the car for a while. Ben was screaming louder now and was beginning to get on Seán's nerves. He had a savage headache, probably from the tablet Kate had given him the night before.

"Shut up, Ben, it's all right! You know me, don't you? It's Seán. Stop it!" he yelled, unable to bear his brother's high-pitched screams.

The louder Seán roared, the more frightened Ben became and the louder he screamed. Seán thought he heard Ben say "Mammy" and laughed.

"Mammy? Your mammy's long dead, Ben, and you're not missing much with her – a whore is what she was!"

Ben began biting his hand until blood trickled down his sleeve causing him to cry even louder.

Seán noticed that Ben was not fastened in his seat and swung his arm back to hold his brother as he took yet another sharp turn off the main road and onto a smaller side-road that he knew no one would think of taking. Ben screamed as though Seán was about to hit him and began rocking back and forth, continuing to bite the hand that was now bleeding heavily. Seán thought about stopping and putting Ben out of the car, knowing someone would find him and bring him back but banished this thought from his mind, amazed that he could even consider this. Are you gone mad? he asked himself silently. He knew that all he needed was a couple of quick drinks after which he'd bring Ben home and face the music. He thought about the look on Kate's face when she saw him driving away, which was priceless. Bitch. He had woken when she slammed the truck door. He looked out through the open curtains and thought he saw Tess standing outside his window, looking in at him with her creepy white face, holding the truck keys in her hand. Seán rubbed his eyes and looked again to find her gone. He wondered now if he had seen her at all. In her place he could see the open truck outside and saw an opportunity to get away for a while. He had slept in his clothes and now quickly put his shoes on. He ran out into the front yard to the truck and found the keys lying on the seat. Ben was in the truck but he didn't wait to put him out. He wondered why he wasn't at school but it was too late then.

Seán pulled over into a driveway and tied a hankie around Ben's hand. He looked at Ben's face for a moment, noticing the fear in his brother's eyes and looked away quickly before he got any notions to turn around.

"Come on, Ben, it's just a bit of fun, okay?" He tried

to put his arm around Ben who flinched and rocked harder, banging the back of his head off the seat and crying even louder. "Shut up, Ben, please shut up! I have a headache and you're making it worse!"

Seán tried to move his hand around his brother to fasten his seat belt but stopped when Ben threw himself forward, biting Seán on the shoulder.

"Fine, suit yourself, ya little bastard!" he said before taking off at high speed.

Seán drove as though in a rally competition along the winding country road, glad that the school buses had been and gone as it was almost impossible to get by them on these roads. When he eventually met up with the main Knockbeg road again, he braked hard and skidded briefly on the muddy surface.

"Whoa! Tight one there, Ben!"

He looked in the rear-view mirror at his brother who was now whimpering, licking his hand through the dirty hankie Seán had tied around it. The main road was quiet except for a few cars pulling trailers and he realised it must be mart day. He overtook the first trailer and settled back into his lane before trying to overtake two more trailers that were driving close to one another. He had to swerve to get back in and looked up in time to catch the second driver shake his fist at him. Seán gave him a two-finger salute but reddened as he realised that the driver was an elderly neighbour he knew well. The embarrassment only lasted a few seconds as Seán attempted to overtake the car again, feeling uncomfortable at the old man's accusing gaze in his rear-view mirror. He stuck his nose out and took off, seeing a clear road ahead of him, overtaking the two trailers and a car full of tourists. Someone beeped at him and he looked around, unable to tell which car the sound had come from.

"Fuck them!" he said aloud to Ben who started to scream once more. "Jesus, Ben, is there anything else in your miserable life that you have learned to do any better than scream?"

As Seán sped towards a dangerous bend, a large tractor and trailer carrying sheep drove out slowly from a side road to the left. Seán swerved to avoid it, narrowly missing a van coming in the opposite direction. He swerved again and tried to straighten the car but spun around, into the path of an oncoming lorry. As his car slid across the road, Seán could see the driver of the lorry brake and swerve to avoid him. He saw the driver's O-shaped mouth, his expression of astonishment and fear merged into one. He glanced sideways to see if Ben was okay while simultaneously trying to turn the truck back in the direction of the traffic. He reversed a little and thanked God the trailer, which had now ground to a halt further along the road, had been going so slowly. He fixed his eyes on the driver of the trailer who had begun to wave his hands frantically at him, warning him.

Seán looked behind him and saw he had reversed too far back. He tried to come forward but somehow shot further into the opposite lane. Everything started to move in slow motion. He thought he could hear his mute brother say something. He could smell burning rubber and could see an articulated truck blurring in his rear-view mirror, the slow sickening screech of its brakes deafening out the sound of his own screams.

Kate stood in the kitchen, Dermot by her side. He had given up on searching for Seán and returned to be with Kate, knowing she would be frantic.

Garda Morris walked slowly into the kitchen and tried to conceal what she had just been told by phone until her superior arrived.

"That was Sergeant Mackey. He'll be here shortly, Miss Byrne."

"Have they found them?"

The policewoman cleared her throat. She had only graduated from Templemore one year ago and hadn't yet come across anything like this, especially in this small country town where she had been stationed.

"I don't know, Miss Byrne, I doubt it," she lied. "We should know more soon."

She felt Dermot watching her closely.

Ten excruciating minutes later Sergeant Thomas Mackey drove up into the yard and walked slowly into the house. He knew the family vaguely but was more familiar with their cousin Liam to whom he had been called out many a night to caution after a hard night's drinking. Before sitting down he asked Dermot was there any whiskey in the house, which Kate thought was unbelievable under the circumstances.

"Not for me," said the sergeant, seeing her shocked face. "You look like you need a shot, Ma'am."

"No, thank you," Kate replied stiffly. She had seen enough drink to last her a lifetime, unaware of the significance of the sergeant's request, a request that was not lost on Dermot who moved closer to Kate, placing his arm around her back to steady her for what he knew was to come.

"Garda," he said, looking directly at the policewoman, "can you find Tess and take her outside for a while? To feed the horse?"

Kate looked at him as the policewoman left the room, but he looked away, unable to bear the pain she was about to face.

The sergeant cleared his throat.

"We found the truck, Miss Byrne, on the main road. I'm afraid there was an accident. Several vehicles were involved."

Dermot felt Kate straighten her spine as though to prepare herself, strengthening her body for the blow. She did not dare speak in case she missed the sergeant's words, in case she wouldn't hear him say they were okay, that Ben was okay.

"It was a bad accident," he began again, pausing enough between each sentence to ensure she could take it in. "Your brother, your younger brother, wasn't wearing a seat belt. I'm afraid the impact caused him to go through the windscreen. The paramedics tried everything. I'm sorry, Ma'am. Truly. They requested I tell you that he wouldn't have felt any pain, that he died on impact."

He paused and looked at the woman whose face stared back at him, disbelieving.

"Your older brother was driving. It seems he lost control of the car. He's in a serious condition in St Patrick's Hospital. I need to be completely honest with you, Ma'am, it's not looking good. We can take you to see him –"

"No! No!"

Sergeant Mackey had been waiting on this, the slow crumbling reaction that occurred when people were faced with such life-changing, life-destroying news. It never got any easier, no matter how often he had to deliver it. He looked towards the man who was trying to hold Kate Byrne up as she slowly folded towards the floor. The sergeant looked down at his shoes. He never knew what to do at this point and was glad someone was with the woman as he had often had to deliver such news to people on their own and had stood holding the person as they cried in his arms. He stood up while Kate Byrne mouthed silent sobs into Dermot's shirt, the man himself shedding silent tears.

The policewoman, sensing that Tess had special needs, had kept her outside for as long as she could but was aware that the young woman was nervous and wanted to return to the kitchen where her sister was.

She took her back and when Tess entered Dermot beckoned her to come to him and all three stood together, arms and bodies entwined, Tess looking into Dermot's eyes, inquiring. Kate's sobs changed to a long, low exhausted moan, her body wracked by howling, buckled into Dermot's body, his arms holding her up. He wanted to whisper words of comfort and reassurance but could think of none. All three remained like this for some time. The sergeant looked down at his shoes and the young policewoman wished she'd chosen any other job than this one right now.

Chapter 42

1981

On the morning after the death, Dermot stood beside Kate inside the small morgue of the general hospital where Seán had been a patient only weeks before. It had been a sleepless night for all except Tess to whom they had not yet fully explained everything. Dermot had spent the entire night with Kate in the kitchen, as she sat rigidly in her chair by the unlit fire, her hands clasped tightly together on her lap as if they were holding her together. She had refused any food and stared into space as though hypnotised. Dermot sensed that while she needed him there, she did not want to talk. They sat silently together through the night.

Deirdre O'Connell had called early in the morning and suggested breaking the news to Tess gently and advised Kate not to be surprised if she didn't fully understand or perhaps didn't seem to care about Ben's death. The two women had then together told Tess who indeed behaved as if she had not even heard what they had said to her. There was nothing more they could do – Tess would have to absorb the shock in her own way and in her own time.

Deirdre had agreed to stay on at the house with Tess while Kate identified Ben's body.

As Kate stood in the mortuary, a short man with an abnormally long pale face asked her if she was ready before pulling a white sheet down enough for Kate to see Ben's sweet face, cut almost beyond recognition. There was a long, evenly stitched cut across his forehead where his face had hit the shattering windscreen. Two smaller cuts on his face, although neatly sewn, looked like deep hollows above his broken jaws and gave him the appearance of a sleeping, dimpled-cheeked boy. His nose, broken and misshapen in the impact looked purple above his swollen lips. For the second time in less than twenty-four hours Kate slumped backwards into Dermot who placed both arms firmly around her.

"I'm with you," he whispered.

Kate nodded to the waiting man, confirming that this was her precious brother, a brother she had raised almost since birth and was like her own son. A brother who was sweet and innocent and did not ask to be born into this world, into this family, and now he was dead, lost to her, and she didn't know where she fitted into the world if not to care for Ben. She moved forward and touched him, shocked by his icy cold skin. Kate wondered what her precious boy went through those last few minutes of his life. Was he crying for her? Was he wondering where she was? She couldn't bear to think about it. She stood back and looked at him again. It was the most peaceful she had ever seen him for even when he was a baby Ben would twitch and kick as he slept. She bent forward once again and kissed him. She wanted to lift him to hug him one last time. Ben had always hated being hugged and for once he would not squirm away from her. She moved to place her arm around his neck to raise him from the cold white slab and into her arms. As if reading her mind the long-faced man moved forward, catching her softly but firmly on the forearm, while simultaneously glancing at Dermot who moved forward and took Kate once again in his arms, both knowing Kate had not seen the dead boy's worst injuries. They remained standing there for some time, the man moving out of sight to give the grieving couple some privacy.

Upstairs, Seán lay in intensive care and had not regained consciousness. Dermot had tried to persuade her to go to him, worried that she might later regret not seeing him but she refused and they left the morgue and headed for home where Tess would be waiting.

In Árd Glen, Tess sat in her room alone while Deirdre made her sandwiches in the kitchen. She took her list from a drawer and adjusted it, running a long black line through Ben's name. She had wanted to apologise to

Ben for pinching him when he was a baby, especially when he could not talk. She planned on apologising by teaching Ben to speak like she had done with some of the small children in the hospital school but it was too late now. Ben was dead and Tess would never be able to apologise.

Dermot Lynch lay awake, stretched out on the Byrnes' sofa. He did not want to leave Kate alone and had stayed even though he knew it would get the town's gossips going. He had wanted to lie beside Kate, to hold her all night and comfort her but felt that under the circumstances it wouldn't be right. Kate had offered him Seán's bed but he declined, saying he probably wouldn't sleep anyway. At the end of the hall, Tess and Kate lay awake in their room, both staring at the shadows moving on the ceiling from the lights of cars passing over the high bend on the road that led to their house.

"Kate?"

Kate did not answer for what seemed to Tess like an eternity.

Kate was lying on her back thinking of Ben. Her body ached for him as she imagined the last few moments of her brother's life over and over, tormenting her mind and keeping her from sleep. Eventually she answered, hoping her sister's questions would distract her tortured mind, if only for a few seconds.

"Yes?"

"If you want to hug Dermot in the sitting room, I won't mind being on my own."

Kate felt a loud gulp rise in her throat and started to sob, tears never being far from her eyes. Her sister's unusual expression of understanding almost seemed too much for Kate to cope with. She had tried to concentrate on caring for Tess since the news, trying desperately to focus on anything other than Ben's death but had found her sister continued to take the news calmly and had remained by Kate's side in the dreadful waking hours since. Tess had even made tea for neighbours who had not crossed their doorstep in many years, calling to console them for their loss.

Kate tried to control her sobs long enough to answer Tess but couldn't.

"We'll be okay, Kate, don't worry. Everything is okay now. Dermot will look after us."

Tess did not know why her words made Kate turn her face to the wall and she could hear her sister weeping into the night.

Kate could not figure out how Seán had got his hands on the keys. She went over the sequence of events in her mind and was sure that she had not left them in the truck. She was sure that she had them in her hand when she went in search of Tess. She could not remember much after that and hoped that Ben's death was not her fault.

At four the phone rang loudly in the hallway. Kate and Tess listened intently as Dermot answered it and spoke quietly to the unknown caller. By the time he knocked on their bedroom door to wake them, both sisters were dressed sitting hand in hand on the same bed. Dermot stood awkwardly in the doorway, knowing by Kate's face that she knew what he was about to say.

"We have to go to the hospital – they've called the priest." Dermot looked at Kate, expecting resistance, but watched as she surrendered to Tess's gentle pull on her hand.

The sisters walked out of the house together and towards Dermot's car.

When they arrived at the hospital, all three were greeted by the hospital chaplain who led them into a small room off the main intensive-care room where Seán had been moved to over an hour before. Tess stared at the breathing tube leading from his mouth to a machine that moved up and down like an accordion. A loud machine beeped repeatedly. A clear plastic bag hung from the side of Seán's bed and was filling with blood. Tess looked away, afraid that she would vomit which, apart from seeing blood, was the second worst thing she feared. All three sat on the seats already placed for them around the bed, Kate choosing the one furthest away, its view of Seán obstructed by the hospital machinery that was keeping him alive. She did not look at her brother and sat with her hands on her lap, head bowed as though in prayer. The chaplain squeezed her left shoulder, moved toward the bed and began praying over her brother's dying body.

Tess, who had always found it soothing to listen to the repetitive chanting of prayers, looked up. Sensing her best behaviour was required, she made a special effort not to begin humming as she often did during Mass as a child. Instead she focused on Seán who lay motionless in the bed. Tess could see something hard and round on her brother's neck which made his head look small. A large bruise ran evenly across his forehead like it had been painted on. His eyes were closed and a long white tube ran up his nose and was taped onto his face. It was attached to a bag filled with white liquid hanging from a hook above his bed. A wire cage covered both his legs which looked as though they had huge bandages on them. The sheet covering him did not reach the end of the bed but was folded neatly about a foot above his bare feet which were not bruised or cut. Tess focused on this and wondered how this could be. She wondered if Seán's feet were cold and worried that if they were, he would not be able to tell anyone, just like Ben could never tell anyone if something was wrong. She stood and moved closer to the brother who had treated her badly since she had returned home. She knew now that she would never know why he had not liked her. If he had told her what she had done wrong she could have tried harder, she could have apologised but it was too late now. It was also too late for Seán to say he was sorry to her as she knew that even if he did wake up, he wouldn't be able to speak with the tube in his mouth. Tess moved closer to the bed and leant close to her brother's ear, her hand covering the left side of her face, obscuring the bag of blood that hung on the tall metal stand beside the bed.

"It's okay, Seán. I forgive you for shouting at me and drinking all the money and for hitting Kate outside the house, and for –"

"Tess!" said Dermot urgently.

The priest, who did not deviate from his prayers, looked up and shifted uneasily from foot to foot. Dermot rose and stood beside Tess who looked up at him, wondering if she was about to be told off.

"Maybe we could say everything we have to say in our thoughts, Tess?" he whispered.

Tess stood silently and mouthed the rest of Seán's sins silently over his body. She tugged at the stiff white sheet, pulling it down enough to cover his feet and smoothing it around him. Kate smiled and stood with her, both silently saying their goodbyes and forgiving Seán for the wrong he had done to them. Kate could not forgive him for what he had done to Ben – she hoped God would do that for her.

At seven thirty, when the late November sun of a fine, frosty morning began to shine through the hospital blinds, two doctors came into the room and removed the breathing tube from Seán's mouth. Tess watched carefully, hoping he would say something. The beeps from the loud machine began to slow down, eventually merging into a long sharp bell. Tess raised her hands to her ears instinctively but moved them swiftly back onto her lap, knowing that Kate hated to see her do this.

Instead she started counting the tiles on the wall, hoping to distract herself from the awful noise. The doctor looked at his watch and wrote something on Seán's chart. The chaplain put a long thin purple cloth around his neck and began praying very quietly over Seán. Kate and Dermot blessed themselves and Tess copied them quickly. Only when Kate began to cry did Tess understand that her older brother was dead. Quietly and without being noticed Tess withdrew her notebook from her coat pocket, drew a line through Seán's name and stared at the last name on her list: Kate.

Kate had not wanted a double funeral for Seán and Ben but knew she couldn't go through the torment of two funerals, coping with the sympathy of people who had never asked after Ben in his entire life and had never visited Kate when they knew she was trying to cope alone. Her "father" still had family in the area but none of them had called to the house since his death, understandably, some might say. Neither did Kate want Seán and Ben buried in the same grave but knew that their mother, who they would be buried alongside, would have wanted this.

Neither had Kate had a wake. It was too painful to bring her beautiful boy home like that, and she wanted to remember him as he was. She did not want a wake for Seán as her fond memories were few and lay dormant now in the back of the mind of the young girl she no longer was. She could not pretend.

She had not slept for the first three nights since the accident, the doctor finally giving her sleeping pills which brought a temporary release to her tortured mind. Sometimes when she woke, she would forget about what had happened, before the nightmare crashed down again upon her, making the day unbearable and longing for the night and the sweet release the pills brought.

As she stood at the graveside, she leant on Tess who had become a rock to her. Dermot stood to one side with his aunt and uncle and looked sadly at her, the worry clearly showing on his face. People who she didn't recognise came and shook her hand. Some kissed her and expressed their sympathy. She remembered seeing Noel Moore there alone, his mother having passed on some months before. He had shaken her hand and asked her to call him if she needed anything. The priest talked about the tragedy and the loss but most of his words became a blur of sound and repetition. Dermot's aunt and uncle, knowing Kate had no family to help, organised refreshments back at their pub, insisting there was no charge. They could see how fond their nephew had become of Kate and wondered if some day they might all be a family. Kate had sat in the stuffy lounge and did not eat, her stomach feeling too sick to eat since Ben's death.

As the sympathisers drifted away, Dermot drove Kate and Tess back to an empty house. Kate had not spoken to him all day and although he knew it was a difficult day for her, he felt there was more to it and was concerned by the distant look in her eye. He offered to stay but she insisted she was fine as she kissed him and gently closed the door behind him.

A few minutes later Kate heard a banging noise coming from the front gate. She looked out the window and saw Tess hammering her *Butterfly State* sign to the wooden post beside the post box, free to do so now that Seán would no longer be bothering her. Kate watched as her sister finished the task.

"What a simple world you live in, Tess," she said aloud.

When Tess came inside, she smiled at Kate and sat silently on the chair beside the range, her favourite.

Kate looked at her and sat down.

"Well, Tess, what do we do now?"

Tess did not reply. She understood it was not a question.

Chapter 43

1981

Sam Moran sat busily typing up his weekly mart report and watched Talbot's son, who had just returned from the States, push his weight around the office. The young Talbot spoke with a slight American drawl which sickened Sam. He always hated when people who were born and reared in Ireland picked up accents as soon as they got off the plane. He had seen it in London where a thick Dublin brogue was replaced within weeks by a cockney accent. Things were going to be different around here now and he was thinking of looking for another job. It would mean driving to Dublin every day as this newspaper was the only one in the area. He had tried to forget about the Byrne murder. He had thought about it every day but the few ideas he had about how to get the information he needed had come to nothing. Talbot had now given Sam and the young office apprentice, Ken, the obituaries, something that bored him even more than the mart report. It was always old Biddies and Paddies who had lived until ninety and he failed to see the newsworthiness of such.

But Seán Byrne's obituary was different. Sam had been to his uncle's funeral in London when the accident happened and he had only heard about it when he returned. By then the story was old news. The newspaper had covered the tragic accident of the Byrne brothers and had, out of decency towards the remaining family members, not raised old wounds by mentioning the murder of the Byrnes' father all those years ago, something Sam would have mentioned without a thought.

As he looked through the photos that often accompanied the obituary pages, he saw the old school photo of Seán Byrne that Ken had managed to get at the local school. He peered closely at the red-haired freckled-faced boy who smiled shyly into the camera before putting the photo back on Ken's desk and going to pour himself a coffee.

He was halfway back to his desk when he turned around and walked quickly back to the apprentice's desk, lifting the photo of Seán Byrne again. He looked closer. He was right.

Seán Byrne was the spitting image of Éamonn McCracken. He took a deep breath and exhaled loudly. Suddenly everything fell into place. McCracken was Seán Byrne's father. He now knew why McCracken had sent him that warning and felt that he also knew who had murdered Michael Byrne and exactly where to go to prove it.

Dermot Lynch had called to the Byrne house every day since the funeral and each time he became more worried about Kate. She was pale and drawn and refused to eat, insisting she had a sick stomach, the doctor saying her nerves would calm in time. On each visit she moved away when Dermot tried to hold her. When he tried to talk to her she retreated to her room, leaving Tess and Dermot alone, both unsure what to do to help. Tess told Dermot she was afraid that Kate had the same illness as her mother who vomited all the time. Dermot, who was not in Árd Glen back then, worried about this and decided he would ask his uncle about it when he returned to the pub. He considered talking to Kate's uncle, her mother's brother, but decided against it knowing Kate would not be pleased. Jimmy Kelly had called twice to the Byrne house since the deaths, his first time to visit since his sister Maura's wake, but Kate had refused to speak to him.

Dermot brought food every day and packed it away, sometimes cooking dinner and trying to force Kate to eat. He checked on the stock which had dwindled in recent years and wondered how the women were going to survive financially now. They could not run the farm alone and, although he had not looked for wages for weeks, they could not afford to hire any more help.

By now Kate no longer spoke to him. His uncle was

not sure what Tess meant by her comment about Maura Byrne always vomiting – as he remembered it, she got some rare brain disease and was as confused as an old woman before her death.

Kate had now taken to sleeping in Ben's bed, leaving Tess alone in the room they had shared. Hard lines began to appear around her mouth and she rarely if ever spoke, even to Tess who was growing more worried every day.

Deirdre O'Connell sat on Kate's bed and tried to tidy up the dishevelled woman. She had organised for the doctor to call and see Kate who was wasting away in front of her eyes. Her hair had not been washed for weeks and her skin was cracked and dry. Deirdre went into the kitchen and lit the range to heat enough water for Kate's bath.

Tess sat alone on the seat beside the range. She had dark circles under her eyes and was drawing on a new sketchpad that Dermot had brought her.

"How are you, Tess?"

"Fine," she replied flatly.

"You're still drawing. Can I see it?"

Tess turned the large page around as a horrified Deirdre searched for words. Tess had drawn a large pool of water that almost covered the entire page. The water was covered by a huge spider's web. The tiny insect drawn in the centre of the web had two giant heads, covered in red hair and snarling. One of the identical heads had a broken front tooth. In the background Tess stood at the edge of the water, the water wetting the toes of her shoes as she looked upward. There were tears running down her face which had an unusual expression, not exactly fear but similar to it. Ben was drawn as a sleeping baby but with injuries similar to those he had sustained in the accident. Deirdre looked closer to see that his face was painted grey and that Tess had depicted him as a corpse. At the edge of the lake, near Tess's feet, a body lay, its face under water, its black hair floating. In a far corner of the page, Kate was drawn sitting on a grassy mound. She wore a white dress which was ripped, showing her underwear. Her hands covered her face from which tears seemed to be flowing. Deirdre O'Connell looked at Tess, unsure what to say but becoming very concerned about Tess's mental health. She wondered if she had underestimated the effect the accident had on the young woman.

"Em . . . I don't have my glasses on, Tess. What is it?"

"It's the lake, Deirdre," Tess replied matter of factly as though this was obvious.

Deirdre thought about asking Tess to explain the two-headed insect but knew this was beyond her training and decided that she would call Dr Cosgrove for his opinion. It was obvious that Kate wasn't able to look after Tess and they might have to look at her being placed in care for a while.

When the doctor arrived he was as shocked as

Deirdre about Kate's weight loss. Kate insisted she was eating, only to be corrected in each lie by Tess who stood in the doorway, as if on guard.

Dr Doyle took blood tests and said he would get back to her as soon as he had the results. He looked around the house which was showing signs of neglect, then at Tess who stood nervously in the doorway. Deirdre signalled to him that she wanted to talk to him alone. On the front lawn, Dr Doyle agreed that unless Kate recovered soon, Tess needed to be placed in care and that he would make the necessary arrangements if Kate hadn't shown signs of recovery within a week. He felt bad about it and felt that separating them might have a detrimental effect on the sisters. Deirdre agreed and said she would call every day and would organise home help to cook and clean. Dermot was looking after the stock as much as he could but Kate would not speak to him and he didn't come into the house any more. Deirdre went back inside the house, unaware that Tess had listened to everything. She looked in on Kate once more who was sitting up in the bed, staring into thin air.

Tess heard Dermot's car on the gravel driveway and stood to open the back door. She knew the different sounds people's cars made and knew who was coming without looking out of the window. Deirdre O'Connell's engine was quiet and did not make any loud noises like Dermot's did and Dr Doyle's car made a rattling noise even though it looked newer than Deirdre's.

When Dermot came into the kitchen Tess stood and hugged him, her arms jutting tensely outwards.

"Is Kate awake, Tess? I need to talk to her"

Tess noticed that Dermot looked upset. She hoped there wouldn't be any fighting.

"Yes, Dermot. She's in bed."

Dermot sighed. It was over a month since the funeral and Kate was not coping any better. He looked around him. The place seemed cleaner and Tess looked like she was okay.

He went down the hallway and tapped gently before entering. Kate lay awake in her bed. Dermot was glad to see she had returned to her own room, Tess telling him that Deirdre O'Connell had made Kate do it. She did not look up when he entered.

"Kate?"

No response.

"Kate, can you sit up please. I need to talk to you. It's important."

No response.

Dermot sat down on the bed, his body touching hers. He loved the feel of her warmth and longed to hold her. He missed her but she seemed beyond reach. He no longer knew what to say to her and, although he prayed she would come out of this, he believed she was lost to him.

"Kate, my father is ill in Galway."

Kate turned her head and stared hard at him, almost as though she had woken to a find a stranger in her room.

"My mother phoned this morning. He suffered a stroke while tending to the stock. I have to go back for a while. I've arranged for John Redmond to check on the stock while I'm gone."

Kate looked at him, tears forming in her eyes. Dermot gulped. He didn't want this to be any harder than it had to be. It was breaking his heart to leave her like this. He wouldn't have gone at all if it wasn't for his mother's pleas down the phone, begging him to come home, for there was no love lost between Dermot and his father. He tried to lift Kate's shoulders from the bed to hold her but she stiffened and stared at him, an accusing look in her eyes that he couldn't comprehend. He stood up, his large shoulders dropping forward as he stood, as though he had given all he had to give to Kate.

"Kate, please say something before I go," he said softly.

Kate took another look at Dermot before turning her back on him. As he left the room he did not see the tears flowing from her eyes as she faced the cold damp wall.

He stood in the hallway for a while, wondering what had gone wrong. They had not fought and he had supported her through every moment of her brothers' funeral. Dermot leant against the wall. He had no idea what he had done to make her treat him that way or how to get her to open up to him.

When he returned to the kitchen Tess told him about

Nurse O'Connell's conversation with the doctor, that if Kate didn't get any better she herself would be taken away. Dermot listened as she asked if he could take care of her, that she didn't want to go to a strange place, and that she wouldn't be any trouble. He looked tenderly at the young woman who meant so much to him. He loved Tess like he loved his own sisters. He felt guilty when he reassured her as he wasn't sure he had anything here to come back to. Dermot gave Tess his phone number and address in Galway and told her to ring him if there was anything he should know. Tess nodded and when he left she went back to her drawing.

When Deirdre phoned Dr Cosgrove to discuss Tess's paintings, Cosgrove told her that Tess had painted that same painting, albeit without the corpse of Ben and certain other details, over and over again during her years at the institution. He had tried to find out its meaning but any time he asked she would put her finger to her lips and say "shhh", like it was a secret she wanted to keep. He told Deirdre that he later tried to bring Tess's mind back to the murder but the process had a terrible impact on her and he'd had to sedate her, later abandoning all forms of therapy as he felt that if she had committed that crime, she had no understanding of it and there was nothing to be gained from going over it with her.

Deirdre listened intently and asked, "Do you think she did it, though?"

Dr Cosgrove exhaled loudly before responding. "No, I don't," he said before hanging up.

Deirdre felt Tess was trying to express a deep hidden memory through the paintings, something she couldn't put into words and possibly didn't even completely remember and she hoped she knew someone who could help her.

Dr Doyle phoned Deirdre and asked her to meet him at Kate Byrne's house as he wanted to have a female with him when he spoke to her and knew that Deirdre had become a friend of Kate's. They arrived at the same time which confused Tess as she couldn't work out who was visiting from the sound of the cars and had to come around the front of the house to see.

Kate was sitting in the kitchen with a blanket wrapped around her. She felt cold although the home-care woman had lit a large fire in the range. Dr Boyle explained to a stone-faced Kate that he had her tests results and asked if it was okay for Nurse O'Connell to sit in. Kate nodded. Deirdre told Tess to go outside and check on the horse, an excuse to ensure Tess did not overhear the conversation. Kate seemed disinterested and not at all worried, as if her heart and soul had left her and nothing mattered now.

Dr Doyle sat facing Kate and began to awkwardly remind her of the blood tests he organised to see why she was so ill, as though Kate might have forgotten.

Kate nodded impatiently. She hated company now

and felt at peace only when left to her thoughts. She spent her days thinking of Ben and where he was now. She imagined him in a heaven where he did not have autism and was playing with other boys his age, her mother looking on lovingly from the distance. Kate could summon this image up at any time and it made her happy, if only for a short time.

"Well . . ." Doyle continued quietly, "your blood tests were fine."

Deirdre O'Connell looked up surprised. She thought she was invited here to comfort Kate because the doctor had bad news.

"You're malnourished, but you know that, Kate." He stalled and looked at both women.

Kate was becoming annoyed. He was drawing this out longer than he had to. "Then what, doctor, what is it for God's sake!"

"You're pregnant."

Marcus Gill looked through Tess's paintings that Deirdre O'Connell had brought to him, making "mmm" sounds periodically.

"They're good, quite good, very dark. You say your friend painted them?"

"Yes, well, it's actually Tess Byrne – remember, the girl here on work experience?"

"Really?" Pascoe replied, surprised.

Apart from her little outburst, she had seemed like a gentle person. It was a pity she hadn't continued with her work experience but he had heard about the family's recent tragedy.

"Do you have any idea what they mean?" O'Connell asked hopefully.

"Why don't you ask her?" Gill asked.

"Well, it's not that simple. You know she is autistic?"

Marcus nodded.

"It means that she finds it hard to express herself verbally or to understand her own emotions. It would be almost impossible for her to tell me what this means to her. I was hoping you might have some idea."

Marcus looked through the lake painting again. Deirdre pointed out who everyone was, telling him as much about the killing of Michael Byrne as she knew.

"Well, you know, sweetie, that we all get different things from each painting, see it differently than the person in the gallery beside us," he said, raising the pitch of his voice higher and becoming more flamboyant as the conversation went on. "It's an individual thing."

Deirdre began to think that she had made a mistake bringing the paintings here. It had taken her ages to convince Tess to let her borrow them, bribing her with the promise of more paints and brushes in return.

"But . . ." he continued, "if you want my humble opinion, I'd say she is a victim in this painting. See?" He pointed to her blurred face. "She has no mouth – it renders her helpless."

"Could it mean she has to keep a secret?" asked Deirdre.

"Mmmm . . . possibly . . . but these insects are interesting. She's telling us they are the 'bad guys' if you want it in simple terms. You see, they are almost identical except that one has a broken tooth. These represent real people that she knows. Very interesting. How much is she looking for?"

"Sorry?" Deirdre asked.

"She's selling her paintings, yes? They'd be worth something. I might even be able to organise a showing. Ask her to think about it or to call in and see me. She has talent." He gazed at the painting thoughtfully.

"Oh, I don't think she'd be interested, but I'll tell her – maybe – I'm not sure."

Deirdre left the shop and placed the paintings in her car. She felt sure they explained what happened all those years ago and although she knew a little more about the painting, she felt she might never know what really happened that day.

Before heading back to Árd Glen she stopped off at the stationery shop to buy Tess the items she promised her. Things were very strained at the Byrne house since Kate realised she was pregnant. Deirdre was expecting any other news except that. Even though it seemed to make Kate snap out of her depression, it had sent her into a state of quiet anxiety. She told Deirdre about her relationship with Dermot, whom she hadn't heard from since he went west. She didn't intend telling him, didn't want him to think he had to marry her, and as yet she had no idea what she would do. She wanted it kept from Tess for the time being; she worked out she was almost eight weeks pregnant so she had time. The vomiting was caused by a condition called hyperemesis gravidarum which Deirdre knew some pregnant women develop, Kate later telling her that her mother had something similar when she was expecting Ben. Kate would need to stick to vitamin treatments or risk spending months in hospital. Deirdre felt Kate had improved, not so much because of her pregnancy about which she spoke very little, but because Deirdre had told her that they might have to find short-term accommodation for Tess until Kate recovered. Kate didn't want this, she felt Tess had been through enough and promised to stick to her treatment plan.

Over the next couple of weeks Deirdre noticed that Kate's physical health was returning – she even had some colour in her face. Her uncle, knowing she had no transport, had given her an old car he had done up himself. Kate had thanked him and reluctantly apologised for being rude when he called during the funeral. The atmosphere between them was still uncomfortable and Jimmy Kelly didn't stay long in the house. Before he left he stood awkwardly at the kitchen door with his cap in his hand. He told her she was the image of her mother and left quickly out the back door. Kate watched him pass the kitchen window as he wiped his eyes with an old dirty handkerchief covered in oil.

Chapter 44

1981

Dermot Lynch sat in his parents' kitchen and dried his soaking feet at the range. He had spent weeks sitting beside his father's bedside and had just returned from walking back through the land that was once his inheritance. Dermot's younger brother had been running the farm alongside their father but he too had great difficulty getting along with the old man. Nothing, his brother confided in him, was ever good enough for their father, nothing ever done right. He told Dermot that he had thought about going to New York where their older sister could get him a job but knew the old man couldn't manage the farm alone so he had stayed.

When the rain settled, Dermot opened the kitchen door that led directly out onto the back yard and smelt the air. He loved the smell that permeated the land after the rain. It wasn't quite the same in Wicklow, he felt. It rained so much more here which made farming harder but there was something about the west that he loved; maybe it was because he was born here, he reasoned. Life was also more laid back here; the people seemed less in a hurry. Even though Árd Glen was a small farming community, the people weren't as relaxed and it was something Dermot had noticed when he first arrived there.

It was difficult to think of Árd Glen without thinking about Kate. He wondered how she was but knew from the last time he saw her that she wanted no more to do with him. He couldn't figure it out; there had been no row, no disagreement. After the funeral she simply cut him out as though he was dead. He hadn't had a lot of experience with women and was always a bit on the shy side but he couldn't understand what had gone wrong between them. For the first few days in Galway, Dermot's heart raced every time the phone rang, thinking it was her, asking when he was coming back, but it was always someone asking after his father. It was hard to see his father like that, shrivelled in the hospital bed, unable to speak. He had been a tall, strong man who in his youth walked a round trip of six miles a day to school and now he would never walk again. When Dermot first arrived in Galway and entered the ward, his father reached out his left arm, his other arm being paralysed, and shook hands with him. He was pleased that his eldest son had returned, even if it was temporary. Dermot had not told his family about Kate as he wasn't sure if there was anything to tell. He didn't know if his aunt in Árd Glen, his mother's sister, had mentioned it in one of her telephone calls back home. He hoped not as he liked to keep his business to himself.

Dermot was also missing Tess. He thought of ringing her but was afraid Kate would answer and would think he had difficulty getting the message she had so obviously given him when he last saw her. Maybe it was all for the best – after all, he was needed around here now. Dermot sat back and listened to the rain fall heavily outside and wondered what they were doing in Árd Glen.

Kate sat Tess down in front of her, making her sister put any distractions away so that she could get her full attention. She was feeling stronger and even though her sickness continued, it had improved slightly. Tess needed her and this kept Kate going. She knew that they were in trouble financially and that they would have to consider selling the farm as there was no way they could work it together. When Kate thought about it, they had been in financial difficulty for some time but she had thought that Seán would eventually stop drinking and she felt like a fool for letting this situation go on for so long. She knew now that she couldn't depend on anyone except herself as everyone in the end had let her down and she wasn't going to give anyone else a chance to do this. Tess had a disability allowance which helped and they received some farming subsidies but it wasn't enough and they needed to make some decisions.

When Kate told Tess that the farm was actually hers, she could see the look of confusion on her sister's face. She didn't tell Tess it was because Michael Byrne was not Seán's father, feeling this would be too much for Tess to take in. She told her she didn't know why he had left it to Tess but that she should be pleased he thought of her. Kate watched Tess's face crumple and crease, knowing her sister was trying to work this news out.

Finally, Tess spoke. "Is that why Seán didn't like me?"

"Maybe, Tess, but none of this was your fault. It's just the way things turned out, that's all."

"Why didn't he leave the farm to you, Kate? You are older than me."

Sometimes Kate felt her sister understood more than she pretended to.

"I don't know, Tess. Like I said, it's just the way it is. What we need to talk about is money. We haven't got enough money coming in for us to live on. We might need, Tess, to think about selling the farm and moving."

Kate stopped talking, giving Tess a chance to digest her words. She could already see the storm brewing in her sister's face.

"No, Kate. I like it here. I like the horse. I like Dermot. I won't go. No." She drew her legs underneath herself and folded her arms tightly.

Kate sighed. She had known this would be difficult. She didn't expect Tess to understand.

"Tess, we might be able to keep some land, maybe keep the house and sell the acreage. Tess, we need money to live. I can't work . . . I . . ." Kate was trying to put off telling Tess about the baby but felt she had to explain why, now that she no longer had Ben to care for, she could not look for work in the town. "Tess, I want to tell you a secret but it's very important that it remains a secret. You can't tell anyone, okay?"

Tess's eyes widened as she nodded.

"I am having a baby. It will be born in summer. That's why I've been sick."

Tess was silent. She lowered her head, lost in thought. She had questions but could not put them into words. She said nothing which disappointed her sister who had expected, or at least hoped, that Tess would be happy about the baby. But Kate couldn't understand why she should expect this when she wasn't even happy about the pregnancy herself. She didn't know how much Tess understood about sex; she didn't know what, if anything, they had taught her at the hospital.

Until Tess finally said, "When is Dermot coming back?"

Kate lowered her head, knowing that Tess did understand. "I don't know, Tess," she replied simply.

Kate had thought about Dermot every day since he left, had hoped he would call her even though she had treated him so badly. She didn't know why she had behaved in that way. Dermot had stood with her every minute during the tragedy and funeral; she wondered how she would have got through those awful days without him. After it was over she felt empty, yet unbelievably hurt. Seán had taken her reason for living away from her. She didn't want anyone expecting anything from her; she had nothing left to give. She wanted to lie in her bed and dream of Ben and she had done this for weeks, unaware that she was neglecting Tess. She flushed thinking about it. How could she have done that?

Now, she felt she had lost Dermot. She decided she wouldn't tell him about the baby; she didn't want to repeat her mother's mistakes. She would keep the child. She wished she could leave Árd Glen. It would be impossible to hide her pregnancy in this small town. But she couldn't leave right now as she had Tess to consider and they had no family anywhere else that they could turn to. She hoped they would sell the farm easily and move somewhere to start a new life before the baby was born.

She realised Tess was staring at her, waiting for a better answer to her question about Dermot.

"Tess, we'll have to go to see a solicitor in Dublin where your – where Dad wrote his will." Kate rarely referred to Michael Byrne as her father now. "We need the deeds of the farm. Deeds are papers that say you own it. We need those no matter what we decide to do."

Tess remained so lost in thought for the rest of the evening that she did not even draw. She had been through enough change and had looked forward to coming home for all those years and now, after only ten months, she would have to move again.

The hospital had sent Tess a follow-up appointment in Dublin and Kate hoped to organise an appointment with the solicitor the same day. Kate worried that Tess might not want to return to the hospital and had not told her yet and tonight was definitely not the right time.

Chapter 45

1981

Dermot Lynch sat at his father's bedside, hating the quiet, white starched world of the hospital ward. It was now six weeks since Dan Lynch's stroke and while he had initially shown signs of improvement, a bout of pneumonia had weakened him. He was asleep almost all of the time but when he opened his eyes he thought Dermot was his own brother who had died of TB as a young man. Although he had regained some speech he was difficult to understand and talked about the war as though it was still happening and asked Dermot had he seen Annie, Dermot's aunt who was long since dead. One night he called for his mother, Dermot's grandmother, as his temperature raged and he did not instantly recognise his wife or any of his children until they reminded him who they were.

Dermot could hear the slow, hypnotic tick of the

large wooden clock that hung on the opposite side of the ward. A statue adorned every windowsill of the long narrow room. Dermot found the silence oppressive and found himself hoping that an end would soon come. He hoped that his father would recover enough to return home or, if this wasn't to be, that he would soon pass away peacefully and without pain. Dermot's father coughed hard and his body shook violently as his face turned red with the sudden exertion. He opened his eyes as the nurse placed the oxygen mask back onto his face.

Dermot slumped back in the hard hospital chair and thought about Kate. So much time had passed now that he was sure he would never hear from her again.

Initially he had been pleased to be back here which surprised him as he had left on such bad terms. It was a chance to work things out with his father whom he felt sometimes knew he was there, beside him. But as time passed his longing for Árd Glen, for Kate, grew. He was surprised at how much he missed the place itself. His initial pleasure in the familiar landscape of Galway had passed and now the heavy rain and incessant westerly winds were gradually getting to him, driving him back where he felt he now belonged.

In Árd Glen Deirdre O'Connell was sitting with Kate in the kitchen, several thoughts burned in her mind. She was glad to see that Kate was recovering and noticed she was starting to "show", a small bulge sticking out from her painfully thin frame. Kate had not spoken once about the baby. Deirdre felt she and Kate had become good enough friends for her to ask questions she would not normally ask in her professional capacity. She finished her tea and, placing her cup onto the table, took a slow deep breath and began.

"Have you thought about the baby, Kate? I mean, thought of talking to Dermot?"

Deirdre knew that she was going about this the wrong way when she saw Kate look crossly at her from across the table.

"Kate, I know it's none of my business but I am worried about how you'll cope on your own. Would you consider talking to Dermot? Telling him you're pregnant?"

Kate shook her head. "I can't tell Dermot, Deirdre. My mother was pregnant getting married and, well, it ruined her life. I don't want him to feel he has to marry me. If he comes back of his own free will and things are all right between us, I'll tell him then."

"Would you not even ring him, tell him you miss him?"

"No. It will have to come from him. I couldn't live my life thinking he pitied me, Deirdre."

"How will you manage for money, Kate?"

"I've been thinking about that. We can't keep the farm, it's too much work for Tess and me and I'll have a child to mind. Anyway, I really don't know enough about running a farm. Seán was taught about it but I mostly helped my mother inside. I know a little, but definitely not enough. Tess has an appointment at the hospital on Tuesday in Dublin and I've made an appointment with the solicitor my father used in Dublin to get a copy of the deeds."

"Did Seán leave a will?" Deirdre asked gingerly, aware that the mention of her older brother still made Kate tense up.

"No, but he didn't have to. Tess actually owns the farm."

"Tess?" O'Connell raised her eyebrows in surprise.

"It's a long story, Deirdre," Kate replied, lowering her head.

Deirdre knew when to back off and changed the subject. "Kate, there's something I have been waiting to discuss with you until you felt a little better. Remember I brought Tess's paintings to the manager in Marshall's Art and Craft Centre?"

Kate nodded, slightly disinterested for she was used to Tess's unusual view of life that she so regularly reflected in her paintings.

"He said they were worth money. He was interested in buying them. Might be worth looking into, Kate."

Kate looked up, surprised. While she could see Tess could paint well, she had always found her sister's paintings a little creepy.

"He said the two caterpillars, or whatever they are, in the painting are people Tess knows."

Kate stared at her and then rose and left the room, returning with the nightmare painting of the lake. She placed it on the table and, sitting, looked closely at the two red-headed insects that stood in the centre of the painting. Then she sat back, amazed. "I think that's supposed to be Seán! I never noticed that before! I wonder why she painted him like that? It looks like he is a butterfly changing into a caterpillar. See how his wings are withering? God knows what goes through my sister's mind. Strange . . ."

"Who is the other redhead? See, it has a broken tooth."

Kate shook her head. She couldn't think of anyone else with red hair. "I don't know," she said, puzzled, shaking her head.

Kate and Deirdre stared at the painting for a few seconds more, neither woman able to make any sense of it.

"Well, I'd better go. I'm heading out tonight," Deirdre announced then.

"You don't sound too excited," Kate replied.

"Well, you know me and my dates. They usually end in disaster!" Deirdre laughed. "Remember the last fellow who wanted someone to look after his mammy?"

Both women fell about laughing. Deirdre had certainly met some strange ones and she and Kate had many a laugh about her "romances" over a cup of tea.

As Deirdre pulled away, Kate felt slightly envious of her friend. She wished she knew that kind of excitement and independence but now, with a child growing inside her, she knew her life would always revolve around caring for others and the lack of freedom that such responsibility brought.

Chapter 46

1981

Kate decided to take the early morning bus to Dublin. She had never driven there on her own before and was worried that the old car her Uncle Jimmy had given her might not make the journey anyway. Black smoke had begun to bellow out of its exhaust and she didn't have the money to get it fixed. She knew she could ask her uncle to look at it for her but her pregnancy was beginning to show and, while she could go to town with a big coat on her, she couldn't do that in the house. She wondered why she was trying to keep it a secret as sooner or later people would find out. "Like mother, like daughter!" she could imagine them saying.

Tess was happy to be taking the bus which would get them into the bus terminus at nine twenty-five. Her appointment at the hospital wasn't until eleven so Kate had promised her tea and scones in Bewleys before they made their way to see Dr Cosgrove. Tess hoped Dr Cosgrove wasn't going to ask her about the lake and had dreamt about it the night before, a dream she had not had since she returned home. They had an appointment at the solicitor's at two which Kate hoped would finish quickly so they could be on the five o'clock bus home. She had checked to see if she would have to pay on the day for the appointment and was relieved when the posh-sounding Dublin secretary assured her that her bill would be posted out by mail.

Dr Cosgrove greeted them warmly and seemed very pleased to see Tess. Kate stayed in the waiting area while Tess went into the office with him and, sensing they would be a while, walked down the corridor towards the main building. Small groups of children sat in rooms where they appeared to be receiving lessons, others walked past her with nurses scolding them for bad behaviour. Kate didn't like the feel of the place. She remembered the two occasions that she had got as far as the foyer but could not come any further. On both occasions she walked the length of the quays while waiting for the last bus home, trying to figure out why she couldn't bring herself to see Tess. Was it guilt at not preventing the police from taking Tess away? For no matter how strange the child had been, Kate didn't believe she had murdered their father. But what could she have done? Tess had been found there, standing over his body.

Kate could hear a child crying which echoed down the long tiled corridor and followed the sound where she found a young girl sitting on the floor outside a wood-panelled room. She had long mousy brown hair and deep green eyes, filled with tears. Kate stooped down and wiped the child's face, feeling her own eyes well up.

"What's wrong, love?" she asked softly.

The child looked up, surprise written all over her little face. Kate could see deep cuts on her arms, old cuts, and wondered who could have done such a thing to this child.

"I want my mammy! I want to go home!" she cried, her chin quivering as she looked into Kate's face.

Before Kate had a chance to answer, a nurse came out of a nearby room and smiled at both Kate and the child who had now suddenly stopped crying.

"Can I help you?" the nurse enquired kindly.

"Oh, no, I'm just waiting on someone. Is – is that child okay? She's looking for her mother."

"Oh, that's Mary," the nurse said casually. "She's fine. She gets like this sometimes."

"Is – is her mother – around?"

The nurse led her away until they were out of earshot and whispered, "No, most of the kids here don't have anyone or, if they do, they don't want them back."

Kate felt an overwhelming urge to cry and put her hand over her mouth to avoid embarrassing herself.

"That's awful, I didn't know . . . I didn't . . . excuse me!" Kate rushed off towards the room where Tess would be waiting. As she ran, loud sobs came from her mouth and filled the empty corridor. She hadn't known what it was like here for her little sister. She had tried not to think of Tess in this place over the years. Had she been calling for her, crying on a cold corridor as that child had been? She couldn't bear to think about it. She had wanted to ask Tess what it had been like but could never bring herself to, worried that what she might hear would confirm her fears.

She found a bathroom to wash her face and stood there for a while, waiting for the redness to leave her eyes. When she returned to Dr Cosgrove's room, Tess was in the waiting area. He asked Kate to come in and speak to him alone.

"It's nice to finally meet you, Mrs . . .?"

Kate was embarrassed that this was the first time she had met the man who had worked hard to help her sister and reddened slightly, wondering what he must think of her.

"Miss . . . Miss Byrne . . . Kate," she said as she sat uncomfortably in the seat her sister had occupied only minutes before.

"How do you feel Tess is settling back at home?"

Kate didn't quite know how to answer him. Tess was Tess. She had good days and bad days, but mostly good days. Kate understood her most of the time and knew, sometimes before Tess did, when she was heading for one of her meltdowns. Kate no longer saw these episodes as a problem. They were a normal part of her sister's life, of Kate's life.

"She's fine," she replied. She could think of nothing more to say but felt the doctor wanted more from her.

"Tess tells me someone wants to buy her paintings?"

"Yes," Kate smiled. "A local art centre. I wish him luck. She'll only have handed them over when she'll want them back!" She laughed and noticed that Cosgrove laughed too. She lowered her head. "Can you tell me, was she . . . all right here? Was she . . ." She didn't know how to finish her question, didn't know what she wanted to hear. "Over the years, I didn't come because I . . . I tried . . . I just couldn't . . ." She searched for words. Tears started to roll down her face. "I couldn't bear to leave here without her. She relied on me and trusted me and I let them take her away. I'll never forgive myself for that. I was young and I think I was more worried about my wedding being ruined than my poor sister."

"You couldn't have prevented it. There was strong evidence that she committed a violent crime and she needed help." He paused. "Do you think she murdered your father?" He was glad to finally be able to speak to someone who knew Tess well.

Kate looked sideways towards the wall and sniffed. It didn't look like she was going to answer and he was contemplating changing the subject when she finally spoke.

"He was cruel to her, to all of us, but mostly he ignored her. She was an embarrassment to him because of her ways. The strange thing is she asked me when he would die only a few days before he was actually killed.

He was drinking heavily since our mother's death and was causing a lot of trouble in the house."

Kate sat silent, aware that Dr Cosgrove was watching her closely, watching her eye movements, her body language, and scrutinising her every move.

"You still didn't answer my question," he said finally, his tone friendly but direct.

"No, I never believed she did it."

When they left his office, Dr Cosgrove told Tess he didn't think he needed to see her again but if she had any problems at all to call him. He gave her a card with his direct line on it. There was something so vulnerable about this young woman. He had an urge to hug her but instead offered her his hand which she shook quickly and weakly.

Tess waved back at him as she walked down the corridor. Together she and Kate walked through the huge building which she knew her way around so well. Kate thought Tess would be nervous here but, although she was quieter than usual, she seemed calm and relaxed. As they moved through the older part of the building, Kate was astounded to see Tess running into the arms of a tall black man who was mopping an identical corridor on the ground floor.

"Leroy!" Tess squealed.

Leroy, looking equally delighted, lifted Tess up, her legs dangling as he waved her about like a rag-doll. Kate stood open-mouthed. Kate had never seen Tess hug anyone before like that

When Leroy finally put Tess down, they stood smiling at each other.

"Leroy, that's my sister," Tess said.

Kate moved forward and shook hands with Leroy.

"I'm Kate, pleased to meet you. Tess has told me all about you." Well, almost everything, she thought to herself.

Leroy smiled back at Kate, knowing or at least suspecting what she was thinking.

"I'm Declan," he finally said. "Tess calls me Leroy. It – it used to be my nickname."

Kate looked confused but didn't ask.

They went to the foyer and talked, Kate leaving the two friends alone for half an hour while they caught up on their news. She walked outside but could see them through the glass doors. She noticed their conversation had quietened down and could see them say the odd sentence and sit smiling at each other. Tess seemed happy. When she returned Tess stood up and almost immediately walked away from Leroy who didn't seem surprised by his friend's unusual behaviour. It was almost lunch-time and Tess was hungry. Leroy smiled as Kate reminded her sister to have manners and he moved closer to hug her goodbye but this time she only permitted a quick sideways hug, her excitement at seeing her old friend obviously beginning to wear off.

"I'll write to you," Leroy said.

"When?" Tess asked. She needed to know because

then she'd know exactly when to expect a letter in her post box.

Leroy laughed. "Friday. That way I can tell you all my week's news."

Tess nodded and made a mental note that the letter would arrive on Monday and walked away from her friend, who was used to her idiosyncrasies, without looking back.

They had time on their hands and walked back slowly towards the city centre. Kate hoped the long walk would give them a chance to talk. There was something that she had to know, something she had finally found the courage to ask.

"Tess, was it awful there – at the hospital? Please be honest with me."

Tess thought about her answer for a few seconds. "I had to bite some kids, Kate. They touched my property."

Kate looked at Tess, wondering if her sister was trying to make light of the situation but she could see by Tess's face that she was being honest.

Kate smiled. "Did you bite them hard?" she asked, laughing.

"Yes, Kate. As hard as I could."

The two sisters laughed as they walked side by side towards the quays, Kate not knowing that Tess had saved her from knowing exactly how hard it had been for her there for all those years. It didn't matter now, they were together and they were safe from biting kids, from Michael Byrne and from the two-headed caterpillar.

Kate explained the purpose of their visit to Simon McCarthy, a new associate at the solicitor's firm. She had brought Seán's death certificate and identification for both herself and Tess who sat nervously in the chair beside her. Kate had often wondered how her mother had come to have the business card of this company in her handbag which had led Seán here all those years ago. She looked around the plush office which was not the sort of place her mother would have felt comfortable in and her family had always used the local solicitor in Knockbeg. Seán said this Dublin firm had never heard of their mother and she had not done any business with them. It was a mystery that Kate felt would never be figured out.

The polite young man said that Tess needed to sign for the deeds which had been changed into her name at the land registry when her father died and her brother had become her guardian. He asked the sisters to follow him down a long hallway while he took the deeds from the locked area. At the end of the hallway he asked them to wait in a small sitting area, the walls of which were adorned with photographs of staff over the years. Tess, who was bored and seemed slightly agitated to Kate, walked along the walls, nosily peering at photographs and paintings as Kate sat, exhausted from the day, in a large comfortable chair. Even though it was a cold day, the sun shone through the long windows on the opposite side of the room. Kate felt as though she could easily sleep, the pregnancy was making her feel so tired. It had occurred to her once or twice that the baby might have the same condition as Tess or Ben, that perhaps they had inherited it from their mother instead of Michael Byrne and it worried her a little. She sat there, with her eyes closed to block out the sunlight, lost in thought when she heard Tess let out a gasp of air, as if someone had punched her. Kate looked up and saw Tess, frozen, looking at a photograph on the wall.

"What is it, Tess?" Kate wearily asked, too tired to get up and see.

Tess simply pointed at the photograph. Kate groaned and stood. Her back ached and she wished she had worn more comfortable shoes. She walked to the other side of the room and as she moved closer to her sister, she could see the look of shock and fear on Tess's face.

"What's wrong, Tess?"

Tess was still pointing at the row of smiling men and women in the photo which looked old, taken at least ten, maybe fifteen years ago. Kate looked and saw Tess was pointing at a smiling man in the front row of the photograph.

Kate peered closer. The sun was reflecting off the photograph and as Kate was at an angle she could not see it clearly.

"What, Tess? What's wrong? Tell me."

Kate was worried. She could see something had frightened Tess badly.

"It's a secret, Kate," she said as her face crumpled with fear.

Kate could see her sister's chin quiver and knew she was about to lose control. She looked closer at the photo, holding her two hands around her face to block out the sunlight. There were about eight people in the photograph which was taken outside the building. They wore 1970s-style clothes with brightly coloured, patterned blouses and wide-legged suits. Kate looked at each face individually before stopping at the man Tess had been pointing at.

He had red hair. He was smiling broadly and she could clearly see his broken front tooth. He was the man in Tess's painting. She turned to look at her sister. Tess knew this man, but how?

"Who is he, Tess? How do you know him? Please stay calm."

Tess had begun to claw at her dress as though it was covered in dirt. She wiped her face roughly as though it too was soiled. She rubbed her hands on her dress and started to rock back and forth as she often did when she felt threatened. Kate was embarrassed. A secretary passing by stopped and asked if everything was all right. The young solicitor had returned and stood staring at Tess who was now sitting on the floor as Kate tried to calm her.

"Tess, please stand up, please, Tess! It's okay, we'll leave here now. Come on, please stand up. Let's go, Tess!"

Tess seemed incapable of hearing her sister's pleas. She continued to rock back and forth and started to emit a loud, low moan.

People started to come out from their small offices and stood looking at Tess whose moaning was quickly turning into a sharp shriek that apparently even Tess herself couldn't stand to hear as she covered her ears with her hands. Finally, two men arrived, the shocked secretary having called them. They were well dressed and when staff moved out of their way to let them through, Kate knew they must be the managers, or perhaps the owners of the firm.

As Tess looked up she started to scream even louder.

"I won't tell, I won't tell! Blood! Shhh, it's a secret, I won't tell, I won't tell. Who's your mother? Wet shoes!"

She repeated these phrases over and over, her pitch rising with every repetition.

Kate turned to see one of the men was the man in the photo, the man Tess had drawn in her lake painting as an insect. Beside Seán. Why? Then a sickening realisation enveloped her. This man was their father.

"I only went to see the butterflies, Kate!"

Kate felt like this whole scene was moving in slow motion. Her heart pounded and a wave of nausea made her shiver.

"You're the caterpillar, you were there . . . you're . . ." Kate knew people were looking at her. "You were at the lake that day. My God, you did it, you killed him!"

Kate felt her sister's hands grab onto her and turned

to see Tess lift herself off the floor. She held onto Kate as though she might break in two. Her legs trembled like those of a newborn lamb and she seemed scarcely able to stand. She buried her head in Kate's coat and did not look at the man who stood motionless, his eyes darting back and forth among the crowd.

Roberts, the senior partner of the firm, who had arrived with McCracken, peered closely at him, questioning.

"What's going on, Éamonn?" he asked, perplexed and resentful of the scene that was taking place in his offices.

McCracken moved his mouth, as if to speak, but sensing the uselessness of this he turned quickly and hurried down the corridor, disappearing through the back door at its end. People who had worked with this man for over thirty years stood staring, uncomprehending. Two other men followed him, not knowing what they would do if they caught up with him and what any of this was about.

Roberts brought Kate and a shivering Tess into his office where the staff could not hear. Over the years Roberts had heard through associates that McCracken was involved in the Republican movement. He had turned a deaf ear to it as long as it didn't interfere with his work and it hadn't. McCracken brought in more business than any other solicitor and four years ago Roberts and his senior partners had invited him to join them. Some of the clientèle he had brought were not quite Roberts' preferred type but they had paid their bills and it was, after all, a business. But this was different. Roberts had no idea what any of this was about but he was about to find out.

Kate explained as much as she knew while Tess sat stunned and mute. She was still shaking and continually turned her head towards the door, afraid that McCracken would come after her for finally telling the secret that he had forced her to keep all those years ago.

"You'll be going to the police, I assume?" Roberts asked, hopeful that his firm could be kept out of it yet knowing how ridiculous this hope was. It seemed McCracken had committed an awful crime and had allowed this young woman to take the blame.

"There's more," Kate finally said, clearing her throat. "I think he might be my father."

Tess was woken out of her terror as quickly as if someone had thrown a bucket of icy water over her. Kate quickly turned and placed her hands on her sister's shoulders.

"Tess!" she said firmly. "I will explain all of this to you later and we'll talk about what we are going to do, okay?"

Tess nodded but was clearly shocked and bewildered.

Kate asked Mr Roberts if they could leave, explaining that she needed to take Tess away from the offices to calm her. He explained however that he needed to call the police as this was a criminal matter. Then he ordered tea and biscuits for the sisters.

After a stressful wait, the police arrived. The tea and

biscuits had distracted Tess and she had by now calmed sufficiently to make a statement. After Kate added hers, they were allowed to go and were informed that detectives would call on them the next day at their home.

As Kate rose, she put her arm protectively around her sister who did not flinch at the touch and moved her from the office.

"Come on, Tess, let's go home."

When detectives called to Kate's home the following morning, she'd had a chance to talk to Tess and find out exactly what had happened that day. The police wanted to hear it from Tess's own mouth which Kate had dreaded, not wanting to drag her sister through it all again. As they sat in the sitting room, Kate assured Tess that she didn't have to keep the secret any more, that she was safe. Tess explained how she had gone to the lake early that morning to see the butterflies as she always did even when Kate got angry with her. She saw her father asleep at the lake and he smelt of whiskey. She told the police that she did not wake him and had stood by the lake and looked at the pretty rock. After a few minutes the man with the broken tooth came towards her and grabbed her and put blood on her dress. She started to cry and he placed his hand over her mouth which put blood on her face so she screamed. He stared into her face and asked her who her mother was and shook her because she couldn't speak. When she at last told him he pushed her back onto the grass and stood looking at her, shaking his head. He put his face too close to hers and told her she had better not tell anyone that she saw him. She had better keep it quiet or something terrible would happen to her. Then he ran away.

Tess stopped talking and looked at the two policemen who stared back at her.

"What did you do then?"

Tess swallowed hard. Kate put her arm around her.

"Then a fisherman came up and he said that Daddy was dead. He called other fishermen who called the police. When they came, they brought me to a police station and wouldn't let me go home to see Kate."

"Tess," one of the detectives said softly, "did you see this man murder your father?"

Tess looked over the seated man's shoulder and replayed the event in her mind again before answering. "No."

The detective sighed. They had motive and could place McCracken at the scene of the crime but the girl had not actually seen him doing it so it was still possible that the smart lawyer would get off with it.

Tess, who had given the details of that day in perfect detail and without emotion, began to cry now, the memory of being separated from her sister overwhelming her. Kate cried too as they sat holding each other, finally knowing what happened that day when their lives changed forever.

The police left a uniformed officer outside the house all night as McCracken was known to them and while he was never convicted of any crime, they knew many of his associates whom they considered dangerous. They didn't tell the women that and said the policeman outside was just a precaution, but this didn't fool Kate as she and Tess faced a sleepless night.

Chapter 47

1981

Sam Moran was finding it hard to ignore what he now knew about Seán Byrne's true parentage. He also knew that even if he proved his theory, there was nothing he could do with the information but if nothing else it would satisfy the one burning issue in his head. How did a country girl like Maura Kelly meet up with Éamonn McCracken? Dublin wasn't far away but she wouldn't have been going that far to dances and, as a single girl, she certainly wouldn't have been allowed to stay in Dublin overnight, not back then. He reasoned that McCracken must have had some connection to Árd Glen and he needed his birth cert to prove it. He didn't know what age McCracken was and if he didn't have an ex-girlfriend working in the Births, Deaths and Marriages office, he would have had no chance of finding it. McCracken was an unusual name so it shouldn't be too hard to find, he reasoned.

He saw Sylvia O'Reilly before she saw him. She had gained about three stone and two chins since he last walked her down the canal for a late-night feel. Her hair, once jet black, was badly dyed and a long white streak ran along her parting making her look like a badger. She reddened slightly when she called the next number and saw him walk towards the counter.

"Sam, how are ya?" she asked in her flat Dublin accent, glancing over her shoulder in case her work colleagues were listening.

"Grand, Sylvia – you look great."

"Liar," she said quietly. "I'm like an elephant. That's what four kids does to ya."

"Who did you marry?"

"Eamo Martin, 'member him?"

Sam tried to think. "Yeah, he was a nutter!" he finally said.

"Still is . . . bastard!" She looked at Sam, wondering what he wanted.

"Well, that's a coincidence as it just so happens it's another Éamonn I'm looking for."

"Oh, yeah?" she asked suspiciously. "Got his date of birth?"

"No but here's his name –"

"Can't do it so."

"Ah, come on, Sylvia, for old times' sake, wha'?"

Sylvia smiled and snapped the piece of paper from his hands.

"It'll cost ya," she said as she turned, her huge thighs quivering as she walked away.

By the time Sam Moran obtained Éamonn McCracken's birth certificate, he had already been located in a safe house in County Antrim and was awaiting extradition to Dublin. Sam, realising it was now safe to run his story, joined the media frenzy outside the police station in Dublin where McCracken was due to be taken that evening. His suspicions had proved right and McCracken's mother's maiden name was Elizabeth Dillon, born in Árd Glen, Wicklow. Following her marriage to McCracken's father, she had obviously returned to Árd Glen for holidays, bringing her son with her. There he had met Maura Kelly, eventually making her pregnant and running off, leaving the girl in the lurch.

Dermot Lynch sat with his family as they watched the life slip from their father. The doctor said it was a blessing as he would never have regained the use of his legs. Dermot knew his father would not have liked to live like that. Despite their differences, they were both men who loved being outdoors, who loved to walk through the land and watch the seasons change.

The funeral was simple and befitting to the man, with Dermot's sister returning from America with her two daughters just in time. His aunt had travelled from

Árd Glen and he had to resist his urge to ask after Kate. He felt she sensed this and told him she had seen Kate in town with Tess, that she had looked well but terribly thin even in a heavy winter coat. Dermot could see his aunt wanted to question him about his plans. She had liked having family in Árd Glen and Mattie missed him helping in the pub. When the house emptied and his siblings went back to their normal lives Dermot felt lonelier than ever. He hung around the farm helping his younger brother who had stopped talking about going to America. He suspected his mother knew about Kate, especially when she asked if he was missing "the people" in Wicklow.

At last Dermot decided he would go back to Árd Glen to see if there was anything there for him to return to. His father's will had not been changed and the farm, if he wanted it, was his. He had a lot of time to think these past weeks. He missed Kate and knew he would spend his life wondering what might have been if he didn't make this one last journey to see her.

The day came when he decided to make the journey back to Wicklow. His mother eyed him from the bedroom door. She missed his father and wanted Dermot to run the farm. He knew this even if she didn't say it out loud. But he knew that what she wanted more than anything was for him to be happy.

She stood and watched him throw a few things in a bag and smiling asked, "Is that all you're taking with you?"

Dermot laughed, knowing she was teasing him.

"We'll see," he said as he threw the bag into the car and headed east. If he made good time, he would be there before dark.

On the Byrne farm, Kate and Tess walked together towards the far field where the row of spruce Seán had planted almost completely blocked out the view of Tess's butterfly lake. And at last Tess opened up and talked freely about the day that had changed her young life. She explained as best she could that because McCracken looked so much like Seán, she thought they might be the same person and drew them together each time she drew the lake. She explained how she thought caterpillars were ugly and nasty things. Seán, she said, had been nice to her but became nasty and she didn't know why. She painted him as a butterfly losing his wings and returning to a pupal state. She tried to explain that she had tried to apologise to Seán so that he would not shout at her but that he would not let her.

"Is that what your list was about, Tess? Making things right?"

Tess nodded. "But it didn't work," she replied flatly. "Sometimes you cannot put things back together, Kate."

Kate thought she could sense some sadness in her sister's voice.

As they walked together through the land, Kate at last explained to Tess how their mother had become pregnant and that because Éamonn McCracken had not married her, she was forced to marry Michael Byrne. Their grandfather had given them the farm as Uncle Jimmy was ill and they did not think he would live.

Tess listened intently to all of these things that she never knew, things that people had kept from her, and decided that she would have to put Uncle Jimmy on her list. They stood there together looking over the land as the December sky darkened and night fell on them like a comforting blanket. Brilliant stars lit up the midnight blue sky. The moon shone down on the lake creating long streaks of light on the almost still water. They could see Venus shining brightly above them and it seemed to the sisters that somehow everything would be different now. Tess looked at her sister who even dressed in her winter coat, showed obvious signs of pregnancy.

"What about you, Kate, will you marry Dermot?"

"If she'll have me," a voice said softly behind them.

Both women turned and in the fading light saw Dermot standing in front of them. Tears sprang in his eyes when he saw that Kate was expecting his baby. Tess ran to him as Kate stood transfixed to the spot, her eyes welling up. She had thought she would never see him again.

"Dermot!" Tess said, hugging him awkwardly. She looked back at her sister and, sensing they needed to talk, walked towards the house leaving the couple alone.

"I didn't think you'd come back," Kate finally said. "I wanted you to, but never imagined it." She was sobbing now, deep gulps of warm heavy tears, the events of the past few weeks suddenly seeming too much to bear. She wrapped her arms around her body, comforting herself and blocking out the cold wind that was now blowing down the valley.

Dermot searched for the words he had rehearsed during the three-hour journey but none of them seemed right now.

"I'd have come back from the first day, if you'd asked, Kate. I meant what I said. I want to marry you. Will you, Kate? Will you marry me?"

Kate put her hands to her face, wiping the tears that flowed freely down her pale face. Dermot walked to her and wrapped her tightly in his arms and they stood for what seemed like an eternity.

"Yes," she finally whispered.

Tess, who had only walked far enough to be out of sight, shouted out "Yippee!" when she heard her sister's answer and ran towards the house. The couple laughed together and walked hand in hand towards the house, towards home.

Chapter 48

1982

In Beech Street Station, Éamonn McCracken awaited his trial for the murder of Michael Byrne. As he sat in his cramped cell, he was already trying to build his defence. He knew no one would believe that he came upon the girl standing over the body, that Byrne was already dead by then and that he had only gone there to warn him off disinheriting Seán from the will. When Michael Byrne came to his office all those years back he was amazed that Byrne did not recognise him. Although Éamonn was a good bit younger than Byrne and had not yet started going into pubs, he had seen Michael around the town. Éamonn acknowledged that he had put on weight over the years but he thought that Byrne would have recognised his face. But he hadn't. Byrne had found the firm's business card in Maura's handbag and had come to the firm in an agitated state. It saddened Éamonn that Maura had kept his number for all those years. He had thought of her too and of their children. He knew a little about the life Byrne had subjected her to and had to exercise a good deal of self-control when he learned that Byrne had come there to disinherit Seán.

McCracken knew it was going to be tough to prove his innocence. A witness had placed him at the scene and he had motive. He considered saying that he had seen Seán there and had kept his mouth shut to save his son, an act of loyalty. Seán was dead now so at worst McCracken would do time for being an accomplice.

He sat back on the narrow bunk and smiled to himself. In a way this was his justice, justice for abandoning Maura when she needed him. There was no point in saying he was sorry for he was under no illusions about himself. He was a weak, spineless man who would do the exact same thing if it were happening today. He laughed aloud to himself and heard someone shout at him from another cell.

He had returned to Árd Glen once in all those years to finally do something right, the one thing he was good at: intimidation. When he arrived on the outskirts of the town that night he had hidden his car by the lower lake and had walked the rest of the way with only the moonlight to guide him. It had been a mild summer night but when light rain began to fall he took shelter in the now abandoned Kelly house, the front door of which was rotting. He could hear pigeons nesting in the roof as he walked down the hallway of the tiny stone cottage to the door of what had been Maura's room. He felt like a giant as he bent his head to enter the tiny bedroom. He stood there for the longest time listening in the quiet for the rain to ease off. Memories of the man he had been resurfaced and seemed at odds with the person now standing in the room where they had first made love, where Seán had been conceived, and he felt that this was somehow symbolic. Memories of another lifetime began to unfold before him, memories of him chasing Maura through the fields, memories of her laugh, her smile. God, she had been beautiful! But he had put his future before her and before their children. He knew Maura had stayed with Byrne to give their son a future and in some way he felt that returning to threaten Byrne might compensate Seán for what he did to her. But his son was dead now and it was all for nothing. He felt that Maura must be laughing her head off at him now and this made him smile to himself in a self-deprecating way.

When the rain finally eased and died, a light breeze blew up from the valley and Éamonn left the cottage without looking back as he walked to the road that ran alongside the lake's edge. He knew Byrne would pass this way sooner or later after a hard night's drinking and that he would be able to approach him without being seen by anyone else. No witnesses, no proof. Éamonn lowered himself into the wet grass and waited.

After almost four long cold hours, he heard

footsteps and hunched down lower into the wet grass. He could not see Byrne on the road but heard him shout out before tumbling down towards the lake's edge. He could hear more footsteps, another person walking on the road and did not raise his head, hoping to remain out of sight until a better opportunity presented itself. The sky was filled with bright silver streaks as the sun made its way onto the horizon. McCracken had hoped to be gone well before daylight and worried now that his car might be seen but he could not risk coming back here again and had to wait it out. The second pair of footsteps seemed to be running towards McCracken so he stood and moved as swiftly and as quietly away as he could but found himself misjudging the landscape and falling down a steep ridge. He placed his hands out in front of him and felt them rip against jagged rocks as he groaned softly. He hid in the long reeds and tried to wipe the blood from his wounds. He could hear Byrne shouting, followed by several dull thuds and knew someone was giving Byrne a going over. He stood and began to walk in the opposite direction but heard the footsteps begin to run through the wet grass towards him and hid again in the long reeds, thankful that the sun had not risen fully and that he might still get away unnoticed. The attacker seemed to fall to his knees and Éamonn thought he heard someone sobbing and then starting to vomit. He did not recognise the voice and could not tell if it was a man or a woman and had no choice but to wait until the person moved away. It would take him at least fifteen minutes to walk back to his car and time was not on his side. This had not gone as he had planned.

When he was sure it was safe he stood up and walked the long way around to the water's edge to wash the blood from his hands. Then he saw her, a young girl the image of Maura standing over the body of Michael Byrne. Looking back now it seemed ridiculous to have approached her but something drew him to her, something that even now he did not understand. He looked at Byrne who was face down in the water as the girl stared coldly at him. She had the strangest eyes he had ever seen. He tried to hide his face but knew it was too late. He wondered if it was her that he heard hitting Byrne and was amazed as the child looked frail and delicate. He didn't care either way and needed to be sure that she would keep quiet. There was something odd about the girl. He tried to talk to her but she moved backwards, afraid of him. He asked her who her mother was but she would not tell him until he grabbed her. Then she began to scream. He tried to quieten her and placed his hand over her mouth but she screamed louder. Éamonn warned her not to tell a soul that she saw him and it seemed that she hadn't, until now.

It had briefly occurred to him that day to silence the girl permanently but he was not a murderer, not then and not now and he knew he was beat. He knew there was no point in mentioning the footsteps he had heard or the noise of Byrne receiving a beating. They would pin this on him and he would spend the rest of his life in jail for something he did not do justice perhaps for all the wrong he had done. The wrong done to this family and especially to Maura.

In east London, Liam Kelly read the Irish newspaper in the cold damp bedsit he had recently rented. He read the article twice, focusing on the section about the upcoming trial relating to a murder that had happened almost eleven years previously and wondered if he could go home now. Even though he had only been here a few months, he knew he wasn't settling into life here and he missed his father. He had fled when the reporter started asking him questions and was worried that the case was somehow being reopened.

He was angry about Byrne taking his dad's farm and had only wanted to scare his uncle that night. Liam knew that he had always been a disappointment to his father and wanted to do something to show Jimmy Kelly that he was a man. He felt angry as he watched his uncle spending money that should have been his dad's in the pub that night and listened as his father recounted yet again the story of how Byrne had taken his livelihood from him, a story Liam had heard throughout his childhood. Liam had been drinking all evening and had followed Byrne from the pub without giving much thought to what he would do when he caught up with him. On the road outside the village, he followed closely behind Byrne which made Byrne nervous and caused him to fall down by the lakeside. Liam remembered laughing to himself as quietly as he could. When he caught up to Byrne he found him bleeding at the side of the lake, a large cut dripping down his forehead. Delighted to find Byrne in such a weakened position, he hit the intoxicated man with his fist twice, but Byrne tried to fight back and held on tightly to his legs and tried to raise himself off the ground. Liam was taken aback by the strength of the man. He became frightened and began to sober slightly, wondering what madness had possessed him to do this. He just wanted to get away and grabbed a rock, hitting Byrne twice in the face to loosen his grip before falling to his knees a few steps from where Byrne lay, still reaching out into the darkness. He vomited a little, sickened either from the drink or the blood that trickled down Byrne's face. He spotted Byrne's wallet on the ground and quickly took fifty pounds that Byrne must have earned in the mart that day, money that would have prevented his father from working long hours on building sites in Dublin and beyond. He moved quickly towards the lower end of the lake but thought he spotted Seán Byrne coming towards him and hoped his cousin did not see him. He ran the entire three miles to his home, his heart pounding and fear choking the breath out of him with each step he took.

When the news broke that Byrne was dead, Liam was shocked as Byrne was still alive when he left and he hadn't meant to kill him. He thought about telling his father that he was there, that he thought he had seen Seán Byrne at the lake but knew it was better to keep his mouth shut. Now that he was sober, he couldn't fathom why he thought his honest God-fearing father would be impressed by his behaviour. The following day he attended Mass in Knockbeg and prayed for forgiveness, discreetly throwing the fifty pound note into the Poor Box.

Liam read about how his cousin Tess had reportedly seen McCracken at the lake and wondered now if it was him and not Seán that he had seen. He felt guilty about letting Tess take the blame for all those years but knew that he couldn't admit it now. Liam couldn't let his father know what he had done that day although he had wondered over the years if Jimmy Kelly had always suspected him, insisting Liam leave the pub with him whenever there was talk about Michael Byrne's murder.

He folded the paper and looked out through the dirty window of his flat and watched as a bluebottle tried to escape from a large web in the corner of the window. He would wait it out. He would lie low until he was sure it was safe to return home, if ever.

Chapter 49

January 1982

Tess Byrne woke early and decided to walk down to edge of the lake, to the area where her father had been killed, for the first time since she had returned to Árd Glen. Kate was still sleeping soundly and Tess delighted in the part she had played in making her sister happy again, scribbling out her sister's name on her list the night that Dermot had returned to them.

As Tess left the house, she noticed a piece of white paper stuck to the tractor, the message that she had left for Dermot the morning of the accident. She removed it and looked at the drawing which depicted Dermot, Kate and herself as a family with no Seán or Ben and she wondered how she knew this would be the way things turned out. She had not meant for her brothers to die. She had only wanted Seán to take the keys that morning so that Kate would make him leave the house and she wouldn't have to be frightened of him any more. Tess stood still for a moment, her head bowed, and began walking towards the lake, walking to the place where it had all begun.

As she stood by the water's edge and stared into the calm blue water, memories of that fateful morning came back to her and seemed clearer to her than ever before, transporting her back to the day when her life changed forever. She could see herself standing there, a little girl wearing her good shoes and dress, knowing she would have to be ready for Kate's shopping trip to Knockbeg that morning. When she saw Michael Byrne asleep beside the lake she remembered feeling frightened as he smelt of whiskey. She did not want to wake him and sat at the water's edge looking for butterflies until she became bored. She noticed the lovely rock beside her father and lifted it to look at the shiny bits as the sun climbed steadily over the mountains. She squealed when she saw the blood on it and quickly rinsed the rock by the water's edge. When the long bright rays of early morning sunshine filtered through the gap in the mountain range, she noticed that there was blood on her father's face and she could hear him making a gurgling noise from his nose which was twisted to one side. She wondered if he had fallen. She hated blood and shivered as she splashed water onto his face to wash the blood off, being careful not to wet her good dress and shoes, but it did not work. She knelt down and lifted his arm up, pushing his shoulder towards the water until she turned his upper body over. Her stomach turned as she put both her hands around his face and turned his head downward into the water, shaking his head around to make sure the blood came off this time. He made another gurgling noise and Tess worried again that he might wake and shout at her but he did not move. Pretty bubbles moved upwards from her father's mouth to the surface of the water which intrigued Tess and she stood and watched them until they stopped. When she tried to turn her father's head around, his arm moved forward into the water. She tried to pull it back but it was very heavy and she could not move him. Her feet slipped and her good shoes got wet so she began to cry, knowing Kate would be angry with her yet again.

She heard a noise and looked up to see a man she first thought was Seán standing above her in the early dawn light. She stared at his face which he tried to hide with his hand. He asked her who her mother was. His tooth was broken which frightened Tess and he had blood on his hands which were cut and dirty. The man was a stranger and Tess was afraid of him and could not speak. She watched as he looked at her father and stared wide-eyed at her before grabbing her by the dress and pushing her back onto the reeds, telling her not to tell anyone she saw him and telling her to stay there until he was gone. He did not seem to care that he had put blood on her dress and that she would be in even more trouble with Kate. Tess's chin quivered as she remembered that morning in detail and realised that nobody had asked her about the good thing she did that morning, trying to clean her dad's face in the water so he wouldn't look so dirty but everyone asked her about hitting him with a rock which she did not do so she didn't know how to answer them. Some of the men asking questions that morning seemed angry and shouted at her so she became frightened and could not speak. She understood that this was her condition but very few people understood that. Very few people except Leroy, Dr Cosgrove, Dermot and Kate knew how to ask her questions in a way that she understood, in a way that she could answer them.

Kate had told her that they should get on with a new life now and that they should try to forget about what happened and Tess thought this was a very good idea. Tess took one last look at the water and threw the drawing of her and Kate and Dermot in, watching it float away in the deep blue water. Her plan had worked and her list was finished. Back at the house her "Butterfly State" sign swayed gently in the breeze. The red-haired caterpillars were gone and she had found Kate a new fiancé who did not want to take her sister away from her. Tess looked down and was surprised to see a caterpillar crawling on the ground near her feet. It was an unusual sight this time of year. She knelt down and picked up the small insect and watched as it crawled around the palm of her hand.

"You'll like being a butterfly," she said softly to it before returning the frightened insect back to safety.

She looked up at the clear blue sky above her. It was going to be a beautiful day.

Epilogue

Éamonn McCracken was found guilty of the murder of Michael Byrne and sentenced to life imprisonment.

Sam Moran covered the case and hit the headlines with a series of exclusive stories about McCracken's connection to the Byrnes.

Jimmy Kelly returned to live in the old stone cottage he had grown up in, after Tess Byrne had it restored for him.

Liam Kelly did well in the construction business in London and did not return to Ireland.

After the birth of their baby boy, Kate and Dermot Lynch decided to stay and farm Butterfly State.

Tess continued to paint the lake, selling her paintings to the art gallery.

The End

POOLBEG *Crimson* 

Also published by Poolbeg

ellen McCarthy

Guarding Maggie

All her life, people have looked after Maggie Breslin. She is happy enough with her quiet life in the heart of rural Donegal. But when a face from her past surfaces, disaster follows, and Maggie is left alone to pick up the pieces.

Who would want to harm Maggie and her family, here in the place she has known since she was a child? Whom can she trust? As tragedy follows tragedy, she doesn't know where to turn.

For the first time, Maggie must take control of her own destiny and find out who her tormentor is – before it's too late.

Fiction with an edge

ISBN 978-1-84223-322-1

POOLBEG *Crimson* 

Also published by Poolbeg

anna kelly

Daniel's Daughter

City girl Angela Brennan is astounded when the father she has never known leaves her a house and land in the country. She is also a little fearful. But it does give her the chance to take her young son Thomas and start a new life, far from their violent and abusive family in Dublin.

But not everyone is happy at Angela's good fortune. It soon becomes clear that behind the friendly faces of her new neighbours there lurks a dangerous enemy.

As their safe haven turns into a living nightmare, Angela finds her very life is under threat.

Can she identify her secret enemy before it is too late?

Fiction with an edge

ISBN 978-1-84223-336-8

POOLBEG *Crimson* 

Also published by Poolbeg

carol magill

Sleep Softly Baby

Handsome, clever, and heir to a fortune – Harry Kavanagh is the dream eligible bachelor. But it is Erin O'Neill – newly arrived in Dublin to pursue a career as a journalist – who captures his heart. And she falls equally in love with him.

But when he takes her to live in Belvedere, the austere family home, things begin to go wrong and they culminate in the arrival of their first child – baby Emily. Erin now finds herself overtaken by nightmarish events where she can trust no one, not even her own husband, and where evil seems to seep out from the very house itself.

A gripping tale of passion, love, intrigue and revenge and one woman's struggle to survive against dark forces.

Fiction with an edge

ISBN 978-1-84223-359-7

POOLBEG *Crimson* 

Also published by Poolbeg

ellen McCarthy

Guilt Ridden

Amy Devine is a successful businesswoman with a beautiful house and a great life which is thrown into disarray when a manuscript arrives on her desk one morning.

The Devine family have a fifteen-year-old mystery. Ruth Devine, Amy's estranged cousin was kidnapped without a trace when she was in college.

The writer of the manuscript lures Amy back to Waterford with information on the tragic childhood she spent there. Questions abound. What was the real story surrounding her parents' death? What guilty secrets can lie at the heart of a country village? What happened to Ruth Devine?

Does the writer know and what has now been planned for Amy?

Fiction with an edge

ISBN 978-1-84223-339-9